TIME REP
CONTINUUM

PETER WARD

DIVERSIONBOOKS

Also by Peter Ward

Time Rep
Note to Self

Diversion Books
A Division of Diversion Publishing Corp.
443 Park Avenue South, Suite 1008
New York, New York 10016
www.DiversionBooks.com

For more information, email info@diversionbooks.com

First Diversion Books edition May 2016.
Print ISBN: 978-1-68230-064-0
eBook ISBN: 978-1-68230-063-3

For Andrea

TEN

There are very few circumstances in which waking up with no memory can be described as a good thing. In fact, not knowing crucial things such as who you are, where you are, what you do for a living, who your friends are, or where to find the nearest kettle is generally described as rather bad. There are exceptions to this rule, of course: if you were a politician, for instance, waking up with no memory that you were a politician would probably be pretty good. Suddenly, you wouldn't feel the need to gesture with your hands unnecessarily every time you spoke, or respond to difficult questions with the answer to a completely different question you would have much rather been asked. You'd be a normal person again, albeit one with no memory.

Geoffrey Stamp wasn't a politician, so the fact that he'd completely lost his memory was not a good thing. As it happened, Geoffrey had a pretty interesting job—he just couldn't remember what it was. He didn't even know he had a job, what a job was, or that his name was Geoffrey Stamp. His name could have been Elizabeth Perkins for all he knew, except his mind was so devoid of any memory that he wasn't aware of the social conventions that meant people had names, or that the name Elizabeth was associated with the female of his species, or that his species had females, or that he even belonged to a species. The only thing Geoffrey Stamp knew was that he was extraordinarily confused.

But Geoffrey was a very fast learner, and he was learning that he was a fast learner very…well, fast. Within moments of waking up, he realized that he had some arms. He thought this discovery was a pretty good start, although he wasn't quite aware yet that they were called arms. He was aware that he could move them a bit just by thinking, and that the arms had hands on the ends of them, but that was about it. The hands moved too, when he thought about it, but something was preventing him from moving them as much as he wanted to. This only added to Geoffrey's state of confusion, and as he became reacquainted with the rest of his physical form, he soon discovered that the reason he couldn't move was that he was lying on his back, restrained to something cold and hard with two thick straps wrapped over his arms and legs. This, along with waking up with no memory, was also something you would rarely describe as being good, unless of course you were into that sort of thing.

He began to squirm around uncomfortably in his restraints, trying to break free. He didn't know why he had the urge to do this; it was just instinctive, a bit like having the urge to run away whenever "Come on Eileen" played on the radio. Above him, a number of big bright things shone in his eyes. He didn't like this either, and began to think of the best way to communicate his displeasure. In the end, he opted to open and close his mouth like a newly born baby discovering how to use its facial muscles for the first time.

"So, has anyone got any ideas?"

Geoff stopped opening and closing his mouth and kept still for a moment. This wasn't because he'd understood any of what had just been said, but because he'd registered a noise. There had been no sound up until this point, and so the discovery of another sensory stimulus had momentarily distracted him from what he was doing.

"Come on—anyone? I mean, this is impossible, right?"

There it was again. That noise. Sounded familiar, but he didn't know why. He decided to turn his head over to see where it was coming from, taking in more details of his surroundings as he did so. Everything he could see was pretty featureless, with the exception of the very bright things hanging above him. When he finished turning his head to one side, he noticed that something else that also had arms and legs was looking back at him. For some reason, though, this thing was not restrained as he was, and was in an upright position. A number of other upright things with arms and legs were also staring at him. Geoff began to fight his restraints again, but they were too strong. Eventually, he gave up and slumped back on the cold hard thing underneath him.

There must be a perfectly good reason why I am restrained in this way, so I will try and keep my composure was not a thought that ran through Geoff's mind as he lay in this primitive mental state. Instead, he started to open and close his mouth again, only this time he discovered that he could make a loud noise.

"Jesus! What's happening? Why is he screaming?"

"I don't know, Dr. Skivinski—can someone give him another shot?"

All of a sudden, Geoff felt something hold his arm down. This was followed by a sharp prick. Then something cool felt as though it were surging underneath his skin toward his head. Then he felt the urge to stop making the loud noise. Then his body went numb. Then he stuck his tongue out and drooled down the left side of his face.

"Okay—is he in a stable condition?"

"Yes."

"And the bullet?"

"We managed to remove it safely," the first noise…*replied*.

Wait a minute—yes, the first noise was *replying* to the second one! And these noises—they were *voices!* These…things with arms and legs…these *people*…had to open their…*mouths* to… to…*speak!* Geoff was listening to a…*conversation!*

This recollection of people's anatomy, the fact that they were talking to each other, and the associated vocabulary to describe everything that was going on was probably the most momentous achievement Geoff had ever known, although at this point he couldn't remember that he'd actually achieved some other pretty major things in the past, like saving the planet.

"Is he going to be all right?"

"I think so—the bullet missed his spinal column by a few inches, and it didn't puncture any major organs. He's lucky to be alive…"

Geoff began to recognize the person who was doing most

of the talking. He didn't quite know who it was, but somehow they looked familiar.

Suddenly, another *person*…a *man*…burst through a door in the far corner of the room and ran over to join the others. This one looked familiar too, but again, Geoff couldn't place him. The man looked exhausted, hunching over for a few seconds to get his breath back before saying anything.

"I don't…believe it," the man huffed, straightening up to look at Geoff. "Is it true?"

"It's true, Tim," the voice Geoff had first heard replied. "What you're looking at is a future version of Geoffrey Stamp."

The man gulped down more air before speaking again.

"A *future version*?" he said. "But how can that be?"

"We've got no idea. All we know is that four hours ago, he materialized on Tower Bridge and collapsed in the street with a bullet in his back. When the police arrived on the scene, they instantly recognized him and brought him to this hospital. The doctors performed emergency surgery on him to remove the bullet, and he's been under observation in here ever since."

Although Geoffrey could hear the words being spoken, at this stage he didn't understand a word of it—his mind was having enough trouble as it was, and in light of this had decided to put speech recognition on the back burner for a moment. Geoff kept listening to them speak, but for all he knew, these people could have been having a debate about what the difference was between a nectarine and a peach, or why men under fifty didn't wear hats with suits anymore.

"Is he all right?" the man said.

"He's fine—we just gave him another shot to calm him down."

"Why is he tied down?"

"We had to restrain him. When they brought him here he was convulsing really violently. It was horrible."

"You tried talking to him?"

"He's only just woken up."

The man walked closer to Geoff and looked down at him.

"Geoff?" he said, narrowing his eyes as he stared into Geoff's empty gaze. "Geoff, it's me! It's Tim! Can you hear me?"

Despite his body feeling numb, Geoffrey was able to stick out his tongue and blow a very small raspberry.

The man looked up at the others and smiled. "He recognizes me!"

"No," one of the others replied. "He's been doing that periodically for the last two hours. He seems to enjoy it."

The man shook his head. "Damn it," he said. "What the hell happened to him? Eric—can't you tell us anything?"

"I'm afraid we know very little," said the other main voice. "Almost everything about this future version of Geoff is a complete mystery. We don't know how he was able to travel back through time, we don't know why he was shot, and we don't know why he appears to have lost his memory."

"So what *do* we know?"

"Well, firstly, he had this in his jacket pocket," the other person said, holding up a small white card. It had some dark squiggles on it. To most people these squiggles would be called writing, but to Geoff they were squiggles.

"Is that…a *Continuum* business card?"

"It is. And it's got Geoffrey's name on it."

"That explains why he's looking so smart. I've never seen him look this well groomed. Where did you find this?"

"Inside pocket of the suit jacket he was wearing."

"Suit jacket? But Geoff doesn't own a suit…"

"Well that's what he had on when we found him. It's hanging up over there."

"Huh." The voice got quieter as the man walked over to the other side of the room. "Let's have a look at this…wait a minute! This is *my* suit!"

"What?"

"See on the left sleeve where one of the buttons is missing? This is an old suit I was thinking of throwing away! What the hell was Geoff doing in it?"

"We have no idea."

"Okay—for now, let's not worry about what we *don't* know.

Let's go through what we *do* know. If Geoff has a Continuum business card with his name on it, then it's safe to assume he leaves Time Tours at some point in the future to go and work for them. Correct?"

"I suppose so…"

"Okay. What else have we got?"

"Well, there's the bullet we removed from Geoff's back."

"What about it?"

"Well, it was very…unusual. It's much larger than any caliber I know of, and made from a material that I've never seen before—a new element that won't register on any of our scans."

"Well, at least a new element gives us something to go on— if this bullet is exotic, we might be able to trace it. So we've got a weird bullet and a Continuum business card. Anything else?"

"Yes—there's this scar on his right wrist."

Geoff watched as the two men leaned over his body and looked closely at something.

"We don't know what it is, but it looks like an injection mark. Six small dots surrounding a bigger dot in the middle."

"Hmm. Any idea what he was injected with?"

"I'm afraid not. But what I can tell you is that judging by the amount of healing, this was done recently."

"Okay. Anything else?"

"Well, there is one other thing."

"What is it?"

"This version of Geoff—he's from just one day in the future."

"A day? You mean he's from tomorrow?"

"That's right. He's just over twenty-four hours older than the present-day Geoff."

"You sure about that?"

"Absolutely. The date on his watch says so."

"Wow—that really doesn't give us much time to figure out what the hell happened here. Where's the present-day Geoff at the moment? We need to speak to him as quickly as possible."

"Sorry I'm late," a new voice said from the door. "What did I miss?"

ONE

In the two years Geoff had been working as a Time Rep, he'd been called to only three emergency meetings, and one of those he didn't turn up to because something interesting came on the television while he was putting his coat on and made him forget why he was going out. The other two meetings didn't turn out to be that important—the first one was after his first week on the job, when he had nearly told his friend Zoë what he really did for a living—that he worked for a company based in the future called Time Tours. He remembered them calling him in for a meeting afterward and holding him in a small room for hours while a very stern man with a thin moustache explained why no one from his time period could know that he met tourists from the thirty-first century and showed them around twenty-first-century London.

"If someone from your time has any knowledge of future events," he was told, "it could create a paradox."

"Ah," Geoff had replied. "Those are very bad, aren't they?"

"Yes, they are. And the reason they are very bad is because they have a nasty habit of destroying everything that has ever existed. Remember?"

"Yes, I remember, I remember. But surely telling Zoë wouldn't be that bad? I mean, at the very worst it would only create a tiny little paradox, no?"

"A tiny little paradox?"

"Yeah. You know, really small."

The man with the thin moustache shut his eyes and sighed.

"The scale of the paradox doesn't matter, Mr. Stamp—big or small, they cause all sorts of problems, like the unraveling of the space-time continuum."

"Oh."

"Yes, 'oh.' And the space-time continuum is not like a sweater, Mr. Stamp—it cannot be easily re-raveled, so let's not let that happen, okay?"

Geoff wasn't sure if a sweater *could* easily be re-raveled (it sounded pretty hard to him the more he imagined trying to actually do it), but decided to keep quiet. He was already in enough trouble as it was, so he didn't think questioning this man's knowledge of sweater construction was particularly wise—he needed to focus on not causing any paradoxes.

If this meeting had been happening at any normal company, Geoff could imagine this conversation being captured in some sort of "personal development" paperwork:

> Objective 1: Improve my networking skills in the wider business.
>
> Objective 2: Offer a quality customer experience to all tourists from the future.
>
> Objective 3: Do not destroy the universe.

But Time Tours was no normal company.

In fact, most people would have described it as pretty unusual.

The second emergency meeting he had attended was a few months ago. This one seemed to be quite a big deal, because it was held in a huge conference room in the Time Tours building, and every Time Rep was there. Over two hundred men and women from throughout history had been summoned, from 3000 BC cavemen to twenty-ninth-century galactic colonists. As far as Geoff knew, it was the first time since the company had started that they had all been in the same room together at once, and seeing such a huge variety of people from across time was quite special. William Boyle, the Time Rep Geoff had met during his introductory tour of the Great Fire of London, was there, along with many other Reps he had heard about.

In this meeting, the chief executive of Time Tours herself, Ruth Ashmore, told them all about a new company called

Continuum, which was also offering holidays to the past. However, unlike Time Tours, which required every tourist to be scanned by a supercomputer before they went back in time as a safeguard to ensure they weren't going to change history, Continuum claimed they had the technology to allow tourists to go back in time and change what they liked, without disrupting anything in the present. Nobody knew how it was possible, but the claims appeared to be true, and as a result a lot of people were starting to book their holidays to the past through Continuum instead. The meeting ended with Ruth asking all Time Reps to keep an eye on things in their native time periods, and to inform them if anything unusual happened. In the months that followed, Geoff hadn't noticed anything particularly different, apart from one week when his local supermarket had decided to stop selling his favorite breakfast cereal. But after having a word with the manager, they put it back in again, so he didn't think that had much to do with Continuum.

Oh, and his neighbor bought a pet rabbit.

Other than that, there was nothing to report.

So here he was for another emergency meeting. Based on his past experience of these things, he hadn't really taken it that seriously when Eric had called and told him to come to the future immediately. In fact, instead of leaving the twenty-first century straight away, he'd brushed his teeth, made himself a cup of tea, and watched the first few minutes of an old *Star Trek: The Next Generation* episode while he drank it. It was one of the many episodes where Captain Jean-Luc Picard kept tugging at his uniform to stop it from riding up, which amused him. After about five minutes, he put on the standard-issue earphones Time Tours had given him to travel back and forth between his own time and theirs, and left. As he arrived in the thirty-first century, though, he began to wonder if perhaps this emergency meeting really was an emergency. After all, it was a little unusual for Eric to call him in person, and he'd detected a hint of nervousness in Eric's voice when he'd told Geoff to come to the future as quickly as he could. And why had Eric asked him to meet them in a hospital operating theater?

"Where's the present-day Geoff at the moment?" he could hear Tim saying as he approached the room. "We need to speak to him as quickly as possible."

"Sorry I'm late," Geoff said, looking around at everyone as he entered. "What did I miss?"

There were at least ten people in here, all crowded around a figure lying on a table. He couldn't make out who it was, but he could see that they were draped with a surgical gown. He immediately recognized Tim—his friend and headhunter for the company, who had nominated him to be a Time Rep in the first place, and Eric—an elderly, double-Nobel-Prize-winning scientist who'd developed the supercomputer that scanned tourists before they traveled to the past. He had no idea who the other people were, but they all wore white coats and looked very concerned about something.

Maybe they were just nervous about the fact that they had to wear white coats, in case they spilled something on them.

"Where have you been?" Eric said, pressing his hands to the sides of his head as though he were trying to mime being stuck in a vise. "You were told to meet us here twenty minutes ago!"

Geoff gulped. Given that he had used time travel to get here (and therefore could have arrived anytime he liked), there really was no excuse for arriving late, but he tried to think of one anyway.

"I, uh…tripped on a thing."

Brilliant.

Eric squeezed the sides of his head a little harder. Nobody else in the room said anything. They all just looked at him awkwardly, as though he'd just suggested they play an impromptu game of strip poker.

"So…what's happened?" Geoff asked, trying to change the subject from his lack of timekeeping skills. "I haven't done something wrong again, have I? I mean, I swear I haven't told a soul what I do for a living, or—"

"Geoff…you might want to come over and have a look at this," Tim interrupted, motioning him to walk toward the table in the middle of the room.

Geoff did as he was told and walked forward. When he got close enough to see the face of the person lying on the table, he stopped still and looked around at everyone.

"Is that who I think it is?" he asked. The man looked to be in his late twenties, with thick chestnut hair, pale skin, and a round face. He was an average height, with a skinny build and narrow shoulders, and the more Geoff looked at him, the more he couldn't help but think he looked extraordinarily similar to the face he'd seen in the mirror two weeks ago, when he'd last brushed his hair.

There was one major difference, though—this man was much better groomed.

His hair had been cut, his face was clean shaven, and for a moment he almost looked...handsome. The man's olive-green eyes were darting erratically around the room, drool was dribbling down the side of his face, and every so often he writhed around in his restraints, but other than that, he looked rather civilized.

"I don't know," Tim said, walking across the room to stand next to Geoff. "Who *do* you think it is?"

"Well, I'm guessing it isn't a lookalike you've hired to go and open shopping centers on my behalf?"

"No, it's not a lookalike."

"And I don't have a long-lost twin brother?"

"No, you don't."

"And there isn't a Geoffrey Stamp costume on sale in stores?"

"A Geoffrey Stamp *costume*?" Tim said. "Do you even need me to answer that?"

"Well, then, that only leaves one other possibility," Geoff said, looking closer at the man strapped to the table. "Is this person me?"

"We think so," Eric said, walking around to the other side of the table and scanning the man with some sort of portable device. "If our theory is correct, this person is a future version of you."

"What do you mean, a 'future version' of me?"

"He's you, only he's somehow traveled back to this point in time from the future," Eric said, examining the results of his scan.

"He looks different from me in some ways," Geoff said.

"We were thinking that too," Tim said. "This Geoffrey Stamp has had his hair cut. He's shaved recently. Washed his face."

"Wow," Geoff said. "So he must be from a few years in the future, then, right? Maybe when I've met the right girl and started taking better care of myself?"

"No, Geoffrey," Eric said. "He's from tomorrow."

"Tomorrow?" Geoff said. In front of him, his future self turned his head and looked him in the eyes. He appeared to be docile and confused, like he'd just been forced to listen to a conversation about sport. "This is weird. You mean to tell me that at some point tomorrow, I'll be lying on that table, looking at me saying the things I'm saying now?"

"If our theory is correct, yes," Eric replied. "Tomorrow you will travel back to today. Understand?"

"What time did his watch say when you brought him in?" Tim asked.

"Three thirty in the afternoon," Eric replied.

"Three thirty?" Geoff looked at his watch. "But that's only twenty-two hours from now!"

"We know," Tim said. "That's why we're all here, trying to figure this thing out. That's the 'emergency' part of our emergency meeting."

"So what's wrong with me?" Geoff said, looking into his own eyes. "Why aren't I saying anything?"

"We're not sure," Eric said. "But according to these readings, you've suffered an enormous memory loss, and only your most basic brain functions are working."

"My most basic brain functions? You mean the part of my brain that knows never to eat quiche?"

"No, your mind is barely active enough to keep you breathing. You're in a massive state of confusion, and it's quite likely the reason you're not speaking is because you don't remember how to."

Geoff swallowed hard. "So do you have any idea what might have caused this?"

"We think it may have something to do with these guys," Tim said. He reached into his pocket and handed Geoff a business card.

It was from that new company Ruth had mentioned a few months ago—Continuum—and underneath the company logo, he saw his name. There was no job title, and when he turned it over in his hand, he noticed the back was blank.

"Continuum?" Geoff said.

"That's right," Tim replied.

"Where did you find that?"

Tim nodded toward a black suit hanging up in the corner of the room. "You were wearing that when you were brought in. We found the card in your jacket pocket."

"But I don't own a suit."

"I know."

"So where did I get it?"

Tim pursed his lips for a second. "It's an old one of mine."

Geoff frowned. "An old one of yours?" he said. "Why would I be wearing that?"

"We're not sure," Tim said. "Maybe Continuum invited you for a job interview, and I let you borrow my suit so you could look smart for it. That would also explain your appearance."

"But how could all that happen in a day? And even if it did, that doesn't make sense. If I was looking to leave Time Tours, why would I tell you? And why would I have an interview with them in the first place?"

"Again, we're not sure. But we do know they are trying to recruit a lot of our Time Reps at the moment. Whatever the reason, it looks as though you choose to go and work for Continuum at some point in the next twenty-two hours. Have they tried to contact you over the last few weeks at all? Arrange a meeting? Anything like that?"

"I don't think so."

"You sure? What about your post? Have they sent you a letter or something?"

"Maybe," Geoff said. "There's quite a lot of unopened post at home, so it's possible they've been writing to me. I can check if you like?"

"You do that."

"So you think what happened to me had something to do with Continuum?"

"We don't know," Tim said, "but for now that's our only lead."

Geoff inhaled some air into his cheeks, held it there for a few seconds, then breathed out again slowly. "Why do you think I traveled back in time?"

"We have no idea," Eric said, "but there are two possibilities to consider. Either you traveled back in time of your own accord, or someone sent you here against your will. And then of course there's the bullet you had in your back when we found you…"

"Right," Geoff said, nodding absentmindedly for a moment. "Wait a minute—someone's going to shoot me?!"

• • •

Geoff spent the next hour sitting in the far corner of the operating theater, staring at the Continuum business card. He had his back to the wall, and his legs were hunched up to his chest. Maybe he could just stay here for a day. If he stayed here, no one could shoot him in the back, right? Then again, what if staying here was what got him shot? Maybe a cleaner who really wanted to mop the corner of the room he was sitting in got so annoyed that he wouldn't move that he ended up shooting him?

This was Geoff's train of thought as he turned the Continuum business card over and over in his hands, creating increasingly ridiculous scenarios that all ended with him being shot in the back. In the end, he reasoned that anything he did could result in someone trying to kill him, so he gave up torturing himself over what fate might befall him and tried to think about what to do.

The others used their time a bit more productively. Eric said something about going off to analyze the bullet, and the other men and women in white coats continued to monitor Geoff's future self for any changes in his condition. From what they could tell, there were signs that his memory loss was only temporary, and that some of his higher brain functions were returning. This didn't really make Geoff feel much better, though. What on Earth was going to happen to him over the next twenty-one hours?

"What are you going to do to him now?" Tim asked one of the people in white coats.

"Once he's in a more stable condition, we'll get him into a ward," they replied.

Tim walked over to Geoff and offered him a hand. "Get up."

"No."

"Come on—sitting there isn't going to solve anything. We need to work out what's going on here."

"Fine," Geoff said, grabbing Tim's hand and pulling himself to his feet.

"Okay—let's go over what we know," Tim said, pacing up and down in front of Geoff. He looked pale, and had to stop walking every now and then to dab his forehead with a handkerchief. "At some point over the next twenty-one hours, you are going to leave Time Tours to work for Continuum. Something is going to happen that results in you getting shot, and you will somehow end up being sent back in time. You will appear on Tower Bridge unconscious at three thirty tomorrow afternoon, and when you wake up, you will have no memory of what happened, nor will you be able to communicate with us."

"Great summary, Tim," Geoff said, trying to reach around to feel his back. "I feel so much better."

"Now—let's think about the unanswered questions," Tim continued. "What would cause you to leave Time Tours and go and work for Continuum? Why would someone try and kill you? How did you lose your memory? Why were you sent back to this point in time exactly? And how were you able to get here?"

"That's a lot of questions."

"Did I miss anything?"

"Yes," Geoff said, handing the business card back to Tim. "Now that I know what's going to happen to me, will this change the fact that I get shot? And what has all this got to do with Continuum?"

"That's what we need to find out," Tim said.

"Who are these people, anyway?" Geoff asked.

Tim looked down at the floor.

"There's a lot about that company that still remains a mystery," he said. "But maybe if we go back to your house, we can start to get to the bottom of this. Didn't you say you might have some letters from them?"

TWO

Geoffrey did indeed have some letters.

In fact, he had about six months' worth, so he was hoping the letter from Continuum would be in there somewhere.

The mound of post lay unopened in a large round pile just inside the front door of 23 Woodview Gardens—the small, inconspicuous three-bedroom house in the suburbs of twenty-first-century London, owned by his employer, Time Tours. At first glance, the pile of letters looked like they might be a piece of modern art, an abstract representation of a bird's nest perhaps, created out of envelopes, fliers, and free newspapers. It looked especially nestlike since the middle of the pile had a large dimple in it, although this had actually been created when Geoff had fallen into it last week and it had taken him three minutes to climb back out again.

Upon arriving at the house, Geoff and Tim did their best to scoop the mail up in their arms and carried it through into the lounge, dumping it on the coffee table in the middle of the room like two detectives about to rummage through somebody's rubbish.

"I see you've been keeping the place nice and clean since I moved out," Tim joked, looking around at the piles of laundry tossed into various clumps throughout the room. The laundry was interspersed with several half-drunk cups of tea placed neatly on the floor in different places, and you'd have been forgiven for thinking for a moment that Geoff was trying to invent a life-sized board game similar to draughts, only using piles of laundry and cups of tea as the pieces.

Tim and Geoff used to live together in this house for four years, before Tim moved out just over a year ago. Geoff had first moved in when he lost his job as a paper boy, and Tim had invited him to live in the house completely rent-free. At the time, Geoff thought this was too good to be true. He had no idea Tim actually worked as a headhunter for Time Tours, and that the invitation to live with him was actually a ploy to keep Geoff under close observation, deliberately reducing his level of contact with the outside world. The fewer friends you had and the less you went out, the more suitable you were for being a Time Rep, since it was less likely that you would cause any disruption to the space-time continuum by behaving differently. It wasn't until two years ago that he had found out the truth. At first he was furious about how his life had been manipulated, and how Time Tours had spent all that time conditioning him to behave exactly as they wanted. But he soon accepted every explanation they gave him for the way he had been treated without question and just got on with what they told him to do: meet tourists from the future, and show them around.

They began to go through the mail. The first thing Geoff pulled out was a leaflet from his local pizza restaurant advertising a brand-new limited-edition meal deal called the Goliath Box. In the box you got a large pizza, four pieces of garlic bread, eight chicken wings, some potato wedges, and a dip. He noticed another leaflet from the same pizza restaurant, only this one was dated a month later. This time, they were advertising a brand-new limited-edition meal deal called the Gladiator Box. In the box you got a large pizza, two pieces of garlic bread, ten chicken wings, potato wedges, and a dip. On top of that were four other leaflets, each one from the same pizza restaurant, each one dated a month apart, and each one advertising a brand-new limited-edition meal deal with a name that usually began with a *G*.

Next, Geoff found a letter from his parents. He had last seen them just over six months ago, when they came to stay for a couple of weeks. They were wishing him well and hoped to see him again soon. His mum and dad had emigrated to America a few years ago because of his father's job, leaving Geoff to fend for himself in England. This had seemed a little harsh at the time, but he felt better now that they were visiting him a little more regularly than they had done in the past. In fact, when they were last in the country, they'd had a really nice time—he'd taken them out for a few meals, been on some nice walks, and his mum even managed to refrain from telling him about any problems she was having with her computer/e-mail account/ lawnmower/neighbors/roof/car/plumbing, which usually became the topic of discussion if they ever ran out of things to talk about.

Best of all, when they'd asked him if he'd found a new job (he'd been unemployed for two years before becoming a Time Rep, which had often been a bone of contention during any long-distance phone calls), for once he could tell them that he had. Of course, he had to feed them the cover story that he told everyone: that he worked as a regular holiday rep, meeting regular tourists on their regular holidays to London. He was careful to leave out certain information, like the fact that the tourists had traveled back in time from more than a millennium in the future, and that there was always the chance in his line of work that he might do something that could destroy the universe. He daren't have told his mum that last bit, even if he were allowed to—she got stressed enough when she once found out he was going to cycle to school instead of getting the bus.

Geoff put the letter from his parents to one side and kept rummaging around for something from Continuum. Tim was searching much faster than Geoff, and for a moment he looked like a contestant racing against the clock on some sort of daytime TV game show. In fact, it wouldn't have surprised Geoff if there really were a real game show where contestants had to rummage through letters, given the quality of shows he often watched in the afternoon. Programs were always about contestants going to an auction/boot sale/flea market/antiques fair/storage yard, buying something for a certain amount of money, and then trying to sell it for very slightly more money, so a show where people had to go through somebody's letters would be completely revolutionary in the world of daytime TV.

A large amount of the mail consisted of unopened bank statements. He hadn't been bothered to look at these because he knew his balance off by heart: zero pounds and zero pence. This lack of funds wasn't due to an extravagant lifestyle in which Geoff constantly spent everything he earned—quite the opposite, in fact. The reason he didn't have any money was that he didn't actually get paid by Time Tours for the work he did. Even when he had saved the entire human race two years ago on his first day (for which any normal person would probably have expected a pretty good bonus), the only thing Geoff got was a pat on the back and a small fruitcake. Someone had piped "Well Done for Saving the Planet" on the top in strawberry icing, but they hadn't written the *e* in *Planet* very clearly, so it looked like it said "Well Done for Saving the Plant." It was a nice gesture, but he would have preferred to have received lots of money. Then he could have bought his own cake, with better piping.

And a Playstation.

But it wasn't just Geoffrey who didn't get paid—the same was true of all Time Reps. In fact, the wage bill for Time Tours was so small, it was even lower than the typical budget for a movie made by the Syfy channel. Obviously, many Time Reps complained about this, but there was supposedly a good reason for it: if Time Reps earned money, there was a danger that they would spend it on things they wouldn't have been able to afford otherwise, which in turn could alter the trajectory of the space-time continuum. Of course, Time Tours understood that their employees couldn't survive without some sort of income, so they developed a special system: instead of having wages, Time Reps could submit requests for anything they wanted. Food, drink, books, clothes, string, pot noodles, anything. The request would then get analyzed by the supercomputer in the future, and if it could be accommodated without disrupting the flow of history, the company would arrange for the item to be delivered within a few days. It was an annoying system, but at least it meant he didn't have to go to ASDA.

"This is the most ridiculous amount of mail I've ever seen," Tim said, examining letter after letter in the hope that he might find one of interest. He paused for a moment and raised his eyebrows, as if he had just remembered something.

"Do you see much of you-know-who these days?" he asked.

Geoff stopped searching through the letters and looked up.

Tim was referring to Zoë—the local postman who had delivered all this mail to 23 Woodview Gardens over the course of the last six months.

"Now and again," he replied, rubbing the back of his head. "We sometimes hang out by the lake, but, you know—as friends."

Zoë and Geoff had met many years ago, when Geoff was still doing his paper round and she was delivering mail along the same route. She was a good friend, someone who always made him laugh, and whom he'd had a crush on for as long as he could remember. Before Geoff was employed as a Time Rep, he'd never had the courage to formally ask her out—after all those years of nurturing a close friendship, he was terrified of ruining things if he expressed his true feelings. But it's funny what a little thing like saving the entire human race from total annihilation does for one's confidence, and after having thwarted an alien invasion, Geoff finally felt ready to tell Zoë how much he cared about her. He would ask her if she wanted to be more than friends. Compared to defeating the Varsarians, this would be a piece of cake, right?

First of all, though, he wanted to be honest with her. He wanted to tell her what he really did for a living, that he wasn't just a lazy slob who sat around the house occasionally meeting tourists from abroad in between his sessions of eating crisps and trying to beat his high score in *Space Commando*. He had an amazing tale of bravery to share with her, one that would make her see him for who he truly was.

Only then would he tell her how he felt about her.

Only then would he tell her that he loved her.

Unfortunately, before he got the chance to reveal anything, he was taken to one side by the man with the thin moustache and told in no uncertain terms that being honest with Zoë was an extraordinarily bad idea.

"But why?" Geoff had asked at the time. "What harm can it do?"

"Mr. Stamp," the man with the thin moustache had said, interlocking his hands over the small gray desk that sat between them. "I know this is a difficult situation for you to be in, but you have to understand—we can't have you behaving differently now from how you would have behaved before. Time must stay as it is. You wouldn't have asked her out if we hadn't given you this job, so you can't ask her out now that we have. And you can't tell her what you really do for a living, or that you saved the planet from an alien invasion. Imparting this knowledge could drastically alter the space-time continuum. Do you understand? If she starts having an intimate relationship with you, she might not end up marrying her original partner."

"Her *original* partner?" Geoff had asked. "Who's that, then?"

The man had paused for a good thirty seconds before answering.

"I'm sorry, Mr. Stamp, but I can't say. You know the rules."

Geoff couldn't believe his luck—this was a real no-win situation. Before he was hired to be a Time Rep, he would never have had the confidence to ask Zoë out, despite being free to do so. Now that he *was* a Time Rep, it had given him the confidence to approach her, but he had lost his freedom; he could no longer behave the way he wanted to behave. Worst of all, he knew that one day, Zoë would meet someone else, and get married.

Damn this job.

He was so busy thinking about the situation with Zoë that he didn't realize he had just uncovered a piece of mail that really stood out from the rest. The envelope was a shimmering silver color with a glossy feel to it, and looked a lot like something you would pull a nomination list out of at an awards ceremony. The top left corner had a strange logo shaped like a *C*, and on the back, just above the seal, were the words:

CONTINUUM

WHAT WILL YOU CHANGE?

Geoff looked at Tim, running his fingers along the edges of the envelope.

"I knew it," Tim said, clenching his fists. "She really is going after every last Time Rep, isn't she?"

Geoff frowned. "*She?*" he said. "Who's 'she'?"

"I meant 'they,'" Tim said, correcting himself. "*They* really are going after every last Time Rep."

"Hmm…" Geoff tilted his head slightly. "Well, shall I open it?"

"No, why don't you just feel the edges of the envelope for the next ten minutes?" Tim said. "We've still got just over twenty hours before you get shot, so there's plenty of time."

"No need to be like that," Geoff said.

He tore the top of the envelope open, pulled out a single, crisp sheet of paper, and laid it down on the coffee table.

It said:

1 Continuum Square
Lower Thames Street
London
EC3 3LQ
21st January, 4678578 OSGMT

Dear Mr. Stamp,

Allow me to introduce myself. My name is Jennifer Adams, and I run a company called Continuum. You may have heard of us—we offer our customers the chance to travel back in time for their vacation, just like your current employer. At Continuum, however, we do things a little differently. Unlike Time Tours, we have the technology to allow our customers to go back in time and change whatever they like. People can alter history to explore the infinite possibilities of the universe, change things to see how their life might have turned out differently. Or if they like, they can just mess around for fun. Ever wanted to know what would really happen if you stepped on that butterfly in prehistoric times? With Continuum, you can find out. And best of all, it's safe. Your current employer is desperate to learn the secret of our technology, but they never will. It's what has allowed Continuum to change the way people travel back in time, and it's why our motto is "What will you change?"

And that brings me to the reason for getting in touch with you. We want to keep making changes. Our business is growing, and we need Time Reps such as you to come and work for us. We know how Time Tours are treating you. We know you are not paid, we know you have to keep secrets from those around you, and we can only imagine how hard that must be.

But there is another way.

If you choose to come and work for Continuum, all of that will change. We believe Time Reps should earn a decent salary, and we believe you should be able to tell those around you what you do. Thanks to our revolutionary technology, all of that is possible. That's why so many of your colleagues have now left Time Tours to come and work for Continuum. Your employer will not have shared this with you, but they are in trouble. Over half of their Time Reps are now employed by us instead, and at the current rate of resignations and lost business, our analysts predict that they will go into bankruptcy in less than a year. But they deserve it. After the way they have treated you, why should you show them any loyalty? Should a company like that really be allowed to remain in business?

So in the spirit of writing a letter that concerns time travel, I will finish simply by asking you to think about the future. Do you want to spend it working for Time Tours, or do you think you deserve something better? We think you deserve something better—we think you deserve to work for Continuum. All you need to do is ask yourself one question: If you're not happy working for Time Tours, what will you change?

If you want to get in touch, our doors are open 24 hours a day.

We look forward to hearing from you.

With kindest regards,

Jennifer Adams
Managing Director
Continuum

Geoff stared at the note for a few moments before saying anything. "Wow," he finally said, leaning back in the sofa and running his fingers through his hair.

"Wow indeed," Tim said, narrowing his eyes. He picked up the letter and read it again.

"Is it true?" Geoff asked.

"Is what true?"

"You know. Is Time Tours in trouble?"

Tim stood up and walked over to the other side of the lounge, stepping over a pile of pants and navigating his way past a number of stray socks that looked like they were trying to organize a prison break from the front room.

"A bit," Tim said. "Tell me—have you noticed anything different about the tourists you've been showing around these past few weeks?"

Geoff thought about this. Now that Tim mentioned it, there had been a few differences. A lot more school trips, groups of students—people going back out of historical interest or educational purposes, rather than to have a holiday per se.

"They do seem a bit less touristy."

"That's the thing—all the proper tourists are going to Continuum," Tim said. "When you've got the choice to use a company that allows you to go back and change whatever you like, why would you ever use us? Unless, of course, you want to see what things were like in an original, unaltered timeline. That's why these days, the only people interested in using Time Tours are historians, or teachers organizing trips for their classes."

"And what's this about the other Time Reps?" Geoff asked. "Is it true that they're all leaving?"

"We *have* had a lot of resignations over the past few months," Tim admitted, leaning against the wall. "We can't compete with what Continuum are offering. A full salary? The ability to go back and change whatever they want? It's incredible."

"But if a Time Rep leaves, why is that a problem for you? Can't you just hire another one?"

"Are you kidding? You know how long it takes to find the right sort of person to be a Time Rep—it took seven years before you were ready for the job. It's not like we can replace these guys overnight. And without a Time Rep to show people around, tourists just aren't interested in visiting a particular destination. The more Reps we lose, the more customers we lose, too. It's a vicious circle."

That was Geoff's least favorite circle, the vicious ones.

"So why can't Time Tours change things and offer us a salary like Continuum does?" Geoff said. "Or at least let us change the past if we want to?"

"Because that's not how our technology works, Geoff. You know how we do things—if we allow any changes to happen to the space-time continuum, the consequences are disastrous. That's why we've got that supercomputer, checking everyone before they go back to make sure they're not going to alter anything."

Ah—the supercomputer. Geoff smiled. This was the machine that was supposedly capable of simulating the precise vibration of every molecule on the planet up to 100,000 years into the future, when humanity had finally left the planet to explore other galaxies, leaving the Earth as a pristine garden world. Whenever somebody traveled back in time, the computer would predict the impact their journey would have on the course of history, then compare it to the precise model of the space-time continuum stored in its databanks. If it detected even the slightest variation from the final second of its model, it would raise an alarm and prevent that person from going back.

It was this computer that had first labeled Geoff as "one of the most insignificant people who had ever lived" when it first identified him as a potential Time Rep candidate. Someone apparently less important to the world than certain types of mushroom. In the end, though, the machine couldn't have been more wrong—in fact, the only way it could have looked more stupid to all its computer friends would be if it had decided to change its operating system to Windows Vista, and then boot up an unpatched copy of *Battlefield 4* for good measure.

When it came to predicting Geoff's insignificance as a human being, it turned out that the supercomputer had a major loophole in its programming, one that was deliberately exploited to make it overlook the fact that Geoff unwittingly prevented an alien invasion in the twenty-first century. Through a series of events that Geoff still wasn't sure he understood, he was eventually able to expose the loophole, alert his friends, and go back in time to defeat the aliens before they invaded in a spectacular space battle. And at one point during this battle, when all hope was lost, it was *he* who had figured out the enemy's critical weakness. *He* was the one who had taken command of the Earth's entire defense fleet and destroyed a key enemy ship by ramming it into oblivion. His quick thinking had ended up turning the battle in humanity's favor that day, and it was no exaggeration to say that if it weren't for him, everyone would be dead. Except the aliens, of course, who would be alive and well, roaming the planet.

So it was especially frustrating not to be able to tell anyone about all of this—particularly Zoë, given how impressed he thought she would be—and talking to her with such a huge secret hanging over his head made it impossible for him to act natural around her. When they met up, he found himself just regressing back to being the *old* Geoffrey Stamp—a nice guy, sure, but a man whose idea of responsibility was making sure he used all the milk before it went off. They talked about films and games and TV shows and the weather and other trivial things, but that was it. He would love to have known how Zoë would react if he ever told her what he really did for a living.

"So…this part where they say I could go back in time and change whatever I like," Geoff said. "Can they really let me do that?"

"Apparently," Tim said. "You thinking about Zoë? If you went and worked for these guys, you could tell her what you really do. You could tell her that you saved the world."

Geoff smiled. "I suppose, but I still don't understand. If I told her the truth about me, wouldn't that change the course of history? She'd start behaving differently, and that would have all kinds of nasty ramifications on future events, right?"

"In theory, that's correct," Tim said. "But somehow,

Continuum are able to send people back in time a special way, allowing them to change whatever they want and return to the future with no consequences whatsoever."

"But how is that possible?"

"From what I understand, when a tourist goes back, they are given a device that allows them to jump back and forth through time and make whatever changes they like. However, once their holiday is over, Continuum doesn't just bring them back the normal way; they *reverse* them back out again, undoing everything the tourist changed on the way back out again. Think of it as erasing a line you've drawn through a maze, back to the entrance. The clever part, though, is the fact that everyone retains the memory of what they changed, despite the fact that it technically never happened."

"Wow," Geoff said. "That *is* pretty clever."

"Tell me about it. Our scientists have been trying to replicate the technology ever since Continuum first appeared on the scene, but so far they've had no luck."

Geoff nodded to himself.

This was fascinating.

"Why do you ask?" Tim said. "You tempted to go and work for them?"

"Tempted, yes," Geoff said. "But I don't think I ever would."

"Why not?"

"Why not? Isn't it obvious? 'Dear Mr. Stamp,'" he said, picking up the letter from the table and pretending to read from it, "'We've got this great job for you at Continuum. You get paid, you can ask out that girl you like, you are given free sweets every day, and in short, everything is amazing. Lots of Love, Jennifer thingy. P.S. We should probably mention that if you do come and work for us, someone will end up shooting you in the back, but hopefully this isn't an issue. See you at the interview!'" He tossed the paper back down on the table. "No thanks. Before I do anything, I want to work out why someone tried to kill me."

"You mean why someone is *going* to try and kill you," Tim corrected him.

"Yes, why someone is going to have tried to...wait, I'm confused—what are you saying?"

"I'm saying it hasn't happened yet. No one has tried to kill you."

"Right—let's start again. I want to know why someone is *going* to try and kill me. Better?"

Tim nodded.

"So let's start thinking about suspects," Geoff said, picking up the letter again. "First of all, who is this Jennifer Adams?"

"Oh, Jennifer Adams...Jennifer Adams..." Tim said, walking back across the lounge and sitting in the armchair opposite Geoff.

"Yes, Jennifer Adams," Geoff said impatiently. "Don't just walk around repeating her name. Who is she?"

"Jennifer is many things," Tim said. "She has a brilliant mind, she's a keen businesswoman, and she's absolutely ruthless."

"You sound like you know a lot about her," Geoff said.

"I should do," Tim said. "She used to work for Time Tours. It was a bit before my time, but everyone in the company knows who Jennifer Adams is. She's a legend at the company."

"She worked for Time Tours?" Geoff said. "Doing what?"

"She's the one who designed our supercomputer."

"Oh, right," Geoff said, taking a moment to digest what Tim had just told him. "Wait a minute—I thought Eric designed it?"

"No, Eric was the one who wrote the algorithm it uses to predict causality. Jennifer was the one who was able to invent a computer with the level of storage and processing power he required to run it."

"How long ago was that?" Geoff said.

"About twenty years, just as Eric was finishing his algorithm. He needed a computer capable of crunching some serious numbers very quickly, and Jennifer was the one who gave it to him. Apparently it was she who came up with the idea of using a lattice of artificial micro-black holes to store that much data. And it was she who worked out how to read information back through Hawking radiation. She's a goddamn genius."

"Funny," Geoff said, "I had no idea. From speaking to Eric, you'd think he was the one who thought up the whole thing."

"Yes, and that was Jennifer's problem too. She thought he took all the credit for their work. She respected him for getting his first Nobel Prize years before they met, when he suggested the initial theory behind his algorithm in a bar, but when he got his second prize the day the facility opened, she was furious. She believed that without her computer, Eric's algorithm would have been nothing more than a nice theory, and she couldn't believe he didn't give her any recognition for her work. Back then, she'd only been out of university for a few years, and the Nobel Prize board questioned how someone so young could have had so much influence on a project already managed by a past winner. Right or wrong, they chose not to award her, and although the decision was down to them, she always blamed Eric for not standing up for her, for not refusing his prize unless she was recognized as well."

Geoff knew how she must have felt, to play such a huge role in something only to have everyone just take her achievement for granted. When he had saved the entire planet from annihilation two years ago, everyone around him pretty much just shrugged their shoulders and got back to watching *Britain's Got Talent*.

"So what happened to her?" Geoff said.

"Not long after the incident with Eric, she left Time Tours," Tim said. "Many think she resigned out of pride—that she couldn't bear to work for a man she didn't respect anymore. But there are others who believe she resigned for a different reason: Some believe that back then, Time Tours was actually working on an advanced time-manipulation device, and that the *real* reason Jennifer resigned was because she was able to convince the key scientist developing the tech to leave and help her set up Continuum."

"What do *you* think?" Geoff asked.

"I don't know," Tim replied. "As far as I can tell, there is no record of Time Tours ever working on any such technology. But regardless of which side of the fence you sit, there is one thing everyone agrees on."

"Which is…?"

"Her last words to Eric as she walked out the door."

"Why, what did she say?"

"It was a vow. A vow that one day she would put Time Tours out of business for good."

"Well, it looks like she might be succeeding," Geoff said, giving Tim a smug grin. "You see what happens when you don't give someone the recognition they deserve?"

"You know, I'm beginning to wonder if it might be me that shoots you tomorrow," Tim said.

THREE

Geoff and Tim agreed that the most logical course of action would be for Geoff to just behave as normal for the next twenty-four hours, despite his knowledge of future events. It took a long time for them to reach this agreement—after all, on the one hand, if Geoff changed his behavior, it might have been the very thing that led to his attempted murder. On the other hand, though, *not* changing his behavior might also have led to him getting a bullet in the back. Since there was no way of knowing how the outcome would be affected by the way Geoff chose to behave, in the end they thought it would be best for Geoff to just carry on with his life as per normal. Geoff tried to argue that this meant he could stay in bed playing his Nintendo 3DS under the duvet for the next twenty-four hours, only emerging from his room to make tea and go to the toilet. This was *kind of* normal for him, he'd argued, so what was the problem?

The problem was that the following day he was scheduled to go and meet a class of thirty schoolchildren and their teacher to show them around London's financial district, Canary Wharf. Apparently the kids were doing a project on twenty-first-century architecture, looking at why every building commissioned at this time was a glass skyscraper of some description. Their working hypothesis was that during this period, all the world's architects had suffered from a case of collective amnesia and forgotten that the last thing they built also happened to be a glass skyscraper. ("Good job with that glass skyscraper, guys! What shall we build next? Why, how about a glass skyscraper?")

The teacher had told him that she wanted to meet at ten o'clock in the morning outside Pret A Manger. Unfortunately, at Canary Wharf, like most areas of London, there were at least sixty-five Pret A Mangers within a mile of each other and Geoff wasn't quite sure which one she'd meant. In fact, the only way she could have suggested a less specific meeting place would have been if she'd just said "outside." He was pretty confident he'd be able to figure out where they were eventually, though. After all, he'd played enough role playing games that neglected to give you a waypoint marker on a ten-square-kilometer map to tell you where your next objective was, so finding thirty kids and their teacher would be a piece of cake in comparison.

When he left the house to walk to the station, Zoë was only about four doors down, slotting the usual mail through people's letter boxes—bills, bank statements, and leaflets for a new pizza meal deal. She had her headphones on, her head bopping away to music, and he only had to lay eyes on her for a split second before he felt a soft warmth wash over him, as though he were stepping out of a shadow into the sunlight. It was then that he realized he *had* actually just stepped out of a shadow into the sunlight, but he still decided to give her some credit for the way he felt anyway.

In terms of how she looked, there was nothing particularly exceptional to say about Zoë today—as usual, her long dark hair was tied back into a ponytail, she didn't appear to have much makeup on (if any), and she was wearing her regular postal uniform that fit loosely around her small frame. When she wasn't working she often wore clothes that disguised her figure—square-cut jeans, long baggy t-shirts, big jumpers. She had very simple tastes in fashion. In fact, if she ever committed a crime and a witness were asked to identify her, her only distinguishing features were the four piercings in her left ear and the tattoo of an owl on her back that was rarely on show. If you didn't know her, you would think that this was a girl who didn't like attention.

However, all that changed whenever she was on stage.

When Zoë wasn't posting letters she played in a band. The band wasn't particularly well known—just a group of girls who got together every week and played down the local pub. Geoff went to watch them most weeks. Zoë was their lead guitarist, and when she was on stage it was like she was a different person—

her normally straight hair would be frizzy and flying all over the place (while still attached to her head, of course), her pale skin would be streaked with flashes of pink and blue makeup, and her high cheekbones would be dusted with a dark blush, making her face look thin and gaunt. To him, it was hard to believe that this normally timid-looking girl was capable of adopting such a different persona when it came to her music, but then again, that was nothing compared to what Zoë would think if she ever found out about Geoff's double life as a time-traveling tour guide who'd once saved the planet from total destruction. It would have been like finding out the cat secretly sneaked off every night to thrill audiences by playing a repertoire of Beethoven's classics on the piano.

"Morning, Geoff!" she called out, taking her headphones out of her ears as she saw him.

"Morning," he replied, giving her a wave.

"You off out somewhere?" she said, stepping over a flowerbed as a shortcut into the neighboring garden, one house closer to him.

"Yeah, I thought I'd go and trample through some people's flowerbeds," he said, looking down at her feet.

"Very funny." She rolled her eyes and dug into her shoulder bag to sift through a few envelopes. "Where are you really going?"

"I'm just meeting some tourists in a little while, showing them around Canary Wharf. Some kids on a school trip, actually."

Zoë laughed.

"What's so funny?" Geoff said.

"Nothing—it's just…"

"Yes?"

"I'm just picturing you wandering around, surrounded by all those big banks, and the people in suits, and the expensive bars. You're, like, the last person I would expect to find showing a bunch of schoolkids around that place," Zoë said.

She was right—he wasn't particularly familiar with the area. It was like asking a horse to show you around the north pole.

"So what are these kids working on?" Zoë said. "Some kind

of economics project?" This time there was a fence in between Zoë and the next house, but that didn't stop her. She grabbed the top of it with both hands and vaulted over in one smooth movement, straightening her jacket as she landed.

"Ancient history, apparently," Geoff said, only realizing after he'd spoken how strange that sounded if you didn't know when these kids had traveled from. He quickly inhaled a lungful of air in the hope that he could somehow suck the sound back in again.

"Ancient history? But isn't Canary Wharf pretty new compared to the rest of London? Why would you go there for a history project, of all places?"

"Did I say ancient history?" Geoff said, trying not to let his eyes look side to side (a classic sign that he was hiding something) as his eyes looked side to side. "I meant business studies. That's it—they're doing business studies."

"Well, that makes more sense," Zoë said, not appearing to notice Geoff flustering. She posted a couple of letters through his neighbor's door and headed up the garden path to the road. "Which way are you going now, then?"

"Down to the station," Geoff replied, taking a few deep breaths. That was close.

"Great—fancy walking with me while I do the rest of this street?"

"Sure," Geoff said. After all, it was the only reason he'd chosen to leave the house an hour and a half earlier than he needed to, but she didn't need to know that.

"So, how have you been?" Zoë asked, lifting a small package out of her bag. It was addressed to the house three doors down. "Anything new happening in your life?"

Let's see, Geoff thought. *I've just learned that in less than a day, someone is going to try and kill me. I've also learned that I'm going to lose my memory, that I get sent back in time for no explicable reason, and that I will have less comprehension about my predicament than a cabbage that's just been entered into a best cabbage competition. Other than that, everything's pretty normal.*

"No, nothing new with me," Geoff lied. "You?"

"Oh, just working on a couple of new songs with the girls, but that's about it. Other than that, things are pretty much the same…"

The last time they'd spoken, a few days ago, Zoë had told Geoff that they'd sent off a couple of demo tracks to a music label, just to see if there was any interest. He assumed the band hadn't heard back, seeing as how she hadn't mentioned anything, but he decided to ask anyway.

"Did anyone get back to you from that record company?" he said.

"What? Oh…no. No, it's only been a few days, so I doubt we'll hear anything yet, if we ever hear anything at all. I'm sure these people get hundreds of CDs through the door all the time."

Zoë looked down at the package she was holding again, opened the gate of the house it was addressed to, and walked toward the front door.

"Well, you never know," Geoff said.

"I just hope we're not wasting our time with all this," Zoë said, posting the package through the letter box and turning back toward the street. "My boss thinks I'm mad, spending so much of my free time with the band. He's worried that all those late nights in the pub might affect my work one day, and that I might as well give up and focus on my career, since we'll probably never make it anyway…"

"You're not wasting your time," Geoff reassured her. "And you shouldn't let other people tell you what you can and can't do. After all, whether you succeed in making it or not, if you don't try now, you'll always look back on your life thinking, 'What if?' At least this way, when you're older you won't have any regrets about not trying."

Zoë smiled, closing the front gate and moving on to the next house.

"Don't listen to your boss at the post office," Geoff said. "He's not your real boss anyway—*you* are."

"You're right, Geoff. Sometimes I just wish I could see into the future, see if this is all just a silly dream. I mean, don't get me wrong—I love playing in the band and I'll keep doing it regardless of whether we make it big, but it would be nice to know whether it's worth getting our hopes up or not. What if I'm making a mistake dedicating so much time to the music? What if I should really be doing something else with my life?"

Geoff didn't say anything. There were so many times when he'd been tempted to use the technology at Time Tours to find out what happened to Zoë in the future—not only to see whether her dreams of making it as a musician came true, but to find out other things as well. Who would she meet in the future? Would she ever get married? Did she end up having any children? Did she lead a long and happy life? He had the opportunity to find out the answers to all of these questions and more, but he just couldn't bring himself to do it.

Part of his reason for not finding out about Zoë's future was just out of respect. He didn't see what right he had to know about her destiny, and any attempt to do so felt a bit creepy, as though he were nothing more than a technologically advanced stalker. The other part that stopped him was fear. Fear of what he'd find out. What if she ended up with a total loser? Someone who didn't treat her right? Or what if something bad happened to her? What if she had an accident or suffered from a disease? Time Tours would never let him intervene in any way, so if there was a problem with Zoë's future and he wasn't allowed to do anything about it, he wasn't sure he would be able to live with that.

In the end, he'd decided it was better not to know anything. If he didn't know what was going to happen, there was always the possibility that everything would turn out fine. This was the same reason he refused to watch the final episode of the *Battlestar Galactica* reboot—if he didn't see it, he could always believe that the writers were somehow able to tie up all the ridiculous loose ends and plot holes in a satisfying way and that they didn't just leave it up to the viewer's imagination to resolve everything that made no sense. Like everything to do with Starbuck from season four onward.

It wasn't long before Zoë and Geoff reached the end of the

street. Zoë needed to double back and do the other side of the road, while Geoff needed to cross over and carry on for another mile or so before he got to the station. Since he had the time, for a moment he considered accompanying her on the rest of her round before heading to Canary Wharf, but he thought this might look a little strange and decided to leave her to it. So they said their goodbyes and went their separate ways.

Had he turned around for one last look at Zoë, he would have noticed a very familiar face waiting for her on the other side of the street: a man smiling nervously in a smart suit, with a clean-shaven face and a new haircut.

But Geoff didn't turn around for one last look at Zoë, so he saw nothing.

• • •

By the time Geoff arrived at Canary Wharf, it had only just gone half past eight in the morning, meaning there was still an hour and a half to go before he needed to begin his grand tour of all the Pret A Mangers in the local area to try to find the class of schoolchildren he was supposed to be meeting. And if the events of yesterday were to be believed, it was less than seven hours before he would leave Time Tours, have a shave, get his hair cut, borrow Tim's suit, join Continuum, get shot in the back, and materialize on Tower Bridge yesterday. How on Earth was he going to do all that in seven hours? He had enough trouble doing the washing up in seven hours, so the thought that he was supposedly about to experience all these events seemed so impossible it was almost reassuring.

As it was quite a pleasant morning, Geoff decided to sit outside a coffee shop to pass the time, sipping on an enormous cup of frothy milk with a faintly bitter aftertaste, or a "grande latte," as it was described on the menu. At this time of day, the streets were bustling with various commuters making their way to work. Many were tapping things into their mobile phones, others were trying to read the newspaper as they walked, and the rest were trying not to be bumped into by the people not looking where they were going.

Zoë was right—Geoff had never really been to Canary Wharf before, and he was struggling to think of what interesting facts he could tell these schoolchildren about the place. When he showed tourists around a particular location, he usually had some historical anecdotes up his sleeve to entertain the crowd—a list of famous people who had once lived there, important events that had taken place on the same spot, that sort of thing. With Canary Wharf, though, the place was so new there wasn't much to say, apart from the fact that there was quite a nice Waitrose and the underground station was the only one in London where commuters politely queued to get on the train, rather than adopting the "huddle around the doors and fight your way onto the carriage" technique that seemed popular everywhere else. He knew the area was one of London's major business districts and everyone gave you a strange look if you went into a bar and ordered a drink that cost anything less than a small fortune, but that was where his knowledge ended.

Geoff was about halfway through his cup of frothy milk, thinking about what he could talk to the children about, when he noticed a man walking straight toward him through the crowd, looking at his watch.

Geoff placed his cup down on the table and stood up.

"William?" he said, looking the man up and down as he approached. Unless he was mistaken, it was William Boyle—one of the Time Reps from the Great Fire of London in 1666. Seeing him here wasn't necessarily that unusual, since one of the perks of being a Time Rep was that you were allowed to go wherever you wanted as long as you didn't change anything, but still—it was unexpected to see him here, of all places.

"That's right, Mr. Stamp," William said, smiling. "It's me." Compared to the William Boyle who had shown Geoff around the Great Fire of London when he'd first gotten the job as a Time Rep, this man looked completely different. Instead of his hair being all messy, it was gelled back. Instead of having dirt smeared on his face and blotchy sores on his skin, his complexion looked healthy, his face clean shaven. He wore a black suit with a white shirt undone at the collar, and his shoes were polished to a fine sheen. For a moment Geoff couldn't believe his eyes—it was like looking at a contestant on *Stars in Their Eyes* after they've been through the makeup department.

"This is a surprise," Geoff said, giving him a frown. "What brings you to the twenty-first century?"

"One moment," William said, holding his finger up and checking his watch again. "Eight thirty-five a.m.," he said, making a mental note. "Sorry, what were you saying?"

"What brings you to the twenty-first century?"

"I was looking for you, actually," William replied. For some reason, William's use of language sounded different from before. When Geoff had first met this man in 1666, he'd spoken in a very precise manner, with a slow, old-fashioned rhythm to his words. Now his voice sounded much more relaxed and modern.

"You were looking for me?" Geoff said. "Why?"

"Because I've got something incredible to show you."

Geoff wasn't getting his hopes up. William Boyle was from the seventeenth century—what could he possibly show him that he hadn't seen before? A new breed of carrot, maybe?

"What's that, then?" Geoff said, trying not to look too uninterested.

William smiled. "I'm going to show you what you're missing, Mr. Stamp. I'm going to show you what you're missing by not working for Continuum."

"Continuum?" Geoff shifted his weight from one leg to the other. "You mean you left Time Tours? You're working for them now?"

"I am indeed," William said, "and let me tell you—it is amazing."

"Is it now?" Geoff said, taking a moment to look around. He started to feel a little bit nervous, as if he were watching a horror movie and expecting a jump-scare at any moment. Could this be the beginning of the very chain of events that nearly got him killed?

"Do you remember when we last met?" William said. "When you were first made a Time Rep?"

"Yes. Yes I do."

"You weren't best pleased with the fact that we didn't get paid, remember? That we weren't allowed to buy our own place, or marry the girl of our dreams? All that stuff?"

"That was two years ago, William," Geoff said. "I'm okay with that now. I understand why it has to be that way."

"Well I don't. I hadn't thought about it until I met you, but ever since that conversation, I've always wondered what it would be like to travel through time without Time Tours watching over my shoulder. What it would be like to be able to go wherever I liked, whenever I liked, and change whatever I liked."

"You've certainly changed your tune," Geoff said. "The last time we spoke, you said you were grateful for everything Time Tours had done for you. Wasn't it you who tried to tell me that despite the fact that you weren't paid, your new life was better than the old one? Thanks to Time Tours, you said, you weren't living in the street or dying from the plague, right?"

William nodded.

"But now you've gone off them?"

"Mr. Stamp. At Time Tours I was a prisoner. But now I am free."

"I don't understand, William—what's brought this on?"

"I was approached by Continuum, Mr. Stamp. They showed me what I was missing out on by not working for them, and from that moment, there was no way I could go back to Time Tours." He leaned closer to Geoff and lowered his voice to a whisper. "No way."

"Okay, William," Geoff said, taking a step back, "I'm going to be honest now—you're really scaring me."

William stood up straight again and smiled. "There's no need to be scared, Mr. Stamp. I'm only here to offer you a demonstration, nothing more. I'm trying to see as many Time Reps as I can—I want to show you all the kinds of things you can do if you work for Continuum."

"Oh, there's no need to worry about a demonstration,"

Geoff said. "I'll just take your word for it: working for Continuum is really, really great." He gave William a thumbs-up. "Got it."

"No, Mr. Stamp," he said, taking what looked like a set of car keys out of his pocket. "You don't get it. I have to show you, otherwise you'll never understand."

Geoff glanced around at the hundreds of people walking past. "Whatever it is, why don't we do this somewhere quieter? You don't want to do anything in front of all these people, do you?"

"Yes, Mr. Stamp," he said, pressing a small button on the car keys. "That's precisely what I want to do."

All of a sudden, a high-pitched engine noise filled the air, and the people who had been merrily walking into each other because they were too busy playing with their phones stopped what they were doing and looked up.

The noise was coming from a flying sports car, descending to where William was standing. The car was silver, with a sleek body, blacked-out windows, and a large spoiler sticking out of the back. The underside was made entirely of reinforced glass so the driver could see beneath them as well as in front and side to side. It was an impressive machine, and Geoff had seen hundreds of similar vehicles in the London of the future. There was just one problem, though—as far as Geoff could remember, antigravity cars weren't going to be invented for another five hundred and fifty years.

As such, revealing a flying car to the people of the twenty-first century really wasn't something you were supposed to do if you wanted the space-time continuum to behave itself.

"Oh my God!" a lady called out, pointing up at the sky. "It's a UFO!"

"What do you think?" William called out over the sound of the engine as the car landed beside him. "This is the kind of thing Continuum lets you bring back with you from the future! Amazing, don't you think?"

Geoff's mouth hung open. He couldn't begin to comprehend the damage William was probably doing to the course of history. Putting aside the fact that a piece of technology from the future was in full view of the public over five and a half centuries before it was invented, all these people had now stopped what they were doing instead of going about their normal routine; they weren't nearly bumping into the people they were supposed to be nearly bumping into because they were all on their phones, or meeting the people they were supposed to be meeting, or having the conversations they were supposed to having. And later on, they weren't just going to go home, eat their dinner, and carry on with their lives as normal, watching the latest episode of *Downton Abbey*—they were going to be on the phone, telling all their friends what they'd seen today. The shock waves from this were probably not just off the chart, but off the desk the chart was on, out of the room the desk was in, in a lift, out of the building, and in a taxi on the way to the airport with a one-way ticket to God-knows-where in its top pocket.

"What the hell are you doing? You can't show that thing to these people!"

"Yes I can!" William said, "I told you—Continuum lets you hire one of these to bring back with you from the future! It's got this autopilot feature that brings the car straight to your location with the tap of a button! Pretty neat, huh?"

"Okay!" Geoff said, walking toward William, "You've made your point—it's pretty neat! Now stop this, okay?"

"Oh, this is nothing," William said, opening the door to the car and climbing inside. He closed the door behind him and wound the window down. "I've had a few modifications installed as well. Watch this!"

Geoff watched as two panels slid back on either side of the car's body, revealing metal cannons that extended out like robotic arms. Then suddenly, the car took off and accelerated through the air toward the skyscrapers of Canary Wharf at a blistering speed, weaving in between the buildings and swooping down at people like an eagle nose-diving toward its prey.

After a few minutes of performing an array of dangerous acrobatics in the air and ruining any chance Geoff thought he might have in explaining the whole incident away to everyone as a very elaborate magic trick, William brought the car around and hovered a reasonable distance from the main cluster of office blocks ahead. Geoff covered his face with his hands and looked up through his fingers. He was completely helpless to stop what William was doing, and he had a bad feeling about what was coming next.

That feeling turned out to be completely justified as a low hum filled Geoff's ears, and he watched as a bright red laser beam fired out from the car, slicing through Canary Wharf's skyline of tower blocks in a single diagonal streak. It was like seeing a samurai sword cutting through some flimsy tissue paper. Then the beam turned off, and for a moment nothing happened.

Everyone stood around in silence.

That was before the law of physics got its breath back and managed to catch up with what had just happened. All around, the buildings began to slide apart where they had been touched by the beam, falling to the ground in giant wedges of steel and glass with a deafening crash.

This was one of the most horrific things Geoff had ever seen, and as was customary with all horrific events, it was at this point that everyone decided it was probably a good idea to start running around screaming.

FOUR

Geoff's body was completely paralyzed with shock. He didn't move. He didn't breathe. He didn't even blink. In fact, he looked so completely lifeless that if he'd painted himself silver and laid a hat on the ground, he probably could have passed himself off as one of those street performers who pretended to be statues in Covent Garden. He wouldn't have made much money, though, since every passerby wouldn't have really been in the mood to stop running for their lives to see if they had some loose change on them.

He simply could not believe what he had just witnessed—a Time Rep from nearly four hundred years ago had been able to show up out of nowhere and lay waste to Canary Wharf in a matter of seconds. What was once quite a nice part of London boasting an impressive sixty-five Pret A Mangers had now been turned into a mountain of broken glass, twisted metal, and crumbling concrete—and what was worse, now there were only twenty-three Pret A Mangers left standing, and only ten of those were still able to serve hot soup. Fires were breaking out everywhere, thick clouds of black smoke were billowing into the sky, and dead bodies were scattered all over the place. He knew William had said that working for Continuum allowed him to travel through time and change whatever he liked, but he'd assumed there were at least a couple of rules to follow, like not going around massacring thousands of innocent people, for instance.

But apparently not—Continuum must have had even fewer regulations than if you worked as a city trader.

"William!" Geoff cried out at the top of his voice, looking up at the flying car. "Are you crazy!? What have you done?"

Through the glass underside of the vehicle he could see William looking back down at him, a broad grin spread across his face. How could he be enjoying this?

Suddenly, William sent the car into free fall toward Geoff, only pulling the nose up at the last minute to come to a stop safely beside him. Once the car had landed, he switched the engine off and opened the door, swiveling around in his seat to place one foot slowly on the pavement, followed by the other. As he stood up to get out of the vehicle, he looked toward the view of London's decimated financial district and leaned over the top of the door, nodding to himself as if expressing some morbid satisfaction with his work. Any people that had been even remotely close to where he had landed were now running in the opposite direction, no doubt terrified as to what this insane person might do next.

Geoff paced over to William, grabbed him by the lapels of his suit jacket, and pushed him across the bonnet of the car.

"Mr. Stamp," William said, lifting himself off the car and dusting himself down casually. "Please calm down."

"Calm down? Look what you've done!" Geoff said, pointing toward a skyscraper behind him as one side of it broke away from the rest of the structure and collapsed across the street below.

Behind William in the distance, Geoff noticed three army trucks skidding to a stop. As the wheels screeched, swarms of soldiers began to pour out of the backs of the vehicles, each one running toward them with their gun at the ready.

"Oh dear," William said, watching as the men and women got closer and closer. "Do you think I'm trouble?"

Geoff looked up as a roar of jet engines echoed all around. Up in the sky, a wave of fighter planes flew overhead, which had no doubt been scrambled in the hope they could provide some sort of defense against whatever had just attacked. "It doesn't matter what century you're in—when you destroy everything in sight, it doesn't do much for your popularity!"

"Then I suppose it's time for us to get out of here," William said, walking back toward the car.

"You're not going anywhere," Geoff said, moving to intercept William. "And what do you mean by 'it's time for *us* to get out of here,' exactly?"

William pulled a gun out from his pocket and pointed it toward Geoff. The gun didn't look like a conventional pistol—it was quite bulky, it had some sort of LED display on the side, and the barrel was strangely wide, as though it fired particularly large bullets.

It took a moment for Geoff to comprehend that he was probably now in quite a bit of danger, but when he did, his mind leapt straight into action, trying to recall if he had anything useful in his own pockets he could point back with.

He had a pen with the cap missing.

Some chewing gum.

His train ticket.

A bit of his coat zip that had broken off a few months ago that he was meaning to get sewn back on at some point.

Well, it was a start. Maybe he could combine the items together somehow like Guybrush Threepwood would have done in the *Monkey Island* graphic adventure games, creating a makeshift device to counteract William's gun?

"I mean you're coming with me," William said.

Geoff was still trying to think of some way to combine all the items in his pockets to create something that would help him get out of this situation. He'd gotten as far as using the gum to stick the zip to the pen before he realized this wasn't going to get him anywhere, and slowly raised his hands in the air.

"But why?" Geoff said, taking a step back. "What do you need me for?"

"I told you—I want to show you something." William motioned Geoff toward the passenger side of the car. "I want to give you a demonstration of what working for Continuum really means. What it *really* allows you to do…"

"So blowing up Canary Wharf wasn't the demonstration?" Geoff said.

"No, no no no…" William smirked, waving his hand at the destruction he'd caused as though he were just dismissing a silly piece of gossip. "That was only the beginning. Now please, get in the car."

Geoff shuddered. If this was only the beginning of what William wanted to show him, what the hell was next?

He looked past William again at the approaching armed forces—there must have been at least fifty men and women dressed in camouflage uniforms, marching toward them steadily in some sort of cover formation. As they got closer, the soldiers split into four separate groups and created a wide circular perimeter around them.

"But—we can't just leave!" Geoff said, trying to stall for time as he made his way around to the passenger door of the car. "Do you have any idea what sort of damage you've just done to the space-time continuum?"

"That's exactly what we're going to find out," William replied. "Now will you get a move on?"

Geoff did as he was told, opening the passenger door to William's car and sliding into the seat. As he sat down, three thick leather straps snapped across his legs and torso from behind, holding his body in place like a snake wrapping itself around something it didn't want getting away. He struggled against the restraints, but it was no use—he couldn't move.

"Okay, are we ready?" William said, sitting down next to Geoff and shutting his door. He wound up his window and pressed a flashing green button on the dashboard of the car, holding the steering wheel with the other hand.

Outside, Geoff could see one soldier barking orders at the rest of the troops, but as the inside of the car was completely soundproof, he couldn't make out a word of what was being said. However, as he watched fifty men and women raise their weapons and point them directly at the car, he started to form a pretty good idea as to what their strategy might be.

"Um…William," Geoff said, making another futile effort to move in his seat. "Don't you think you should maybe surrender now?"

"Surrender?" William said, tapping a few more buttons on

the dashboard. Geoff felt the car vibrate as the engines roared to life. "Why would I want to do that?"

Geoff nodded toward the circle of guns trained on their position. "Because we're about to have the shit blown out of us?"

"Don't be silly," William said. "The safety features of this car are designed to protect us from a fall from ten thousand feet. The windows are reinforced, the body is armor-plated—they could drop a bomb on this thing and it wouldn't make a dent. Now, would you like some music?"

"Sure! You got anything relaxing to take my mind off things, like maybe the theme tune to *Sesame Street*?" Outside, he watched as the soldier who had been talking raised his hand up in the air, then swung it down in their direction. As he did so, the army opened fire from all around, muzzles flashing as a hail of bullets hit the car from every direction.

Geoff shut his eyes. This was it.

Only it wasn't it.

Not even remotely.

With his eyes closed, he couldn't sense anything. There was none of the searing pain he was expecting from his body being shredded into a million pieces by the onslaught of firepower, no noise from the guns, not even the slightest vibration from the bullets hitting the car. In fact, it was so peaceful he might as well have been relaxing in the bathtub with a flannel over his face.

As he opened his eyes again, he could see bullets ricocheting off every surface outside, harmlessly bouncing away as though the army had accidentally replaced their ammunition with ping-pong balls. It was strange for such an intensely visceral thing to be happening with no accompanying sound, and for a moment it was like watching an action movie with the volume off. This was actually Geoff's preferred way of seeing many action movies, so he didn't have to listen to the horrendous dialogue (*The Transporter* in particular was much more bearable in silence, he'd discovered), but in this instance it felt strange, like he was somehow detached from reality.

William was nonchalantly fiddling with the radio, completely unfazed by what was happening outside. "Here we are," he said.

"Let's Dance" by David Bowie had just started to play. William turned the volume up and smiled. "You like David Bowie?" he said over the funky intro.

"Uh...yes. Yes I do," Geoff replied.

"So do I," William said. "In fact, I like all music. Before I was made a Time Rep, I'd never heard a single piece of music. Nothing. I'd never heard an orchestra; I'd never even heard anyone play an instrument. All I knew of music was when people sang in the streets, and those were usually songs about death. And do you know what all songs about death have in common, Mr. Stamp?"

Geoff shook his head.

"They're all crap."

The army was still firing at the vehicle, but they didn't appear to be doing any damage, despite the fact that they were trying *really* hard. Even the odd grenade thrown in their direction didn't do anything as it exploded against the windshield.

William released what looked like a handbrake to his side and pulled down on the steering wheel. As he did, the car began to ascend into the sky.

"Can you imagine that?" William continued, turning to Geoff. "Can you imagine never having heard a piece of music your whole life? That's what it's like for most of the people in my time, yet here you can put thousands of songs in a little box and listen to them anywhere you like. People in the twenty-first century take so much for granted, it's unbelievable."

Geoff turned his head to look out of the window as the car climbed a few hundred feet in the air. Down below, the army had stopped firing, although the man who had been barking orders at the rest of the troops was now shouting something into a radio attached to his shoulder.

"Where are you taking me?" Geoff said, turning his attention back to William.

"Well," William replied, "you asked me if I knew what

damage I'd just caused to the space-time continuum, and the answer is no, I don't. So that's what we're going to find out."

Geoff sighed and looked down through the glass floor at the city. He could see flashing lights everywhere, with police cars, ambulances, and fire engines tearing through the streets toward the ruins of Canary Wharf.

"Look at this." William nudged Geoff and pointed ahead through the windshield.

Geoff looked up and saw three Harrier jump jets maneuvering themselves directly in front of them, their engines rotating down to allow them to hover in the sky. They were only a few meters ahead, the nose of each plane pointing straight toward them.

The plane at the front of the formation edged forward. Inside the cockpit, the pilot lifted up the visor on her helmet. She then pointed toward them and then to the ground, repeating the gesture a number of times. Presumably this meant she wanted them to land, although what she was doing did also resemble that dance move from *Saturday Night Fever*.

"What do you think she wants?" William asked.

"I suspect they might want you to give yourself up."

"Hmph," William hmphed. "I don't think so."

And with that, he jabbed a small red button on the dashboard and pushed the steering wheel to the right. The car responded immediately, shooting forward at an incredible speed and banking to the right. Unfortunately, William didn't quite manage to avoid one of the Harriers, clipping the wing of the plane as the car accelerated away.

"Shit!" Geoff screamed, watching in horror as the jet spun out of the sky in a spiral of smoke and smashed into a street below, the wreckage tearing through rows and rows of traffic in a blaze of fire and molten metal.

He hadn't seen a parachute.

Despite the damage they had done to the plane, the car they were flying was completely fine. This thing was strong.

"Whoops," William said, leveling the car off as it continued to accelerate away. "Didn't mean to do that!" He looked through the glass beneath him as scores of people scrambled away from the crashed plane. "Sorry!" he called out.

And then a missile shot past them.

Geoff looked around, his eyes following the missile's vapor trail back the way it came. It led to the wing of one of the two remaining Harriers, which had both turned around to give chase.

"They're firing on us!" Geoff screamed.

"I know!" William said, banking the car to the right as another missile whistled past. "Isn't this amazing? Bet you never thought you'd be doing this today!"

William pushed down on the steering wheel, sending the car soaring up through a layer of cloud and high up into the atmosphere. The Harriers were struggling to keep up, but every so often a missile narrowly missed them, indicating that they weren't too far behind.

"Okay, let's see what these guys can do," William said, pushing the steering wheel forward. The car responded by entering a steep dive, piercing the thin layer of cloud again and hurtling toward the ground at an incredible speed. As they descended, another missile shot past, missing its target again but exploding against the roof of an apartment block directly ahead of them. Or was that beneath them? With all the sudden changes in direction, Geoff was more disoriented than the time he'd tried to take a shortcut through IKEA to avoid following the path around the all showrooms.

Just as they were about to hit the ground, William pulled the steering wheel down hard, leveling the car off a few hundred meters in the air. Behind them, the two pursuing Harriers weren't able to maneuver out of their dive fast enough, and Geoff watched in despair as they crashed into the ground in a ball of flames.

"William!" Geoff cried out, "Please, you've got to stop this!"

William laughed, wiping a tear from his eye. "I knew it was worth renting one of these things."

"William!"

"All right, all right," William said. "I'll stop."

Geoff shut his eyes and tried to focus on his breathing.

Air in.

Air out.

This couldn't be happening.

It was impossible.

It had to be a nightmare.

Or a horrible dream.

No, wait—that was the same thing as a nightmare.

Focus on breathing.

When he opened his eyes again, the car was hovering in midair with an aerial view of London in front of them. Over in the east, Canary Wharf was shrouded in plumes of smoke. William held a small device in his hand. At first glance it looked a bit like a tablet computer—a thin, rectangular thing with a large touchscreen. William was pressing a few buttons on the screen.

"What are you doing?" Geoff said.

"You'll see," William replied, tapping away. Once he had finished his tapping, he put the tablet to one side, reached into his pocket, and pulled out a syringe. "Now, hold still, will you?"

"W-what's that?" Geoff said, trying his best not to hold still at all. The syringe looked pretty serious. It was filled with a red liquid and ended in a cluster of six needles, which in turn surrounded a larger one in the middle. William bit the plastic safety cap off the end and spat it to the floor.

Geoff hated injections. Particularly ones administered to him under duress by lunatics.

"Wait!" Geoff said, his body shaking as William held his right wrist down and pressed the tip of the syringe against his skin. "I'm really not a fan of needles!"

"I'm sorry," William said, plunging the needles into Geoff's arm. "But unless this serum is inside you, you won't get to experience the next part properly."

"N-next part?" Geoff said, wincing as a shot of pain seared through his body. "What next part? And what is that stuff?"

"Don't worry," William said. "It's perfectly safe." He withdrew the syringe and tossed it behind him.

Looking back, Geoff could see a number of empty syringes lying across the back seat.

"How many other Time Reps have you visited?" Geoff said, glancing down at his wrist. He could see six small pinpricks of blood on his skin, surrounding a larger one made by the central needle.

"Oh, just a few," William said, reaching for his tablet again. "Now, watch this."

William pressed a symbol displayed on the tablet's screen. The symbol looked like a bit like a fast-forward button you would get on a video remote, and as William held it down, the world around them began to react as though it were indeed being fast-forwarded. Time appeared to be speeding up before their very eyes—the sun started to set quickly, then rise again, then set, the movement getting faster and faster the longer William held the button down. Clouds quickly transformed from calm brushstrokes of white into pools of liquid spooling across the sky. And down below, traffic moved at lightning speed, with streaks of headlights flashing on and off on the roads as the days and nights rushed past.

In the distance, Geoff watched in fascination as Canary Wharf started to regain its form. In a matter of moments, the cloud of black smoke dispersed, all the rubble was cleared away, and the skyscrapers were rebuilt twice as tall.

It was a truly incredible sight.

"Amazing, isn't it?" William said, holding up the tablet for Geoff to see. "This thing is standard issue when you join Continuum. The damn thing allows you to control time however you like! Can you believe that?"

Geoff was about to ask William what he meant by being able to control time however he liked, when suddenly there was a bright flash. Despite still being restrained, he instinctively tried to reach up to cover his eyes, but just as quickly as the flash had appeared, it was gone again. And once it had, all that was left behind was a decimated city. Time continued to wind on forward with the sun rising and setting every few seconds, but no matter how long they waited, nothing was rising from the ruins. Buildings were not getting rebuilt. It looked as though London had been completely destroyed, and no one was left to pick up the pieces. Or put the pieces back together again, which would have been much more useful than just picking them up.

"Whoa." William took his finger off the tablet's screen. "Did you see that?"

Geoff swallowed hard as time returned to normal speed. "My God," he said. "What have you done?"

"I'm not entirely sure," William said casually, as though he'd just been asked a tricky Trivial Pursuit question rather than being made to answer for the annihilation of a city, "but this definitely didn't happen in the original timeline. I guess something I did must have caused it."

Geoff shook his head. "You guess?!" he said. "You *guess*!?"

"Huh," William said, reading something from the tablet. "It says here that the British media blamed my attack on foreign terrorists, which in turn led to an extremist regime being elected into office a few years later. In the decades that followed, London was rebuilt, but Britain changed in its attitude toward the rest of the world, becoming far more defensive and less tolerant toward other cultures. This all came to a head at the turn of the twenty-second century, when they launched a preemptive nuclear strike against another country they incorrectly suspected to be an aggressor. The other country responded with a nuclear strike of its own, and London was destroyed. England's remained a wasteland ever since."

After what he had seen, Geoff barely had the strength to speak.

But he managed five words.

"How do you know that?"

"The device gave me a summary of the how the new timeline reacted to the changes I made. A bit like that supercomputer at Time Tours, but small enough to fit in your pocket! Clever bit of kit, don't you think?"

Geoff let out a long, deep breath.

"Well, there you go," William said. "You asked me if I had any idea of the damage I'd caused to the space-time continuum by destroying those buildings, and now we know. It caused a chain reaction that ultimately wiped out the whole city. Pretty interesting, huh?"

"Pretty interesting!?" Geoff screamed, writhing around in his chair. "Pretty interesting!? William—you just killed millions of people! You may have just caused the end of the world!"

"Oh, there's no need to worry about all that," William said, pressing a few more buttons on his tablet. As he did, a small icon appeared in the bottom right-hand corner of the screen. It said REWIND.

"Now—look what happens when I do *this*," he said, pressing the icon. When he did, the screen displayed a message:
PLEASE CONFIRM HOW FAR BACK YOU WISH TO REWIND

Beneath the message was a horizontal slider, with an arrow hovering over the far right-hand side. Geoff watched as William touched the arrow and dragged it to the left. As he did, a number of dials at the bottom of the screen showing years, days, hours, minutes, and seconds began to count backward. William stopped moving the slider once the date matched when he had first shown up at Canary Wharf, but the time was set to midnight. Geoff noticed that he had only moved the arrow back about a tenth of the way across the screen.

"Okay. What time was it when I first came to see you?" William said, touching the dials at the bottom of the screen that corresponded to hours and minutes. "Eight…thirty…five… a.m., wasn't it?"

Once he'd finished adjusting the slider, a green button that looked like the rewind symbol started flashing.

"There we go. Are you ready?"

"Ready for what?" Geoff said.

"This," William said, pressing the button.

Then something very strange happened. Geoff no longer had any control over his body.

Next to him, William began unpressing all the buttons he had been pressing, unsliding the slider he had been sliding. Then they began having a very strange reverse conversation as William began reading the text about the destruction of London backward. Soon after that, the sun began setting and rising again at the same speed it had done before, but in reverse.

Setting and rising.

Setting and rising.

Then there was the flash again. Afterward, though, London was completely undamaged.

And this was how the next few minutes continued, with Geoff watching time reverse itself. Everything that had just happened was unhappening, except Geoff could perceive the rewinding of events as though they were still constructing a forward narrative in his mind. It was incredible. The taller skyscrapers of Canary Wharf unbuilt themselves, the fighter jets unchased them, and Canary Wharf undestroyed itself as the lasers fired by William unfired from his car, which disappeared back into the sky as if it had never arrived.

There was one thing that wasn't quite the same, though— Geoff noticed that when William unplunged the syringe into his arm, the red liquid didn't come out again. And when he had removed the needle in reverse, the marks still remained on Geoff's wrist.

Other than that, everything undid itself exactly, and before Geoff knew it, he was sitting down at the table outside the coffee shop again, picking up his coffee in reverse (which actually meant putting it down) as William walked backward away from him into a crowd of people, looking down at his watch.

And then Geoff was able to move again.

He jerked suddenly, as if he had just been resuscitated, and looked down at his own watch.

Eight thirty-five exactly.

As was Geoff's habit when he was very surprised about something, he leapt to his feet, looked around a bit, then sat back down again.

No one was paying any attention to either of them anymore. After all, there was no reason to. Canary Wharf was exactly as it was before William had blown it up.

"There," William said, looking up from his watch. "You see? No harm done."

Geoff didn't know what to say. He just sat there, taking large sips of his coffee, his eyes wide open.

"Well?" William said. "What did you think of that?"

Geoff couldn't speak. He took a few deep breaths and blinked about twenty times. Then he did some more blinking. He wanted to stand up and punch William in the face, but that would only have served to draw attention to them again, and potentially start changing the space-time continuum.

And he'd had just about enough of that for one day.

"I just undid everything I did since I came here!" William said. "Isn't that incredible?"

"How did you do that?"

"Like I said, when you work for Continuum, they give you one of these things." William held up the tablet computer as if it were some sort of trophy. "With this, you have the power to change time however you like, and the best part is, if you don't like what you change, you can just undo what you did and try something else! This is what allows a tourist traveling with Continuum to go back and change things. With this, you have the freedom to go wherever you want! Change whatever you please! It's no wonder nobody's using Time Tours anymore."

"Wait a minute," Geoff said. "If you just undid everything, how come we remember what happened?"

"Ah—that's all thanks to that serum I gave you," William replied.

"You mean the one you forcibly injected into me," Geoff said, rubbing his sore wrist.

"Whatever," William said. "Anyway, from what I understand, that stuff is immune to the effects of time manipulation. No matter how this device is used to alter the flow of history, the serum stays inside you, shielding your mind and body from any changes to the flow of time. That's why the liquid didn't come back out of your arm and into the syringe when I made time flow in reverse. It's amazing stuff—whether time is being accelerated, slowed down, reversed, or paused, it keeps your body and mind separate from what is happening, allowing you to perceive the effects of time manipulation from a normal perspective. Admittedly, if time moves backward, your body is still forced to undo everything it did, but thanks to the serum, you still remember everything."

"But what about everyone else?" Geoff said, pointing at the people around him. "What happens to them?"

William laughed. "As far as everyone else is concerned, nothing we just experienced ever took place. There was no flying car. I never destroyed those buildings. And no one got hurt."

Geoff sighed. Despite none of it ever having technically happened, it still didn't feel right. And why hadn't William just told him all this from the start?

"Are you okay?" William said.

Geoff looked at William and shook his head. "What happened to you, William?"

William frowned. "What do you mean?"

"The William I knew would never have done anything like that—killing all those people—regardless of whether it could be undone or not. What the hell has gotten into you?"

"But I didn't kill anybody! Don't you see? None of that happened!"

"I understand," Geoff said. "I guess I just don't see how undoing your actions makes them okay in your conscience. Have you considered that having this power to undo time and change things however you please might have warped your sense of right and wrong?"

"Geoff, since joining Continuum I've traveled backward and forward millions of years. I've seen civilizations rise and fall. I've seen wars, I've seen famine, and I've seen death and destruction. The one thing I've learned is that no matter what the catastrophe, things move on. Most setbacks in human history are only ever temporary, and life bounces back. Believe me— what I did today is nothing compared to some of the things I've seen." He leaned forward. "Nothing."

Geoff didn't know what to say to that, so he chose to pull his trusty stalwart expression of inflating his cheeks with air, which he often used whenever he was at a loss for what to say.

"So, you gonna check out Continuum?" William asked. "See if they'll give you a job?"

Geoff let the air out of his mouth very slowly, like a balloon with a very small leak.

"We'll see," he said. As much as he was intrigued, he still wasn't that keen on the fact that all this led toward someone trying to kill him.

But he had the feeling it was already too late to stop that.

William turned to leave. "Well, I think my work here is done. Next stop, the Middle Ages—there's a Time Rep back there who's gonna absolutely love this when I show her!"

"William," Geoff said. "Why are you doing this?"

William lowered his head. "I want to set us free, Geoff. Once a Time Rep witnesses firsthand how much better it is working for Continuum, once they see the kind of stuff they let you do, they'll be leaving Time Tours in droves. And they'll be free to explore time however they want, just like I am. Isn't that great?"

"So how many Time Reps are you trying to visit?"

William smiled.

"All of them," he replied.

FIVE

"All of them?" Tim said, slumping across his desk and folding his hands over the back of his head. "That's what he said?"

Geoff really liked Tim's office. It was incredibly spacious, with a high ceiling, dark, wood-paneled walls, and a soft green carpet that looked like a kind of show lawn you would expect to find at a garden exhibition. The room was decorated with an assortment of beautiful Victorian furniture—it had a big wooden desk, two high-back wing chairs, and a little coffee table that looked like it belonged in a doll's house. Each of the offices in the Time Tours building was specially designed to represent a different era, and Tim's was made to look like the late nineteenth century. Leatherbound books were stacked high on dark mahogany shelves, oil paintings hung from every wall, and two tall sash windows looked out onto the London skyline. It was strange having a view of such a modern city outside, with futuristic buildings and flying traffic whizzing in every direction. In here, Geoff felt like he was trapped in a little bubble from the past, watching the world move on without him.

Then again, that's how he felt all the time, whether he was in this room or not.

Trapped in a little bubble from the past.

"Hello?" Tim said, sitting upright in his chair again. "Will you stop gawping at this room like you always do and answer me?"

"Sorry," Geoff said. "Yes, that's what he said. That he was trying to see every Time Rep he could."

"And after he left, you came straight here? You didn't mention this to anyone?"

"That's right."

"So talk me through this again. He just showed up, destroyed half of London for your benefit, and then just undid it all?"

"It was horrible, Tim. He destroyed everything."

"You said. But then he just made it all go back to normal?"

"That's right. Like I was saying—he seemed to be able to control the flow of time with this tablet thingy."

"And then there's this serum."

"That's right."

"Can I see where he injected you?"

"Sure." Geoff held out his arm and rolled up his sleeve. The circle of dots from the injection had started to heal, but they were still easily visible on his skin.

"Son of a bitch," Tim said, pressing his thumb against the marks. "It's coming true."

"What is?"

Tim sighed. "Your future self has these marks in this exact same place. Eric's been trying to work out what they are, but I guess now we know."

"I tell you, Tim—that was some weird stuff he put in me."

"Oh, we know all about that serum," Tim said. "Our scientists have been analyzing samples of it for months, trying to work out how it protects itself from the manipulation of time. So far we've got absolutely nothing. What we do know is that it's the key to how Continuum can safely allow people to go back in time and change whatever they like. At the end of the holiday, they can just reverse everyone back out of the timeline again and return everything back to normal. And what's even more remarkable is that people can retain memories of what they experienced. It really is incredible stuff. "

"But if you knew about the serum, why didn't Eric make that connection when you saw the marks on my wrist?"

"It's not normally injected," Tim said, standing up from his desk. "From what I hear, you're supposed to just drink it. In your case, I guess William assumed you'd resist, so he had no choice but to inject it into your bloodstream."

"There were a lot of syringes on the back seat of that car. He must have already seen quite a few people."

"Yes, you said. Which means someone is giving him a steady supply of that serum. Someone is *encouraging* him to do this."

"Do you think it's that Jennifer Adams lady? The boss of Continuum?"

"It wouldn't surprise me. But there's one thing that doesn't make sense…"

"What's that?"

Before Tim had a chance to answer, there was a knock at the door.

"Come in," Tim called out.

The door opened with a creak, and a young woman walked in. Geoff recognized her immediately—it was Isabel, a Time Rep from the fourteenth century. Geoff had met her a few times at the odd work party. She was about twenty years old, and when she wasn't showing tourists around the medieval countryside, she worked on a farm. Normally she wore clothes sewn together from bits of rags and old sacks, but when she came to the future she liked to wear bright colors, knee-high boots, and jeans. She strode into Tim's office smiling, with her head held high.

"Hey Geoff," she said, giving him a nod. She was holding a letter in her hand.

"Isabel," Geoff said.

"You leaving too?" she asked.

"What do you mean, leaving *too*?" Tim said, staggering forward and resting his weight on the back of one of the chairs. "Isabel, do you mean to tell me that…?"

"That's right—I'm here to hand in my resignation," Isabel said, offering the letter to Tim.

Tim looked at Geoff for a split second before looking back at Isabel again. "Isabel, come on," he said, not taking the letter. "Think about this…"

"Oh I've thought about it," she said. "I've thought about it a lot, while I've been trudging around in the mud, or sitting out in the rain gathering hay, or scooping up horse shit. I've thought about why I'm not living here instead, earning money. Eating out. Going to the theater. Traveling the world. But no, I'm not allowed to do any of those things because it might change history. Well, guess what? Continuum just offered me a job, so now I can do whatever I like."

"At least take a week or so to think about it, okay? Geoff and I are really worried something might not be right with Continuum. We're worried you all might be in some sort of danger."

"The only person in danger here is you," Isabel said, holding the letter out farther. "In danger from me, that is, if you don't accept this."

"Fine."

Tim took the letter but didn't open it. He could already guess what it said, since he'd read at least twenty others just like it that week.

"Good," Isabel said. "Look, I'm sorry to do this to you, Tim, really I am. But when Continuum is here offering me everything I ever wanted, it's kind of hard to refuse them, you know?"

"I understand," Tim said. "Just be careful. And for what it's worth, it was a pleasure working with you."

"Likewise." Isabel paused for a moment as if reconsidering her decision, but soon brushed her long hair back and turned to leave.

Geoff touched her arm as she began to walk out. "Was it William who came to see you?" he asked.

"That's right," Isabel smiled. "Why, has he been to see you too?"

"Yeah," Geoff said. "And to be honest, I'm still recovering from it."

"I know!" Isabel said. "I couldn't believe it either. He looked so cool! And when that flashy car of his appeared, I didn't know what was going to happen. He totally scared the hell out of me at first, but once I saw what he could do thanks to his job at Continuum, I was sold."

"If you ask me, I thought what he did was totally insane."

"Yeah, it was pretty crazy, wasn't it?"

"No, Isabel—I'm not using the word 'insane' in a complimentary sense. I mean that what he did was literally insane. I don't know what William did when he came to see you, but when he came see me in the twenty-first century, he quite happily killed thousands of innocent people and destroyed an entire city without even a twinge of guilt. And I don't care if he was able to undo everything afterward—the fact that he even did it in the first place makes me worried for the guy. It's like this technology to undo time has completely warped his sense of right and wrong. When someone never has to worry about the consequences of their actions, when they have the power to undo every mistake or wrongdoing, then surely that must change them?"

"What are you saying?"

"I don't know. Just don't let this new power corrupt you like it's corrupted William. And be safe."

"You too, Geoff," she said, and left, closing the door behind her with a click.

"Well, that's just great," Tim said, tossing the letter on the floor. "Another one gone."

"What were you about to say before she came in?" Geoff asked.

"What's that?"

"Before Isabel came in, you were saying there was something that didn't make sense. What was it?"

Tim walked around in front of the chair he had been leaning on and sat down. "Have a seat," he said, pointing at the chair opposite.

Geoff sat down.

"Here's the thing," Tim said, leaning forward. "If the whole point of Continuum is for tourists to go back and change history, why do they need Time Reps?"

Geoff thought about this for a second.

"Do you see what I mean?" Tim continued. "The whole point of having Time Reps throughout history is for them to show tourists around their native time periods. Tell them things they don't know. Show them the sights. But with Continuum, Time Reps aren't required. People aren't going back to learn about history—they are going back to change it. From what you're telling me, all the information they need is provided by that tablet device they are given, so a Time Rep would be no use to them whatsoever."

"You're right," Geoff said. "But if that's the case, why is Continuum offering us all jobs? Why are they making it their mission to tempt every Time Rep to work for them instead?"

"That's what we need to find out," Tim said. "In fact, maybe that's what your future self discovered. Maybe that's why someone tried to kill you."

"You mean why someone is *going* to try and kill me, remember? It hasn't happened yet, right?"

"Right."

Geoff looked at his watch. It was now eleven forty-five in the morning.

If events were continuing to transpire as they had done originally, there was just less than four hours to go before his rendezvous with a bullet.

And the person that fired it at him.

"Well, I don't know about you," Geoff said, rubbing his hands together, "but I'm quite happy not knowing the answer to that little mystery. Shall we just put it down as one of those things we'll never solve and move on?" He stood up and rubbed his hands. "So I guess I'll be going home now, okay? See you tomorrow!"

"Geoff, wait. We need to get to the bottom of this."

"No," Geoff said. "I need to get to the bottom of a nuclear bunker, and stay there for the next few hours."

"Come on, Geoff—you know there's something very fishy going on here, and we need to work out what it is."

Geoff sighed. "Look, Tim—you know I'm always happy to help, but in this instance, I've got to be honest—I have a very strong urge to book a flight to Hawaii and lie on a beach until this blows over."

"You can't go to Hawaii."

"A *very* strong urge."

"Geoff," Tim said, standing up from his chair. "Don't you get it? There is a plot at work here. Continuum is up to something, and we are the only ones who can find out what it is."

"So what do you suggest we do?" Geoff said. "We can't exactly turn up and say, 'Excuse me, but we suspect you guys are up to no good—can you tell us what it is, please?'"

"Perhaps you could go and pretend you're there for a job interview," Tim said. "Since they've invited you in anyway, it wouldn't raise any suspicions…"

"Not a chance," Geoff said. "That plan has 'dead Geoff' written all over it."

"More like 'severely injured Geoff.' You weren't killed, remember?"

"Is that supposed to make me feel better?"

"Oh, come on," Tim said. "All you've got to do is—"

But before Tim could continue his sentence any further, the phone on his desk rang. Like the rest of the room, the phone was quite old-fashioned, with a separate earpiece and receiver. Geoff was astounded that they still used regular telephones in the thirty-first century, but then again, they still used tin openers, too. After all, no matter what century you were from, a tin opener was the best thing to use if you wanted to open a tin, so a phone must have been the best thing to use if you wanted to make a phone call. Wait—did that make sense?

Tim picked up the receiver and lifted the earpiece to his ear.

"Good afternoon, Tim Burnell speaking," he said.

Suddenly his face went pale, his eyes widened, and he snapped his gaze toward Geoff.

"Oh no," Geoff said, getting to his feet. "It's not one of those annoying recorded messages about claiming mis-sold PPI insurance, is it? Do you still get those in the thirty-first century too?"

"You're not going to believe this," Tim said. "It's you."

SIX

"Hugh?" Geoff said. "Who's Hugh? Do I know him?"

"Not *Hugh*, you idiot," Tim said, "It's you! *You*!"

"*Me?*"

Tim rolled his eyes. "Yes! It's the future version of Geoffrey Stamp! The future one from the future! He's calling from the hospital!"

"My God!" Geoff ran over to Tim, leaning his head as close to the phone as possible. "Is he all right? ARE YOU ALL RIGHT?"

"Hang on a second," Tim said, turning away and pressing the earpiece closer to his ear. "Geoff," he said into the receiver, "hold on a minute. I've got the other Geoff here as well. Are you sure it's okay to talk like this with him here?"

Tim listened to a reply for a few seconds, nodding. Geoff tried to hear what was being said on the other end of the line, but couldn't make anything out. It was like trying to listen to pirate radio through a wet sponge.

"I see," Tim said. He turned to Geoff. "He says he remembers being in the room when I was on the phone to his future self, so it must be okay for you to be here now."

"So I can stay?"

"Apparently."

Tim listened to the phone again for a few seconds, then turned to Geoff again. "But he says I told you to sit down over there," he said, pointing back toward the chairs in the middle of the room.

"Okay," Geoff said, not sitting down.

Tim looked at Geoff in silence, waiting for him to move.

"Oh," Geoff said. "Does that mean I have to sit down now?"

"Yes," Tim replied. "And don't worry—the Geoff on the other end of this phone says he'll talk to you later."

"Okay. But is he all right?"

"He's fine. Looks like his memory came back quicker than we were expecting."

Geoff still hadn't sat down. He was kind of hoping Tim had forgotten to tell him to leave them alone to their conversation, so he could eavesdrop on it.

"Please, Geoff," Tim said. "Sit down."

Geoff stamped his feet all the way back to the chair and lowered himself down into it slowly.

Well, this was annoying.

He really, really wanted to know what Tim and his future self were talking about, but instead he was just sat in this chair, alone. He felt like a kid at a dinner party for grown-ups, made to sit at a smaller table by themselves, eating chicken nuggets while everyone else enjoyed a five-course meal and had interesting conversations about things he wasn't allowed to know about.

"Okay," he heard Tim say. "You can talk now."

Despite Tim being quite far away, Geoff could just about make out his end of the conversation. Unfortunately, what followed was a long period of silence, which wasn't exactly helpful.

"Who told you this?" he heard Tim say eventually.

A pause.

"You met with Jennifer Adams herself?"

Another pause.

"I knew it," Tim said. "So what did they ask you to do for them instead?"

Now a very small pause.

"Nothing?"

And now a slightly longer pause. These pauses were getting a bit tedious.

"I see. So what happened next?"

Next there was an unbearably long pause, which must have lasted at least two or three minutes. Geoff began to get agitated.

One thing that Geoff found quite useful when trying to

figure out what his future self was saying was how the expression on Tim's face changed as he listened. Geoff found himself studying his friend very closely, as his mannerisms were quite a good bellwether for the tone of the conversation. At the start of the phone call he had looked entertained. Then he looked extremely happy. Then in the middle he looked quite shocked, and then he looked extremely sad. In fact, he looked devastated, his entire body slumping against the window for a few seconds. By the end he straightened himself up, but it was quite obvious that he was worried about something.

Then finally he looked angry.

Extremely angry.

"That bloody…" he trailed off, as if he'd suddenly remembered that the present-day Geoff was still, well, present. He took a deep breath. "Well, that certainly explains everything," he said. "But how come—"

Tim stopped speaking and listened, as if the future Geoff had already anticipated the question and was answering it.

"I see." Tim looked over at Geoff. "Well, I think you and I need to get over there right away, don't you?"

A pause. Future Geoff was speaking.

"Of course—you're right. We need to let your past self do his thing first, otherwise you won't be speaking to me now. Good thinking."

"Okay," Geoff said, getting to his feet. "I've had just about as much of this as I can take. Will someone tell me what the hell is going on?"

"Geoff," Tim said into the phone. "Your past self has lost his temper over here. Didn't you say you were going to speak with yourself?" He listened for a few seconds, nodding. "Okay," Tim replied. "After I send Geoff to Continuum, I'll come and pick you up from the hospital."

Another pause.

"Good thinking," Tim said. "After I come and get you, we'll go over there and explain the situation. Hopefully they should be able to help us."

Another pause, very brief this time.

"Uh…sure."

And another bloody pause.

"No, I won't forget! Look, here's Geoff for you." And with that, Tim handed the phone over to Geoff.

"Hello?" Geoff said, putting the earpiece to his ear and holding the receiver stand up to his mouth.

"Hello, Geoff," came a voice at the other end of the line. Geoff flinched. He hated the sound of his own voice—particularly when he could hear how it sounded to everyone else.

"Hello," Geoff said again. Now that he'd put up such a big fuss about wanting to know what was going on, he didn't really know what to say.

"I know how you're feeling," his other self said. "Now that you've put up such a big fuss about wanting to know what's going on, you don't really know what to say, do you?"

"There's not much point in lying and saying I know exactly what I want to ask you, is there?"

"Not really. I can still remember your half of the conversation pretty well. Next you're going to ask me if I can tell you everything I just told Tim, and the answer is no. Then you're going to say 'drat.'"

"*Can* you tell me everything you just told Tim?"

"No."

"Drat."

"I'm sorry, Geoff, but if I share any information with you about the future, it might make you behave differently. And it is critical that things transpire for you exactly as they did for me. That you follow the same path I did. I know you're frightened about the things that await you, but you just have to trust me. Everything will be all right."

"So what am I supposed to do now?"

"Tim is going to ask you to go and pretend to accept a job at Continuum," future Geoff said. "But all the while, he'll want you to actually be an inside man for Time Tours, spying on your new employer and reporting back."

"I'm not sure I like this," Geoff said. "In fact, this is starting to sound exactly like the kind of thing that might get me shot."

"It *is* the exact thing that gets you shot," future Geoff said. "And the reason you get shot is because you uncover a horrible truth about that company—a truth that needs to be exposed, for the sake of…well, I'm probably saying too much. Needless to say, it's important you do as Tim tells you."

"Can't you just tell me what it is I find out to save me having to find out for myself?"

"No, Geoff—if I do that, you won't go to Continuum and then I won't be able to tell you what you find out. We'll create a paradox."

Bloody paradoxes, Geoff thought. *Always getting in the way of things.*

Geoff looked down at his watch again and exhaled into the receiver.

Midday.

Three and a half hours to go.

"You still there?" future Geoff said. "Damn it—I thought to myself I wouldn't ask that since I already know you're still there, but I still did it."

That was a silly thing to ask, Geoff thought, given he must have known he was still here. He made a mental note not to ask himself that question.

"I suppose I've got no choice, then. I'll do it," Geoff said. "But this conversation hasn't exactly been the reassuring exchange I was hoping for. Isn't there any advice you can give me? Anything at all?"

"Well, I remember myself telling me one thing," future Geoff said, "so I suppose I can do that."

"Yes?"

"When the time comes…"

"Yes?"

"It's difficult for me to say…"

"Say what? Come on!"

There was a sigh at the other end of the phone.

"When the time comes," future Geoff said, "don't save Zoë."

And with that, the phone went dead.

"Well?" Tim said, taking the phone from Geoff and putting it back on his desk. "What did he tell you?"

Geoff tried to open his mouth to speak, but no sound came out.

"I'm not sure…"

"You need to go work for Continuum," Tim said, not looking Geoff in the eyes. "And when you get a job there—"

"—you want me to spy on them. Report back. I know."

Tim swallowed. "Your cover story is that you're responding to the letter they gave you. Jennifer Adams herself said their doors were open twenty-four hours a day, so here you are, ready for an interview. Nothing suspicious about that."

"Sounds like a plan."

"But you can't go dressed like that," Tim said. "You need to look like you really want that job, not like you're there to fix the coffee machine. Don't you own anything smart?"

"Nope. Don't you remember my interview with Time Tours? I hardly made any effort for that."

"That's right—you turned up in the same clothes you'd slept in, didn't you?"

"Tim, I'm not like that anymore. My standards of personal hygiene are now marginally better than they were back then."

"That may be true," Tim replied, "but I still can't believe you don't own a single suit. That interview was two years ago. Do you mean to tell me that in two years you haven't requested we get you any smart clothes?"

"I haven't requested any new clothes, smart or otherwise."

"Unbelievable. Okay, so you don't have anything smart to wear. But don't worry—"

He stopped talking.

"What is it?"

"I was about to say—you can borrow an old suit of mine if you like."

Geoff smiled. "At least we now know why I was wearing it. Maybe I should get my hair cut and have a shave as well, just to fall in line exactly with what my future self looked like. What do you think?"

"I think it would be rude not to. Now, do you want to run through any practice questions for this interview before you leave?"

"No, I'm okay," Geoff said. "After all—interviews are my speciality."

SEVEN

"I'm here for a job interview," Geoff said to the receptionist. For someone who just sat behind a desk in the lobby of the Continuum office and let people know when a guest had arrived, this girl looked absolutely stunning. Not that receptionists weren't allowed to look stunning, but we were talking supermodel looks here, as though she'd just stepped off the catwalk after a photo shoot and been hired by Continuum to be the first face you saw when entering the building. Her long blonde hair was tied in a thick braided ponytail behind her back, her skin had not one blemish anywhere to be seen, and her eyes were hazel brown and looked as though they could disarm any man who walked through the door, even if they were there to complain about the superficial nature of Continuum's receptionist-hiring policy.

"You must be Geoffrey Stamp," she said, looking him up and down. There was a slight look of mischief in her eyes, as though he were being a bit naughty for turning up and it was their little secret. But there was something else going on here as well. Was she checking him out?

"That's right," he replied, suddenly conscious of his appearance. He couldn't remember the last time he'd made so much effort for anything. He'd showered, cut his hair, and even had a proper shave. And once his scraggy hair had been tamed and he'd slipped on one of Tim's suits, he actually looked quite dapper. Whatever that meant.

"I'm Jeanette," she said.

"How do you know my name?" Geoff asked.

"Come on," Jeanette said, leaning forward and twirling a few strands of hair around her fingers. "Everyone's heard of you. You're the Time Rep for the twenty-first century, aren't you?"

"That's right," Geoff said. He'd forgotten that Time Reps were treated a bit like celebrities in the future. Given the decline of Time Tours over the last few months, he was surprised anyone still recognized him or even cared about what he did. He thought by now his celebrity status might be comparable to that of a forgotten star trying to revitalize their showbiz career by going on a reality TV show, but he guessed he was mistaken. Apparently people still knew who he was.

"Ms. Adams will be so pleased you decided to come," she said. "Of all the Time Reps she's contacted, I'm told you're the one she's wanted to meet the most."

"I am?"

The receptionist picked up a phone and began to dial a number.

"Please, have a seat," she smiled, resting the phone against her shoulder and pointing across the room to a row of black leather chairs. "We'll be ready for you in a moment."

He looked down at his watch.

Two fifty.

Were there really only forty minutes to go before he got shot? He could barely believe it. Everyone here had been quite friendly so far, so he'd have to do something pretty bad to take such an amicable environment and let it deteriorate to the point where someone would try to kill him so quickly. Then again, he was pretty good at ruining the mood in certain situations at the drop of a hat, like that time he literally dropped Zoë's new hat under a bus by mistake.

Geoff made his way across the busy lobby toward the seating area, weaving his way through a relentless flow of men and women walking in all directions. The Continuum building really was a hive of activity. There were people standing around in groups chatting excitedly, others dashing into different elevators at the far end of the hall with bundles of paperwork in their hands, and over near the entrance, a number of companies had set up stands advertising things you could do on your holidays. Geoff stopped to look at these for a moment. One company let you take canoe equipment back to go whitewater rafting in the prehistoric jungle. Another one was offering advanced weaponry for people to go back and start wars for fun. And one particularly sadistic stand was showing off a range of flying cars that had been modified with weaponry, which you could take back in time and use to cause whatever havoc you pleased.

Just the sort of thing to do with the kids during the school holidays.

Geoff eased himself into one of the few remaining seats. This was not to say that there weren't many remaining seats because someone was taking them all away; they were just mostly occupied. As he sat down, he felt his stomach rumble—with all the excitement today, he'd forgotten to have any lunch.

To take his mind off of his hunger, Geoff took a moment to examine Continuum's lobby in a bit more detail. You could really tell the company must have been doing quite well at the moment, because the whole place screamed of money, and screamed even louder of money being spent. The floor was made from solid marble, thick beams of sunlight shone down on everyone through tall, stained-glass windows, and right in the middle of the room stood a huge golden *C* at least ten meters high, mounted on a square pedestal. This was the logo of Continuum, and although it wasn't obvious at first, the logo was actually rotating around slowly, the golden surface reflecting on a different section of the room's perimeter as time passed.

Next, Geoff turned his attention to the other people seated in the waiting area. There were about ten or twelve men and women here. Some were dressed in suits, others looked more casual. Geoff was pretty sure he recognized half of them, and figured they were probably other Time Reps, no doubt hoping to be hired by Continuum. A few looked back as though they recognized him, too.

"Mr. Stamp?" came a voice to his right.

Geoff looked around. A smartly dressed woman was standing next to him, smiling.

"Yes?" Geoff said, getting to his feet.

"Allow me to introduce myself," the woman said, extending a hand for him to shake. "I'm Jennifer Adams."

"Pleased to meet you, Ms. Adams." Geoff shook her hand. She had long, thin fingers and a firm grip, but not so firm as to imply any kind of dominance. Strong, but not too strong, like a good cup of tea. "Oh, call me Jennifer," she said.

"Right…Jennifer," Geoff said. He stood a little awkwardly, as though he had a stone in his shoe.

So this was the boss of Continuum. Jennifer Adams looked to be in her mid-to-late forties, though at first glance you might have been forgiven for thinking she was a few years younger. It was only when she smiled that telltale wrinkles emerged around her eyes and mouth. Standing a little shorter than Geoff, she seemed to keep herself in good shape, with a thin frame and narrow shoulders. She wore her long brown hair down past her shoulders with a neat parting combed into the right-hand side, kept her makeup to a minimum, and had a steely gaze to her eyes that suggested a no-nonsense attitude. Wearing a dark gray trouser suit with a pale green blouse, she looked like your regular sort of businesswoman.

"So you finally decided to see what we're all about?" she said, leading him across the lobby toward an elevator that was being held open by a security guard. As they walked, a few passersby looked around, as if seeing the head of the company walking through the lobby was quite a novelty.

"Yeah, I had a visit from William," Geoff replied. "His demonstration of what you allow people to do when they go back in time was very memorable."

Jennifer laughed. "William Boyle? The Time Rep from 1666? Yes, he's done a great job for us in spreading the word." As they approached the elevator, Jennifer stepped to one side and invited Geoff to go first. "Please, after you, Geoff," she said. "May I call you Geoff?"

"You can call me what you like," Geoff said, stepping inside the elevator. He was followed by Jennifer and the security guard.

"Basement," Jennifer said.

"Actually, I would prefer it if you called me Geoff."

"No, I was telling the lift where to go. Haven't you ever been in a voice-activated lift before?"

"O-of course," Geoff said. "I guess I'm just a little nervous."

"Nervous? There's no need to be nervous."

"I suppose not," Geoff said. Unless of course you took into account the fact that someone was going to shoot him in thirty-seven minutes, he thought.

The doors closed, and the lift began to move.

"So tell me," Jennifer said, folding her arms across her chest. "After all this time, what made you decide to finally come and meet us? We've been trying to get in touch with you for months, sent you letter after letter, but up until now we've had no reply. Why the sudden change of heart?"

"I don't know," Geoff said, trying to quickly think of a reason other than the fact that he was there to spy on them.

But once he'd thought of spying, that was the only reason that went around his mind.

Spying.

I'm here to spy on you.

I thought I'd do a bit of the old spying.

Spy, spy, spy.

Spy.

"Come on, there must be something."

"I guess I'm just fed up of not being able to do what I want," Geoff said eventually. "I want to be honest with the people I care about and tell them what I really do for a living, but because I'm a Time Rep, I'm not allowed. I just have to do what I'm told all the time in case I change something. The truth is, I'm sick of lying to people every day. Pretending to be someone I'm not."

That's rich, he thought to himself, *considering you're actually here to spy*. But at least there was some truth to what he was saying.

He was fed up with being told what he could and couldn't do, and how he was supposed to live his life.

Jennifer nodded. "That's what a lot of you say. What's her name?"

Geoff smiled. "Zoë. How did you know it was about a girl?"

"With the men, it's always about a girl," she replied.

EIGHT

Jennifer's office wasn't what Geoff was expecting at all. Considering how successful Continuum was, he was expecting it to be a huge, palatial room, tastefully decorated with expensive art and large enough to accommodate its own swimming pool, private golf course, and nine-screen cinema. In reality, though, her office was very small. It had no windows, felt a little cramped, and was poorly illuminated by a single naked bulb hanging from the ceiling. Above all else, the room was a complete mess—books were scattered on the floor, various blueprints and paperwork were spilling out of rusty filing cabinets, and every surface was coated by a thin film of dust. It was as if the place had never really been cleaned, unless the cleaner didn't know the difference between a vacuum cleaner and a leaf blower.

On the wall to Geoff's left was a large blackboard, scrawled with notes and long, complex equations. On the right, a row of bookshelves was packed with tatty old engineering textbooks and, strangely, a book about baking.

Then a thought struck Geoff—beneath this professional exterior, was Jennifer Adams a bit of a slob? Was she actually a bit like him?

"Please forgive the mess," Jennifer said, tossing her suit jacket over one of the hooks on the back of the door and shrugging on a white laboratory coat. She walked over to a desk on the far side of the room, brushed some screwed-up notepaper aside, and sat down.

"This is your office?" Geoff said, pulling a chair up.

Jennifer smiled. "A hangover from my days working as a researcher," she said, attempting to tidy a few more papers into an already-crammed drawer. "Back at university, I had to spend most of my days in an underground lab. Writing out formulas on the walls, sitting cross-legged in a corner surrounded by textbooks. At first I couldn't bear it—it was just so claustrophobic. But after a while, I started to like it. Made me feel all cozy being surrounded by clutter. At Time Tours it was the same—whilst I was building that supercomputer underground, I needed to have a small office nearby, so once again I found myself cooped away, out of the light."

"And you liked that?"

"When I first set up this place, the board tried to make me take an office on the top floor. That was what they expected from the boss of the company. I did it for a few months to appease them, but after a while I realized that I missed the security of being in a small, enclosed space. The solitude of it all. I knew where I wanted my office. Not up on the top floor in full view of the world, but down here where it's quiet. Private. Not too much room. This is how I like to work—out of the limelight."

"Huh," Geoff said. "Well, everyone's different, I guess."

There was a knock at the door.

"Come in," Jennifer said.

The door opened, and a man came in holding two mugs of tea.

"Tea, Ms. Adams?" the man asked.

"Excellent," Jennifer said, waving the man inside. "Just put them down on the desk, will you?"

The man did as he was told, then left.

"Milk and two sugars, right?" Jennifer smiled.

"How did you know that?" Geoff said, picking up his mug and taking a sip. The tea was exactly as he liked it—quite strong and sweet.

"Just a lucky guess." Jennifer picked up her own mug and warmed her hands against the side of it. "Anyway—where were we?"

"We were talking about your office," Geoff said, taking another sip of his tea. It really was a very good brew.

"Were we really? How frightfully dull. Why don't we talk

about you instead? That's a much more interesting subject, wouldn't you say?"

"Me? There's nothing that interesting about me."

"Come now, Geoff," Jennifer said, giving him a crafty wink. "There's no need to be modest. I've been wanting to meet you for quite a while." She gulped down a mouthful of tea and placed the mug back on the desk. "Quite a while indeed."

"Yes, your receptionist—Jeanette, was it?—said something about that. Why have you been wanting to meet me so much, exactly?"

She looked at him for a moment as if she were carefully considering her reply.

"I know what happened two years ago, Geoff," Jennifer said, leaning back in her chair. "I know about the alien invasion, the changes in the timeline—everything."

Geoff shifted his weight in his chair. "You do?"

"Oh, yes. You're a hero, do you know that?"

"A hero?" Geoff could feel himself blushing. No one had ever called him a hero before. He'd been called many things, but never a hero. "You sure about that?"

"Well, how else would you describe someone who singlehandedly saved the entire human race from extinction? If it wasn't for you, those Varsarians would have wiped us all out. Every single person on this planet owes you their life. Isn't that right?"

"How do you know about that?" he said. "Time Tours told me that they'd managed to cover it all up. Keep it a secret."

"They did keep it a secret." Jennifer picked up her mug of tea again to take another sip. "But I still have a few friends there. They feed me all the juicy gossip."

"Even so, I thought that unless you were someone who actually experienced all the changes we caused in space-time continuum firsthand, you shouldn't remember anything that happened."

"Is that so?" Jennifer smiled.

Geoff looked down at his watch.

Three o'clock.

His stomach rumbled again—the tea was doing a good job of filling him up a little, but he was still pretty hungry.

"I can't believe that buffoon Eric didn't realize what was going on," Jennifer said, looking down into her mug as she swirled the tea around inside. "Explain to me again how his algorithm was tricked?"

"You want me to explain it?" Geoff tugged at his shirt collar. He wasn't sure how comfortable he felt sharing that kind of sensitive information, but if he wanted to maintain the illusion that he was fed up with Time Tours, he figured he had no choice.

He thought back to his first day on the job, when all of this had happened. It was quite a long time ago, but he was pretty sure he could remember everything. Then again, he'd felt equally confident about remembering the rules to Boggle after a two-year gap, and yet he'd still managed to wind up in A&E with his arm stuck inside a traffic cone the last time he'd tried to play it.

"Well, you know how his computer worked before he fixed the loophole in its algorithm?" Geoff asked.

"Correction," Jennifer said, holding up an index finger. "It's *my* computer. *I* designed it. Only the algorithm it ran was his, and we all know that code wasn't exactly a flawless masterpiece of programming."

Geoff looked down at his watch again. He knew he'd only just looked at the time a little while ago, but he couldn't help it. It wasn't long now before someone was going to put a bullet in his back, and things like that had a way of making you check your watch a little more often than you might have done otherwise.

It was one minute past three.

Twenty-nine minutes to go.

He looked again.

It was still one minute past three.

Still twenty-nine minutes to go, and a few fewer seconds.

"Okay, let me rephrase that," Geoff said. "Do you know how his *algorithm* worked, before he fixed the loophole?"

"Yes, yes," Jennifer replied. "It created a precise model of the space-time continuum, calculating the exact vibration of every molecule up to something like 100,000 years into the future, right? Then it took a snapshot of that moment in time, when Earth will have apparently been deserted by mankind to explore new worlds. Then, the computer compared that moment to a simulation of history which took into account the impact made by the tourist wishing to travel. If the computer detected any changes, it stopped them from going back. Correct?"

"That's right," Geoff said, looking down at his watch again.

Like before, it was still one minute past three.

He really needed to stop looking at his watch so much before Jennifer noticed.

"Something wrong with your watch?" Jennifer said.

"What? No, nothing. What were we talking about?"

"You were about to tell me how Eric's algorithm was tricked."

"Right. Basically, the Varsarians worked out that after going back and wiping out humanity, as long as they terraformed the planet 100,000 years in the future to make it look identical to final snapshot in the original timeline, right down to the last molecule, the computer would let them go back to change the outcome of their aborted invasion in the twenty-first century."

Jennifer laughed. "It was such a stupid flaw. Even a child could have spotted that loophole. You know he actually won a Nobel Prize for that algorithm?"

"Yeah, I think he might have mentioned it once or twice," Geoff said.

Jennifer placed her mug down on the desk and stood up.

"Anyway, that's all in the past. Welcome to Continuum, Geoff."

Geoff tilted his head slightly and frowned.

"What do you mean?"

"I mean you're hired."

Geoff stared at Jennifer for a second in silence. This was just like his interview with Time Tours all over again. What was it with people just hiring him out of the blue for no reason whatsoever?

"You okay?" she said.

"Yes, but I mean, you're hiring me just like that? No proper interview? No entrance exam? No ringing around my references to make sure I really am Geoffrey Stamp and not just some chump who's just walked in off the street *pretending* to be Geoffrey Stamp?"

"No, no, no. There's no need for any of that." She reached into her desk drawer and pulled out a business card. "Trust me—I know it's you all right."

"You do?"

"Here," she said, handing the card to him. "I've had this waiting in my desk for a long time. Waiting for the day you would join us."

Geoff froze as she showed it to him. It looked just like the one his future self had had on him. No job title, just the word *Continuum*, and his name printed in block capital letters below the motto WHAT WILL *YOU* CHANGE? Hands shaking, he took the card, examined it closely, and then put it in his jacket pocket.

"You okay?" Jennifer said.

"Me?" Geoff's voice had decided to go very high-pitched all of a sudden. He cleared his throat. "Yes. I'm fine."

"Good." She got to her feet. "Now, will you follow me, please?"

"Wait a minute," Geoff said. "Before I start, I did have a question, actually. I mean, as long as that's okay with you."

"Of course it is!" Jennifer said, making her way toward the door. "Ask away."

"What exactly is the job?"

Jennifer stopped and looked at him.

"I'm impressed," she said, walking back across the room and sitting down at her desk again.

"About what?"

"You're the first Time Rep to ask me that. So far, all the others have assumed I was hiring them to be a Time Rep."

"But that wouldn't make any sense. If the whole point of going on holiday with Continuum is to go back and alter the course of history, to see the effects of different changes, it wouldn't make sense for there to be tour guides based in different time periods."

"That's right," Jennifer said. "In fact, there's no need for us to employ any of you at all."

Geoff knew what he wanted to ask next, but it was now getting dangerously close to half past three, or as he was now calling the time in his head, bullet o'clock. What if this next question was the one that nearly got him killed?

But it was too late in the conversation now to just drop the topic. He couldn't just say "Never mind—I've just realized that I'm not curious about that at all!" and skip merrily out of the room.

He had no choice but to ask.

"So, why *are* you employing Time Reps?" Geoff asked, his face contorting into a wince as though he'd just asked her to hand him a live grenade.

Jennifer let out a long, deep breath.

"I'm hiring as many Time Reps as I can for one reason, and one reason only. Without Time Reps, Time Tours will go out of business. And the day I left that company, I promised them I would do just that—put them out of business."

"Why do you hate them so much?"

"Because they cheated me, Geoff. " Jennifer looked down at her hands. "That algorithm was completely useless without my computer. The kind of processing power needed to run that thing was astronomical, and I mean that literally—I had to practically create a scaled-down universe of miniature black holes to process and store the amount of data required. Took me three whole years of my life, sourcing the right materials, working out the physics, solving the problem of reading information back through Hawking radiation, sacrificing my personal life to hit deadlines, and what thanks did I get? Nothing. Well, I say nothing—they got me a box of chocolates and a card that said 'Thanks.' And it was one of those annoying cards where no one knows what to write, so all the messages were variations on the same thing, like, 'Thanks for doing such a *good* job,' next to someone who'd written 'Thanks for doing such a *great* job,' next to someone who had just written 'Great job!'"

"Were the chocolates nice at least?"

"Not really. They were Turkish Delights. And I hate Turkish Delights."

"I like Turkish Delights."

"I think we're drifting away from the subject here."

"Oh, yes. Sorry."

"Anyway, the day we launched our first selection of holiday destinations, I found out Eric had been awarded another Nobel Prize for giving time tourism to the world. I get a crappy box of chocolates, and Eric gets worldwide recognition, and the highest honor that can be bestowed by the scientific community. So, as I'm sure you can imagine, I felt a little bit underappreciated, you know? That prize should have been shared between us, but instead he took all the credit."

"So you were annoyed?"

"You could say that, yes," Jennifer continued. "From that moment on, I vowed I would one day invent something that would render that computer obsolete. After all, since I was the one who built it in the first place, I should be the one that decided when it was no longer needed, right?"

"Right," Geoff said. "Only…"

"Only what?" Jennifer said, narrowing her eyes.

Geoff was about to ask about the rumor Tim had told him, that Jennifer hadn't actually invented the technology used by Continuum, but had convinced a key scientist who had been developing it to leave Time Tours and work for her instead. However, given that he was trying his best to avoid getting shot, he felt it probably wasn't wise to antagonize her.

"Nothing," Geoff said. "I just forgot what I was going to say. You ever get that?"

"No," Jennifer said, standing up from her desk again. "I never forget anything. But never mind. Let me show you the reason why we invited you here."

Jennifer led Geoff out of her office and down a series of narrow winding corridors that felt as though they had been designed just to annoy whoever was trying to navigate them. Many pathways double-backed on themselves, others just ended for no reason, and all in all, the layout of the place was nearly as bad as the level design in *Duke Nukem Forever*.

Eventually, they stopped outside a room with the words DEPARTURE ROOM A written on the door.

"Here we are." Jennifer turned the handle and opened the door. "Come on in."

"Okay," Geoff said, following Jennifer as she stepped inside.

There wasn't much to say about the interior of the room. It was about the same size as Jennifer's office, with gray walls and no real features to speak of. The only thing of note was a small wooden table placed in the middle of the room. On it were two small bottles with some sort of red liquid in them, and a tablet computer that looked identical to the one William had been using to manipulate the timeline when he'd paid Geoff a visit.

"I'm sure you recognize this," Jennifer said, walking over to the table and picking up the tablet. "My greatest invention—the Sat-Nav."

Geoff laughed. "The Sat-Nav? Is that really what that thing is called?"

"What's wrong with that as a name?"

"Well, I thought a Sat-Nav was the thing that shouts the wrong directions and falls off your car windshield all the time if you don't stick it there properly."

"No," Jennifer said. "Sat-Nav is short for Space and Time Navigator. It's the device we give all tourists when they go back in time. With this, you can rewind time, fast-forward it, and even..." She trailed off.

"Yes?" Geoff said.

"I don't want to spoil it," she said, handing it to Geoff. "You'll get to explore all its functionality during the tutorial."

"Tutorial?" Geoff said. He hoped it wasn't like those boring tutorials you found in every single first-person shooter, where the opening level was conveniently designed to have a bit where you need to jump so it can say "Press A to jump," and a bit where you need to crouch so it can say "Press B to crouch," and a bit where you need to sprint so it can say "Hold down the right stick to sprint." He hated those sorts of levels.

"That's right," Jennifer said. "The first thing all tourists experience on a holiday with Continuum is a tutorial, demonstrating all the features of the device. We send you right the way back to the beginning of time and give you a taste of what you can do—how you can change whatever you like, and how you can send shock waves of causality through the space-time continuum with no harmful consequences to yourself whatsoever. You'll basically have the powers of a god, someone able to change the course of history however you wish. Trust me—you're going to love it."

"And what's with those bottles?" Geoff said, pointing at them.

"These?" Jennifer said, picking one up. "This is the serum that links you to your Sat-Nav. Drink this, and your mind and body will be shielded from however you choose to manipulate the timeline. Whether you leap forward a thousand years or slow time down to a crawl, your body will age normally. And if you rewind time, while your body will be forced into reverse, your mind will remember everything that transpired, even once the events you witnessed have been undone."

She unscrewed the cap and handed it to Geoff. "Drink it."

Geoff smelled the bottle. It smelled a bit metallic.

"But William has already injected me with this stuff," Geoff said. "Do I really need more?"

"Each serum is coded differently," Jennifer said. "The one he gave you was linked only to his tablet, and he would have unlinked you from his device the moment he returned things back to normal. Otherwise, you'd still be moving through time in line with what he is doing now."

"I see," Geoff said. He didn't know a liquid could be uniquely coded. This stuff probably had more artificial ingredients in it than any number of diet soft drink brands that would no doubt sue the living daylights out of anyone who mentioned them in an unfavorable context.

"Well? What are you waiting for?" Jennifer said. "Drink it."

Geoff looked at his watch.

Three fifteen.

"I don't get it," Geoff said, still holding the full bottle. "Before I drink this, do you mind telling me what the deal is here?"

"What do you mean?"

"I mean you still haven't answered my question. If you're not hiring me to be a Time Rep, then why are you hiring me at all?"

"It's simple," Jennifer said. "All I want is for you to take that Sat-Nav and disappear into history forever. Spend the rest of life on vacation, moving through time and changing things as you please. Maybe you could use your new powers to go back and win the lottery. Or perhaps take your chances with this Zoë girl. Whatever you choose to do, with the Sat-Nav, you'll never make another mistake again. Everything you do can be undone. Every happy memory can be relived. I'm asking all Time Reps to spend the rest of their lives in paradise; I'm asking you all to go back and enjoy yourselves. Forever."

Geoff narrowed his eyes. "Sounds too good to be true. What's the catch?"

"There is no catch. Just go back in time, and enjoy the rest of your life however you please."

"But this makes no sense," Geoff said. "What do you get out of all this?"

"Simple—I get to watch Time Tours go out of business, and I get to see a lot of Time Reps free themselves from the shackles of their old job. Their old life."

"That's it?"

"That's it. It really is a win-win situation."

Geoff had to admit, it sounded like a pretty good deal. In fact, the only way it could have been any better would be if he used the opportunity to go back and time and change history so that quiche was never invented. He hated quiche.

At this point, he knew he should probably have immediately gone back to tell Tim what was going on, but part of him was extremely curious to try this out. This was his chance to find out what Zoë's reaction would be if he asked her out, to see the look on her face when he revealed the truth about who he really was. It was too good an opportunity to miss.

Of course, he would eventually get around to telling Tim all about Jennifer's plans, but not just yet.

First of all, he wanted to have some fun.

He looked down at the bottle, lifted it to his lips, and drank the serum. Just as he had detected from its scent, the liquid tasted slightly metallic. There definitely must have been some artificial colors and flavorings in there.

"Good," Jennifer said, picking up the other bottle and handing it to him. "Here's a spare batch in case you want to share the experience with someone else."

"How do I use it?" Geoff said, taking the bottle and putting it in his pocket.

"The Sat-Nav will tell you what to do," Jennifer replied.

Geoff looked down at the tablet. It was quite light, about the weight of a small book. On the screen, a big green button appeared that simply said BEGIN.

"Okay," Jennifer said. "From the moment you press that button, your Continuum experience will start."

Geoff looked at his watch one last time.

Still no sign that anyone was going to try and kill him.

But then everything started to fall into place in his mind. He'd been looking at this all wrong—at the moment, there was no reason for anyone to try and kill him. He was harmless. He'd done nothing wrong. But what if he discovered something while he was away, then used the Sat-Nav to eventually come back to this exact moment in time? Maybe he was going to reverse his way completely back out of everything he was about to experience, returning to this spot with new memories. And maybe it was something about those memories that nearly got him killed.

He must have been about to uncover a secret that was worth killing to protect, like what was going to happen in the remaining *Game of Thrones* books.

But what secret could that be? And having figured all this

out, why would he willingly return to this point in time if he knew it meant someone was going to shoot him?

"Are you all right?" Jennifer said.

"What's that?"

"You keep looking like something's bothering you."

"It's nothing. I'm fine."

"Well then, what are you waiting for?"

"Right," Geoff said. "Here I go."

He took a deep breath and held the air in his lungs, his finger hovering over the BEGIN button on the screen. Somehow, he had a feeling he'd be back in this room sooner than either of them would expect.

"From now on," Jennifer said, "the fate of the world is in your hands. All you need to do is ask yourself one question: What will *you* change?"

NINE

Geoff breathed out slowly and pressed the BEGIN button on the tablet, and in that moment, everything around him changed. The walls of the Continuum building melted away, the sky went dark, and in front of him, huge volcanoes appeared on the horizon, spewing out lava and pumping thick, black smoke into the air. Instead of standing in a small underground room, he now found himself on an outcrop of rock, surrounded by bubbling rivers of lava. He removed his finger from the button on the tablet and tugged at his collar—it was baking hot.

"Welcome to your Continuum tutorial session," a voice said from behind him.

Geoff spun around.

He knew that voice.

It was Jennifer Adams again.

Or at least, it was a holographic representation of Jennifer Adams, projected a few feet in front of him to make it look like she was standing there with him. Her physical form was slightly transparent and seemed to be constructed out of a blue light, and as she moved, millions of floating pixels darted around within the rough outline of her body to animate her movement. She kind of reminded him of Cortana from the *Halo* games, except she actually had some clothes on.

"Jennifer?" Geoff said, taking a step forward. The ground beneath his feet felt hot even through his shoes, a bit like when you're on a beach and it's sunny, and you think it would be nice to walk around barefoot until you realize after two steps that the soles of your feet feel like they're on fire.

"Jennifer?" he said. "Is that you?"

The hologram of Jennifer Adams didn't appear to react to

Geoff's question; its eyes just looked straight through him as if he weren't there. This was actually how a lot of women tended to react to Geoff, so it wasn't an unusual experience for him. He reached out to touch the image, but his hand just passed straight through it.

Now that *was* unusual. He'd never actually just reached out to touch a woman without warning before, but he assumed the normal reaction in that instance would be to get a slap.

And then get arrested.

Geoff's stomach rumbled again.

Roughly translated, this meant "please insert food immediately."

The hologram of Jennifer spoke.

"You are now standing at the earliest known point when the Earth could sustain oxygen-breathing life forms, billions of years ago," it said. The image of Jennifer appeared to be prerecorded, reciting a standard script. Geoff assumed this was what every tourist saw on their first trip.

"At this time, most of the planet is still covered in lava," it continued. "There is barely any plant life, and the first vertebrates will not exist for many, many years."

Great, Geoff thought. If that was the case, he didn't fancy his chances of finding a conveniently located Pret A Manger nearby. He would just have to put up with being hungry a little while longer.

The hologram turned to face the vast range of volcanoes in the distance, extending its pixelated arms toward them. "In front of you," it said, "the Earth is still a volatile planet, with the continents you know today still yet to be formed. But over time, forests will grow. Oceans will rise and fall. And mountains will climb high into the sky."

And ultimately, Geoff thought, *the human race will appear on the scene and offer many contributions of its own to the evolution of the planet, like the wheel, foldable cutlery, and squeezy Marmite.*

Once the hologram finished speaking, it disappeared in a puff of blue dots.

Geoff stood there for a moment, staring blankly at where the hologram had just vanished into thin air.

Was that it? What kind of tutorial was that? He'd just been given one of the most sophisticated pieces of time-manipulation devices to do with as he pleased, and yet when it came to being told how to use it, all he'd gotten was a quick lecture about how the planet had lacked a lot of basic amenities back when it was still developing into the world he knew today. It was like turning up for a flying lesson only to learn that the instructor was a small dog holding an interesting story about the Wright brothers in its mouth.

But just then, something began to happen. Time appeared to speed up before Geoff's eyes, and he watched in total amazement as the landscape of the planet began to change form in a matter of seconds. It was as though he were watching a piece of time-lapse photography set over billions of years, like that really cool special effect in *Star Trek II: The Wrath of Khan* where Kirk watches the video demonstrating how the Genesis device could transform a barren moon into a lush planet in just a few days. He watched in awe as tiny saplings in the ground grew into towering trees in a matter of seconds, and then watched as a cycle repeated itself of trees decaying away, falling down, and being replaced by other trees. To his right, a few trickles of water swelled into a surging river, weaving its way through the landscape like a winding snake. And in the distance, Earth's tectonic plates crashed into each other like two angry giants, the scars taking the form of beautiful snow-capped mountain ranges that soared into the sky.

He couldn't understand how this was happening. Who was controlling his journey through time at the moment? It was only then that he thought to look down at the Sat-Nav. On the screen, the date was spinning forward, and the words TUTORIAL MODE were displayed underneath.

The device must have been doing all of this automatically.

At least, he hoped that was the case—otherwise he was in big trouble. It would be just typical if he'd broken the bloody thing already.

Eventually, the flow of time returned to a normal speed. Geoff let out a deep breath, took a few steps forward, and looked around. He was standing in the middle of a tropical jungle, with all kinds of strange and exotic animal noises emanating from his surroundings.

Geoff looked down at the tablet again. On the screen, the date said 200,000,000 BC.

In front of him, the hologram of Jennifer Adams appeared again. "Now, let's take a look at your Space and Time Navigator," it said, "or as we like to call it at Continuum, the Sat-Nav."

Geoff sniggered. He still couldn't believe they'd called this thing a Sat-Nav. As far as the naming of a product went, it was nearly as bad as when Kellogg's briefly renamed Coco Pops to Choco Crispies before changing it back again. Didn't they realize nothing rhymed with *crispies* if they wanted to use the same jingle in their TV adverts?

"The Sat-Nav is a remarkable device, allowing you not only to have complete control over your exact position in time, but also in three-dimensional space. It is small, compact, and easy to use, with a simple, intuitive interface. It also comes in eight different colors, and for additional security, the screen took a scan of your fingerprint when you first pressed BEGIN, making you the only person now capable of using it."

The Sat-Nav was all very impressive, Geoff thought, rubbing his stomach, but could it help him find the nearest restaurant?

"At present, your Sat-Nav tutorial program has sent you to two hundred million years BC, in the middle of what will one day be known as the Amazon rainforest. If you look at the display, you can see the date clearly."

Geoff could indeed see the date. This interface seemed pretty straightforward and easy to use so far, although that's what he'd thought the first time he'd used Windows 8.

"You are now on the WHEN screen," the hologram said. "The WHEN screen has two main functions—it tells you when you are, and you can tell it when you want to go. Now, you will see three icons at the top of the screen. One has a question mark, one has a clock, and one has a crosshair. The question mark represents the WHAT screen, which we will get to later. The crosshair represents the WHERE screen, which we will look at now. Go ahead and press the icon with the crosshair."

Geoff did as he was told. As he pressed the icon, the screen below changed to show a map of his location. As he played around with the screen, drawing on it with his finger to navigate, he realized you could zoom out for a full view of the planet, or right down to the individual blades of grass beneath his feet. It was like Google Maps on steroids, only minus the blurred-out faces and markers for minicab companies.

"This is the WHERE screen. Just like the WHEN screen, the WHERE screen also has two functions—it tells you where you are, and you can tell it where you want to go. Used in conjunction with the WHEN screen, you can use the Sat-Nav to transport you wherever, and whenever you want."

Geoff raised his eyebrows. Despite the stupid name, this device was seriously impressive. It was so sophisticated it made Apple's iPad look like it had no more functionality than an actual apple.

"Now, let's say you wanted to travel forward in time, and appear on another continent. First of all, go back to the WHEN screen by pressing the clock icon."

Geoff pressed the clock. The current date appeared on the screen.

"Next, use the dials to change the year to one hundred and ninety million years BC."

Geoff did as he was told.

"Now move to the WHERE screen again, and zoom out. Spin the Earth so the crosshair is over the northern hemisphere, then zoom in. The image you see is a real-time snapshot of the moment in time you intend to travel to, so you can be sure you won't materialize in the middle of a mountain, or in the path of anything moving toward you. The Sat-Nav will also perform a safety check of your destination before transporting you, and will prevent you from traveling anywhere that might put you in danger."

Except in my case, Geoff thought, *when I'll eventually use this thing to go back and get shot. Great!*

He followed the hologram's instructions, scrolling around the map and zooming in on a beach somewhere in the northern hemisphere. When he had decided on a location, another icon appeared at the bottom of the screen. It said EXECUTE.

"When you are ready to travel," the hologram said, "press the EXECUTE button. There will be a short delay while the Sat-Nav performs its safety checks, and once that is done, you will be transported instantly to the time and place you selected."

Geoff pressed the EXECUTE button and waited. In the top right hand corner of the screen, a little hourglass spun around. Then before he knew it, he wasn't standing in the jungle anymore. He was on the long sandy beach he had chosen, looking out across the ocean, the sky overcast and swirling with huge gray clouds up above. It was like standing in the middle of a magnificent Constable painting, except there were no horses wandering onto the scene.

This thing was incredible.

"Next, we have the WHAT button," the hologram said, appearing in front of him again. "This is the third icon at the top of your screen, with a question mark on it. The WHAT button provides the user with a live stream of information, allowing you to understand the consequences of any changes you make to the course of history. For example…"

Without warning, Geoff's surroundings suddenly changed, and he found himself standing in the middle of a lush evergreen forest. Above him, huge pine trees rose high up into the sky.

"Welcome to London," the hologram said, this time walking out from behind Geoff, which he found to be a little disorienting. "Or rather, welcome to the site where London will one day be built, one hundred and ninety million years in the future."

Geoff shook his head. For a moment, he couldn't believe how different everything looked from the London he knew, but then, he was still struggling to comprehend just how far back in time he was. It wasn't like this place was going to get bulldozed in a few weeks and converted into a nice high street with several apartment blocks (and Pret A Mangers, of course). He was *one hundred and ninety million years* in the past.

"Now, we've all heard of the butterfly effect," the hologram continued. "This is the theory that a small change made long ago could potentially have a huge ripple effect on future events. You're going to test that theory. In a few moments, a butterfly is going to land on the ground in front of you. When it does, please stand on the butterfly and kill it."

Just as the hologram had predicted, a large butterfly with violet wings soon fluttered around in front of him before landing right at his feet. Geoff looked down on the insect. It was a beautifully delicate creature, with an intricate purple pattern spread across each wing like a piece of decorative calligraphy, designed by nature itself.

He trod on it and twisted his foot into the ground, killing it instantly.

"Now, on the WHEN page," the hologram said, "you will notice a button with a fast-forward symbol on it, much like the fast-forward button you would find on a video remote."

Geoff recognized this button. It was the same one William had pressed to see the future consequences of his actions when he destroyed Canary Wharf.

"Holding down this button will begin to wind time forward, and the harder you hold it down, the faster time will pass. Try it now and see what the consequences will be of killing that butterfly."

Geoff held down the fast-forward button and watched as time began to speed up. Just as the hologram had said, the more pressure he put on the button, the faster time passed, until the rising and setting of the sun was just a blur. He watched as the years began to count up on the Sat-Nav's display, and within a few minutes he was racing through thousands of years every second.

"Now, you may be wondering how you are able to occupy the same space while time is moving forward, and not be impacted by any physical changes in the environment," the hologram said.

Geoff was actually thinking about whether it was too soon to have another cup of tea when the opportunity presented itself, but now that he thought about it, this was a good question. While traveling through time, would it appear to everyone else that he was just standing still? And what happened if something bumped into him while he was standing still? Like a speeding bus? He suddenly felt a little nervous.

"While you are in this state," the hologram explained, "your body is phased outside of regular space-time, meaning not only are you invisible to people in the normal world, but physical objects pass straight through you."

Well, that's good to know, Geoff thought. The last thing he would want to happen would be to travel forward a few millennia only to discover that someone had stolen his trousers six hundred years ago.

As he got closer and closer to 0 BC, he took a little pressure off the button, causing time to pass a little slower. He had yet to see any sign of human civilization, although some structures began to appear on the landscape that he didn't recognize. But time was just passing too quickly for him to catch a glimpse of any people.

One thousand years AD came and went, and London started to take form. But as Geoff slowed down the passage of time more and more, he noticed a number of significant differences in this new timeline.

For a start, the dominant species on the planet did not appear to be *Homo sapiens* anymore. Instead, the major species was a catlike race with stumpy tails and large feet, walking around on their hind legs and wearing clothes much like humans. As a result of this, the passage of history was very different from the way he remembered it, and he observed with interest as the catlike creatures became more and more technologically advanced. Over the years, this race built a city on the same site as London, but they chose a very different architectural style, with several dome-topped cylindrical towers of different heights being the main type of structure.

It was like a city of giant scratching posts.

Once Geoff reached the twenty-first century, he took his finger off the fast-forward button and stood in the street. All around him, the catlike creatures stopped and stared back at him, as though he'd just materialized out of thin air. Some began to panic and run away. Others seemed to be approaching him with caution. It was really strange—these creatures had so many qualities similar to human beings, but they were feline. What the hell was going on? How had stepping on that butterfly turned the world into a Saturday morning cartoon with anthropomorphized cats everywhere?

At that moment, time paused, and the hologram of Jennifer Adams appeared in front of him. "You're probably wondering why everything looks so different," it said.

No shit, Geoff thought.

"This is where the WHAT button comes in," the hologram said. "Press it, and the Sat-Nav will explain the exact consequences of any changes you have made."

Geoff pressed the WHAT button and watched as the screen filled up with text. Just as the hologram had said, the Sat-Nav provided a real-time explanation as to why the Earth was now dominated by a catlike species rather than human beings. It turned out that stepping on the butterfly in 190,000,000 BC had caused a chain reaction, altering the course of evolution in the favor of a feline species. In short, stepping on that butterfly had wiped out the entire human race.

Good job no one had mentioned that to the Varsarians two years ago. If they'd known it was that easy to defeat humanity, they would have just turned up in prehistoric times with a can of insect repellent and waited.

"Finally, we have the rewind button," the hologram said. "This is probably the most important feature of the device. In the WHEN screen, you will see a symbol in the bottom right-hand corner of the screen, much like the rewind button on a video remote. Press it."

Geoff did as he was told.

Just as had happened on William's Sat-Nav when he'd

pressed the button, a new line of text appeared on the screen:
PLEASE CONFIRM HOW FAR BACK YOU WISH TO REWIND.

Beneath this text was a horizontal slider, and a series of dials for years, days, hours, minutes, and seconds.

"The slider in front of you represents your own personal continuum, as experienced from your point of view," the hologram explained. "The far right of the bar represents the present moment, and the far left represents the moment you ingested the serum linking you to the Sat-Nav. To rewind time, all you need to do is drag the slider to the left as far back as you want to go. The dials below will change accordingly, and if you want to fine-tune the period of time you want to go back to, simply touch the dials to change them manually. In this case, we want to go back to the moment before you trod on the butterfly, which was three forty-five p.m. on the third of March, one hundred and ninety million years BC. Simply slide the arrow accordingly, or touch the dials to enter the date and time manually. Once you are done, press the flashing green button at the bottom of the screen."

Geoff entered the date and time he'd been given and pressed the flashing button. The moment he did, time began to flow backward, and just as he'd experienced when William had done this, his body felt paralyzed, as it was forced to move exactly as it had just done, only in reverse. He watched as he unentered the date and time he had just entered on the Sat-Nav, then passively observed the events he had caused by stepping on the butterfly undo themselves. The catlike civilization regressed back into a primitive state, and the impressive city of vast cylindrical towers shrank back to nothing. Then the reversal of time began to speed up, no doubt reflecting the speed at which Geoff had fast-forwarded time when he perceived it flowing forward. Then, finally, time slowed down, he felt himself lift his foot back off the undead butterfly, and as he regained control of his body again with a jolt, he watched the butterfly fly away unharmed. He sincerely hoped that butterfly was going to take good care of itself and that it had a decent pension plan—the future of the entire human race depended on its survival.

He thought about what had just happened. It was strange—even though he had just undone all the changes he had made to the space-time continuum, he could still remember all the details of the alternate future he had created.

"Finally," the hologram said, "if you have chosen to bring along some spare serum so a guest can join you on your travels, you will need to know how to use it."

Geoff felt his pocket to make sure the bottle was still there. He knew exactly who he wanted to give this to, so he was sure to listen carefully as the hologram gave its explanation.

"Using a spare serum is very simple. First, your guest will need to ingest it. Once this happens, they will automatically be linked to your Sat-Nav, meaning they will have the same experience of time being manipulated as you. They will be connected to your Sat-Nav indefinitely, and will be able to move along the timeline as far back as you ingested your own serum. If for whatever reason you wish to sever the connection, simply hold down the small red button on the rear of the device for three seconds. But be careful using this feature—once your guest is disconnected, they will no longer be able to move through time with you unless you are rewinding time, and even then they will no longer be able to retain memories of anything they unexperience."

So it was a bit like disconnecting a Wii remote to the main console, Geoff thought.

"Be warned, though—once your guest is severed, they will not be able to reconnect to the Sat-Nav until they ingest more serum, and rewinding events will cause them to lose all memory of the changes you experienced together."

Geoff nodded to himself. Like the rest of the tutorial, that sounded pretty straightforward.

"So I will leave you now to explore history however you please," the hologram said, flashing a pixelated smile vacantly toward him. "We hope you enjoy your Continuum experience, and wish you a safe and pleasant vacation."

With that, the hologram disappeared in a puff of blue dots again, only this time the dots seemed to get sucked into the

Sat-Nav. Was that where the projection had been coming from all along?

So this was it.

He needed to decide what he was going to change.

He stood in the forest alone for a moment, closing his eyes to listen to the wind ruffle through the surrounding vegetation.

Geoff imagined most people being completely spoiled for choice when it came to choosing where to go and what changes to make, but in his case the decision was made instantaneously.

He knew exactly where he wanted to go, and what he wanted to change.

He wanted to go to a restaurant, and change the fact that he hadn't eaten anything all day by ordering a large cheeseburger.

He might order some chips, too.

And then he would find Zoë.

TEN

Because Geoff couldn't wait to tell Zoë what he really did for a living (after having eaten his cheeseburger, of course), he decided that the best moment to talk to her would be immediately after he'd seen her that morning when he was on his way to Canary Wharf. In his excitement, it didn't occur to him that it might seem a bit strange for her to see him waiting on the other side of the street right after she'd just said goodbye to a past version of himself, or that he now looked quite different. Although from Geoff's point of view he hadn't seen Zoë for a few hours, to her, it would appear as though he'd instantly changed into a nice suit and altered his appearance so he didn't always look like he was about to audition for a part in a film set in a world where all self-grooming products suddenly ceased to function.

But this didn't really cross Geoff's mind—all he wanted to do was see Zoë, and tell her the truth about himself for the first time in two years.

Geoff felt his hands shaking slightly. He had waited so long for this moment, and now it was finally here. He could show Zoë who he really was, confess to her how he really felt. He didn't know how she would react, didn't know if she would tell him that she felt the same way, or if she would find the whole thing a bit awkward, but right now he was just excited about being honest with her. And if this all went horribly wrong, he could always rewind time and try again.

Which was quite handy.

But how on Earth would he start the conversation? *Hi Zoë! Guess what? I'm actually a time traveler!* No—that sounded a bit weird. *Hey! Interesting story about me that I might not have told you—did you know I saved the world once? And that I'm a time traveler?* Hmm.

That also sounded a bit weird. *Hey Zoë! I was just thinking—how would you like to go and see a dinosaur?* No, no, no. These were all weird ways to start up the conversation. But then, that was the problem with being a Time Rep. As careers went, being a Time Rep was weird.

Weirder even than those people whose job it is to separate the girl chicks from the boy chicks on farms by squeezing poo out of their bums.

Well, he needed to think of something to say quickly, because Zoë was now walking right toward him. In the end, he opted for the ever reliable "Hello," but just as he was about to open his mouth to speak, she put her headphones in, started humming along to her music, and walked straight past, rummaging around in her bag for the next batch of mail.

She hadn't even seen him.

Geoff turned around on the spot and watched her walk away.

Well, that didn't exactly go as planned.

Should he go after her? Tap her on the shoulder to get her attention?

No—that would scare the hell out of her (Zoë was very jumpy), and this was a big moment for him.

He wanted it to be perfect.

Maybe he should try that again.

Rewind.

TEN

Because Geoff still couldn't wait to tell Zoë what he really did for a living, he once again decided that the best moment to talk to her would be immediately after he'd seen her that morning when he was on his way to Canary Wharf. He was still excited, so it still didn't occur to him that if Zoë saw him waiting on the other side of the street right after she'd just said goodbye to a past version of himself, it might come across as a bit weird. And he'd still forgotten that he looked completely different.

Geoff was shaking slightly. He had waited so long for this moment (plus a few extra seconds since the last attempt went wrong), and now it was finally here.

Again.

If Zoë actually saw him this time, he could show her who he really was, confess to her how he really felt. He still didn't know how she would react, didn't know if she would tell him that she felt the same way, or if she would find the whole thing a bit awkward, but right now he was just excited about being honest with her, albeit a little less excited since the last attempt had backfired slightly. He was still feeling nervous about what would happen when he told her, but once again he reassured himself that if this went wrong again, he could always rewind time and try again.

Which was already proving to be quite handy.

In fact, if he wasn't careful, rewinding time to correct his mistakes could become quite addictive.

He'd put a bit more thought into how he would start the conversation this time, though, and before Zoë had a chance to put her headphones in and block out the world, he was ready with his opening.

"Hey, Zoë," he called out, giving her a wave.

Zoë looked up and stared at him for a few seconds. It seemed to take her quite a while to realize who she was talking to.

"Wait a minute," Zoë said, looking up and down at him. "*Geoff?*"

"Yup," he said, taking a couple of steps back. "It's me."

"But I…" she pointed back down the road. "And you were…"

"Ah," Geoff said, suddenly looking at the situation from her perspective. "You were just talking to me a moment ago, weren't you?"

Zoë nodded.

"So I suppose this must look a bit weird."

"You could say that!" Zoë put her post bag on the ground and took a few deep breaths. "How the hell did you change clothes so quickly? And how did you make yourself look so…"

"…clean?"

"Different. How did you make yourself look so different?"

"Oh," Geoff said, just beginning to remember how he looked. He ran a hand across his smooth jawline and smiled. "I had a shave."

"I can see that!" Zoë said. "And a haircut! How the hell did you do that so quickly?"

Geoff raised his hands to calm her down.

"Zoë—there's something I have to tell you."

"There is?"

"Yes—listen. This will explain everything. You know how I work as a holiday rep, showing people around London?"

"Yes."

"Well, that's not the whole picture. You see…these tourists…" he trailed off.

Zoë tilted her head to one side and waited for him to speak again.

"Yes?" she said.

"Let me put it another way," he said. "What would your reaction be if I said that these tourists were from…" he trailed off again.

"What would my reaction be if you said these tourists were from…where? Sunderland?"

Geoff rubbed his eyes. "This is very difficult for me to explain," he said.

Geoff sighed. He wanted to tell her everything—how he was employed as a Time Rep, how he had traveled as far back as prehistoric times, how he had defeated the most aggressive alien race ever encountered by humanity; but it was so difficult. He just didn't know where to start.

He started to formulate a decent explanation in his mind, but by now it was too late. Zoë was beginning to give him a strange look. In fact, she looked a little worried for him, as though he'd just come up to her and told her he was having romantic thoughts about the cat.

This hadn't gone to plan at all.

But he could always try again.

TEN

This time Geoff understood that it might seem a bit strange for Zoë to see him immediately after she'd just said goodbye to a past version of himself, but he decided to use this to his advantage. If he were clever, he could use this as proof that he could travel through time. After all, how else could he have gotten changed and had a shave and a haircut so quickly?

"Hey Zoë," he called out, giving her a wave.

Zoë looked up and stared at him for a few seconds. It seemed to take her quite a while to realize who she was talking to, but since she had no memory of their previous last two encounters, he supposed that was understandable.

"Wait a minute," Zoë said, looking up and down at him. "*Geoff*?"

"That's right," he said, taking a couple of steps back. "It's me."

"But I..." she pointed back down the road. "And you were..."

"I can explain," Geoff said, "I know this must look a bit weird."

"You could say that!" Zoë put her post bag on the ground and took a few deep breaths. "How did you change clothes so quickly? And how did you make yourself look so..."

"Different?"

"Yes, different. How did you make yourself look so different?"

Geoff raised his hands to calm her down.

"Zoë—there's something I have to tell you."

"There is?"

"Yes—listen. You know how I work as a holiday rep, showing people around London?"

"Yes…"

"Well, that's only part of the story. You see, the tourists I show around London aren't from around here."

Zoë blinked. "I know that, Geoff," she said. "That's why they're called tourists."

"That's not what I meant," Geoff said. "Okay—let me put it this way. You know how a regular tourist is from the same time period as we are?"

Zoë frowned. "The same *time period*?"

"Yes. You know how a regular tourist is from the twenty-first century?"

"Yeees…."

"Well, these ones aren't. The tourists I meet are from the future."

"And what do you mean by that exactly?"

"I mean they travel back through time to go on vacation. From the thirty-first century."

"The thirty-first century."

"That's right," Geoff said.

Zoë looked at him in silence.

He knew that look.

It was the same look she'd given him when he'd accidentally dropped that hat of hers under that bus.

"You don't believe me, do you?" he said.

"Not particularly," Zoë replied.

"Why not?"

"Why not? Time travel is impossible!"

"No it isn't," Geoff said. "And I can prove it."

"Maybe another time, Doctor Who," Zoë said, picking up her post bag and looking through it. "Besides, I'm sure your TARDIS must be coming to the end of its time on the parking meter."

TEN

This was getting ridiculous. He was on his fourth attempt now, and he still couldn't get this right.

Maybe he should just kiss her.

TEN

Okay, so he knew not to just kiss her.

"Hey, Zoë," Geoff called out to Zoë, giving her a wave. His jaw hurt a little when he moved it to speak, but fortunately you couldn't see a bruise.

Zoë looked up and stared at him for a few seconds. "Wait a minute," she said, looking up and down at him. "*Geoff?*"

"I know what you're thinking," Geoff said, his voice quickening with impatience. "You're wondering how it is I'm able to be here talking to you, when you've only just said goodbye to me a few seconds ago."

Zoë opened her mouth to say something, but no words came out.

Geoff stepped forward and smiled. "I know this looks weird, Zoë," he said. "And I know I look different. But please—don't be scared."

"Your hair…" she said. "And your face…"

"I've scrubbed up," Geoff said.

Zoë pointed behind her to where she had just said goodbye to the other Geoff.

"I don't understand," she said. "How did you get over here? And how did you change your clothes so quickly?"

"Listen, Zoë," Geoff said, stepping forward. "I have something amazing to tell you, something that will explain all of this. But before I do, I want to ask you a question."

"Y-yes?"

"Do you trust me?"

"What?"

"I said, do you trust me?"

Zoë looked him in the eyes as if to check whether this really was the Geoffrey Stamp she knew talking to her. He reached out and held her hands, and as he did so, he felt her relax. Somehow, despite however crazy this situation must have appeared, he could tell from her eyes that she knew it was him.

"Yes," Zoë said, dropping her post bag to the ground. "Yes, I trust you."

"Okay. That's all I needed to know."

Zoë smiled. "What is it you wanted to tell me?" she said.

Geoff let out a sigh.

"This is going to sound crazy," he said, letting go of her hands and taking a step back, "but you have to promise to hear me out, okay?"

"Okay…"

"It's like this. You know how I work as a holiday rep, showing tourists around London?"

Zoë nodded.

"Well, that's only part of the story. You see, the tourists I show around London are very different from your regular tourists. They travel back in time from the future, visiting different historical periods for their vacation."

Zoë narrowed her eyes.

Geoff knew this look. This was the first stage of her skeptical look. He needed to do something quickly before the look entered stage two, which involved tilting her head to the left slightly. Once that happened, he would be only a hairsbreadth from her pursing her lips, and then it would all be over. There would be no chance of convincing her that he was telling the truth.

"They travel back in time from the future," she said.

"Yes."

As Geoff had feared, she tilted her head. They were now at DEFCON 2.

"Visiting different historical periods for their vacation," she said.

"Uh-huh. Like I said—I know it sounds crazy, but it's true. I'm not a holiday rep. I'm a Time Rep." She untilted her head. Whatever he had just said must have intrigued her. "A *Time* Rep?"

"It's like a holiday rep, only instead of being a tour guide for a certain country, I'm a tour guide for a certain time period. In my case, the early twenty-first century."

"I see," Zoë said, tilting her head again. It had only been a small reprieve. "And what year did you say these tourists are from?"

"They don't measure time in Earth years where they're from."

"They don't?"

Geoff could see Zoë's lips beginning to purse. He needed to make sure that whatever he said next wasn't too weird, otherwise he'd lose her.

"No, they use something called Outer Galactic Mean Time Spiral something something. I can't remember exactly. But basically, they're from the mid-thirty-first century."

Geoff thought about what he had just said. If there was ever an award for the last thing you would want to say to someone to convince them you weren't insane, that sentence probably would have won it.

But it was true.

"Okay, Geoff," Zoë laughed. Somehow, his talk of Outer Galactic Mean Time had disarmed her. "Very funny."

"What's very funny?"

"This story," she said, reaching to pick up her bag again. "It's funny."

"I'm not joking," Geoff said.

"Yes, you are."

"Okay—how else do you explain this?" he said, gesturing to himself. "How else do you think I was able to be standing here, just a few seconds after you said goodbye to me?"

"I have no idea," Zoë said. "You have a twin brother. It's magic. I'm dreaming."

"No. It's because that man you just spoke to was a past version of me. I was him a few hours ago, and now I've traveled back in time."

"Geoff—I'm sorry, but…"

"Please, Zoë," Geoff said. "You said you trusted me. Will you give me one chance to prove it to you?"

"I don't know…"

"Oh—I should point out that you'll need to drink this weird serum," he said, taking the small bottle of red liquid out of his coat pocket and showing it to her. "But don't worry—it's totally safe. I had some a few moments ago, and as you can see, I'm perfectly fine."

Zoë narrowed her eyes, tilted her head, and pursed her lips.

That was it.

DEFCON 1.

"No chance," she said, and walked off.

ELEVEN

Okay, he was getting fed up with this now. He thought telling Zoë was going to be a special moment where she would just happily accept everything he said without question.

"You meet tourists from the future? That's amazing!"

"I know. And I've saved the world, too."

"Wow, Geoff—I had no idea! You're incredible!"

But that conversation was just a fantasy.

He knew Zoë better than that.

Zoë was smart, and when you went up to someone smart and told them you met people who traveled back in time from over a millennium into the future, it was only natural for them to be a tad skeptical about your sanity. As he was discovering, he needed to navigate his way through this conversation very carefully, and for a moment he felt as though he were in one of those annoying video games where you have to choose the right dialogue options, otherwise you get sent back to the beginning of the level.

Then he realized he didn't need to go back to the beginning of their conversation. Toward the end of their last exchange, Zoë was thinking it over. He had been so close—in fact, for a while she looked like she was about to say yes. It was only when he'd mentioned the serum that she'd decided against it, so maybe if he didn't mention that, she would give him a chance to prove that he was telling the truth.

There was only one way to find out. He took the Sat-Nav out of his pocket, pressed the rewind button, and dragged the slider back a few seconds, to just before he'd messed up the conversation. Then, after pressing the flashing green button at the bottom of the screen, he watched as he un-took out the tablet from his pocket, un-jumped up and down holding his foot, un-kicked the lamppost, un-swore, then looked up at Zoë as she marched back toward him. Then she said "ecnahc oN." Finally, Geoff un-mentioned the serum, and then Zoë was un-tilting her head from one side to the other.

Then time began to flow forward again.

TEN

Zoë's head began tilting from one side to the other. Once again, she was thinking about giving Geoff a chance to prove he was telling the truth about being a Time Rep.

This was the moment he needed to say something that would nudge her decision in the right direction—something that didn't mention serums, or anything else that might put her off. Like paradoxes.

"Come on," he said. "Didn't you say you wished you could look into the future? What if I told you I could take you to any time, any place? We could go wherever we liked, with no one telling us what we can and can't do."

Zoë stopped tilting her head and looked Geoff in the eyes.

"Isn't that worth taking a chance on? And besides, if I'm joking, so what? You have absolutely nothing to lose."

Zoë began nodding to herself. "To hell with it," she smiled. "I know you're probably pulling my leg, but whatever. Let's do it."

Geoff let out a long sigh. "At last," he said.

"Fine," Zoë said, picking up her post bag. "If you're going to be like that, maybe I won't let you show me."

Needless to say, Geoff undid that last comment.

ELEVEN

It took Geoff another eight attempts to adequately explain to Zoë how the Sat-Nav worked, and another fifteen to convince her to drink the serum. As it happened, the correct conversation path was to first of all invite her back to his place for a cup of tea, sit her down on the sofa, and then gently introduce the idea that she would need to drink a serum as well. He then needed to do a bit of reconvincing that this whole time travel thing was a good idea, tempting her with ideas like the fact that she would be able to see if her band ever made it, and that he would take her back to visit her favorite time period, which just so happened to be ancient Egypt. Then they had to talk about how amazing ancient Egypt would be to visit, and then Geoff had to listen to an anecdote about how Zoë had actually been to Egypt quite recently and lost her phone. Then the conversation took a detour to talk about what the best phone was to get these days, then they talked about Angry Birds, and finally the conversation returned to the subject of time travel. All in all, it took about two hours and three cups of tea for Zoë to finally understand how the Sat-Nav worked, and to agree to drink the serum so that her mind and body were synchronized with the device.

"That tasted awful," Zoë said, handing the empty bottle back to Geoff.

"I know," Geoff said. "But it will be worth it—trust me."

"Just for the record, I still don't believe any of this," Zoë said, wiping her mouth. "But since you seem so convinced by all of this, I'll humor you."

"I do appreciate it," Geoff said. "And I promise—I won't let you down."

"So what happens now?" Zoë asked.

"Now, I'm going to show you something I did two years ago," Geoff said. "Not long after I was hired to be a Time Rep. It's something I've been desperate to talk to you about since the day it happened, something you are not going to believe."

"And what would that be?"

"Well, you might have a little trouble believing this, but two years ago, I saved the world from an alien invasion."

Zoë looked out of the window for about fifteen seconds before appearing to register what Geoff had said. She seemed distracted. "Sorry—I thought I saw a starling. You don't see many of those around this time of year. What did you say?"

"You heard me. I saved the world from an alien invasion."

Zoë took a sip of her tea. "Uh-huh."

"I'm serious," Geoff said, getting to his feet and walking over to the other side of the room. "They were called the Varsarians, and two years ago they sent a massive fleet of spaceships across the galaxy to wipe out the human race. The only thing that stopped them doing that was me."

"You stopped an entire fleet of spaceships from wiping out the human race."

"Yup. That's correct."

"And how did you do that exactly?"

"I broadcast a message over the Internet while playing a computer game called *Space Commando*. And when the Varsarians heard it, they thought it was meant for them."

"What did you say?"

"'I see you alien fuckers, and the Death Bringer is coming your way!'"

"The Death Bringer?"

"It's a weapon in *Space Commando*."

"Right."

"Of course, I had no idea they had picked up this message, but the second they heard me say this, they called off their attack to make sure they hadn't underestimated humanity's technological capacities. It took them two hundred years to realize their mistake, but by the time they sent their fleet back to wipe us out, we had invented time travel. So this time, when the Varsarians turned up again, we projected a portal into space sending the entire alien fleet forward in time by six hundred years. When they materialized in the future, the human race had massively improved its military capabilities, and the invading forces were defeated."

Geoff paused for a moment to catch his breath. He wasn't sure his explanation was making a huge amount of sense, especially since Zoë looked more confused than a protestor at an antiprotest protest rally.

"Are you with me so far?" he asked.

"I think so," Zoë said.

"Good," Geoff said, "because the next part is where it gets pretty complicated."

"The next part?"

"Yes. You see, some of the aliens survived the battle, and spent the next couple of centuries hiding on Earth in human form, infiltrating different aspects of society. One particularly nasty alien called Tringrall managed to put himself in charge of Time Tours, and once he was there, he began plotting a way to use the time tourism industry to change the outcome of the failed Varsarian invasion."

Zoë leaned back on the sofa. She appeared to only be half listening. "So…what did this Terlingown do?"

"Tringrall."

"Right, Tringrall. What did this Tringrall do?"

"Well, once he knew it was my Internet broadcast that was responsible for delaying the original invasion in the twenty-first century, he realized that if he could stop that from happening, the Varsarian invasion would succeed. But there was just one problem—all time travel was strictly monitored by a powerful supercomputer to stop anyone going back and changing history. However, the supercomputer did have its uses to him—it showed Tringrall that with the exception of stopping the Varsarian invasion, my life was completely insignificant to the space-time continuum."

Zoë laughed.

"Now *there's* something I don't find hard to believe," she said.

"Oh yes," Geoff said. "In fact, if you must know, that computer said I was less important to the world than certain types of mushroom."

"No kidding."

"Anyway, that was when Tringrall came up with the idea for Time Reps—hiring nobodies from throughout history to meet tourists from the future. But the project was invented for one reason—it was a cover to allow Tringrall to get to me. You see, Tringrall figured out a loophole in the supercomputer's programming—one that would allow him to stop me from broadcasting the transmission that stopped the invasion. Fortunately, we were able to realize enough of what was going on before it was too late, and Earth's entire battle fleet was sent back in time to the twenty-first century to defend the planet."

"Wow," Zoë said, standing up from the sofa in that way people do when they kind of want to leave. "That's quite a story."

"It's quite a story that isn't finished yet," Geoff said.

"Oh," Zoë said, sitting down again.

"You see, there was one last problem. By this point, we still didn't know who Tringrall really was, as he was continuing to hide in human form. This meant he was able to get on board the *Concordia*—the flagship of the battle fleet sent back to the twenty-first century to defend Earth—without raising any suspicion."

"Whoops," Zoë said. She didn't look like she was taking this story very seriously.

"Right, whoops. Anyway, in the middle of the battle, he sabotaged a computer that was controlling most of our spaceships, sending the entire fleet into disarray. His actions nearly wiped us out completely, but at the last minute, when it appeared all hope was lost, I figured out a way to undo everything he had done. I worked out a way of identifying the ship that had Tringrall's ancestors on it, took command of the ship, and destroyed that ship by ramming it with the *Concordia*. The moment that happened, Tringrall ceased to exist. The damage he had caused never happened, all our ships instantly repaired themselves, and the tide of the battle was turned back in our favor."

Zoë looked at Geoff in silence.

"That it?" she said eventually.

"That's it," Geoff said. "The planet was saved."

"You know I don't believe you, right?"

"I know," Geoff replied, placing the Sat-Nav on the table. "That's why I'm going to take you there right now."

"Oh, this I've got to see," Zoë said.

"Right," Geoff said, pressing the WHEN button. After entering the correct date, two years ago, he pressed the WHERE button. Fortunately, he was able to zoom the map of Earth out far enough to get a view of outer space, and as he did, he could see a visualization of the battle taking place just as he remembered it, a few thousand kilometers away from the planet.

"You see?" Geoff said, showing the screen to Zoë. Explosions were flashing against a backdrop of stars, ships were flying around everywhere in a torrent of laser beams and missiles, and the burnt-out wreckages of several destroyed craft were drifting lifelessly around like corpses made from scrap metal.

"Wow," Zoë said.

She didn't look particularly impressed, but then that was understandable. To her, this probably just looked like some sort of basic computer game.

If he truly wanted her to believe him, he would need to take her there.

But where should they go? He zoomed in on the battle again to get a good look at the different ships. He wanted Zoë to see him at the moment he took command of the fleet, but he didn't think plonking them on the bridge of the *Concordia* was a great idea—he couldn't just show up out of thin air, turn to the past version of himself, and say, "Don't mind us, Geoff, you just carry on!" No—that might be a tad distracting at such a critical moment.

He needed to think of something else.

Perhaps if there was another ship he could get on board,

one that was near enough to the *Concordia* so that they could see him take command on the bridge, maybe that would be enough?

He thought back to the battle and remembered a ship that had drifted right in front of the path of the *Concordia*, just as he was trying to ram Tringrall's ancestors. Maybe if they were on that ship, it would be close enough for Zoë to see him on the bridge when he was in command.

It wasn't hard to find the ship he was thinking about—it was one of the last remaining craft toward the end of the battle, just as the *Concordia* was about to set its collision course toward the ship with Tringrall's ancestors on it.

Geoff looked at Zoë.

"Here we are," he said, using the Sat-Nav to select an empty spot in a corridor on the starboard side of the ship that he knew was going to drift in front of the flagship while he was in command. The corridor looked a little bit damaged from the battle, with hairline cracks beginning to appear across the ceiling, but it still looked safe and had huge windows, which he hoped would give them a perfect view of the *Concordia*'s bridge as they drifted by. He stood up, took Zoë's hand, and pulled her to her feet. "You ready?"

"I'm ready," Zoë said, throwing her arms up in the air in mock excitement. "Beam me up, Scotty."

Geoff smiled, pressed the EXECUTE button, and the next moment, he and Zoë were standing in the corridor on the spaceship, right where he had intended.

For a second, Zoë didn't say a word. She just looked at Geoff in silence as though they'd just gone out for a walk and she'd remembered that she'd forgotten her handbag.

"Well, we're here," Geoff smiled, reaching for her hand "You okay?"

"Agggggggggggggggghhhhhhhhhhhhhhhhhh!" was Zoë's response, screamed directly at Geoff's face at the top of her voice.

TWELVE

Zoë's legs gave way immediately, her limp body spilling across the floor as though her bones had instantly been replaced with overcooked spaghetti. Geoff tried to catch her as she fell, but failed quite spectacularly and ended up lying on the floor with her in a tangled mess of arms and legs. The whole episode reminded him of the last time he'd been ice skating.

"Hey hey hey hey hey!" Geoff said, grabbing Zoë by the shoulders and pulling her body upright, seating her with her back against the window. "Keep calm, okay? Everything is fine."

"Keep calm?" Zoë leapt to her feet and pressed herself against the wall on the other side of the corridor as though she'd just seen a big spider crawling toward her. "Keep calm? What the hell just happened? Where are we?"

"I told you," Geoff said, standing up. "We're in space."

"Space?" Zoë cried. "Space? How can we be in space? We're in space? This is space?"

"Yes, this is space," Geoff said, "and we're in it. I told you this was going to happen a minute ago, remember?"

"I thought you were joking!"

"Yeah, I know," Geoff said. "But I wasn't."

Zoë started murmuring something incomprehensible to herself. Geoff sometimes found it difficult to read women, but in this instance he thought he knew what was going through Zoë's mind: sheer panic. "It's okay, Zoë," he tried to calm her down.

"Oh, it's okay, he says," Zoë scoffed. "We're in space and that's fine. It's normal."

He walked over to the window and looked outside.

"We won't be here for very long. I just want to show you one thing, and then I'll take you back to Earth."

Zoë looked at him in silence.

"I'll even make you another tea."

She still looked at him in silence. He had a feeling that the promise of a nice cup of tea afterward wasn't quite enough to calm her nerves.

"Look," Geoff said, pressing his hands against the window. "This is the moment I was telling you about, the moment I took command of an entire fleet of spaceships and defeated an alien invasion."

He peered through the glass at the war raging outside, trying to work out at what point they had arrived. Just as he'd intended, the Sat-Nav had brought them to a point in time near the end of the battle. In front of him, the charred remains of thousands of Earth ships drifted lifelessly through space, with the Varsarians conducting an all-out assault on the remainder of the fleet. The cosmos were littered with dead bodies and space debris, with flying saucers gleefully whizzing in all directions, and laser beams and missiles were exploding everywhere like some sort of nightmarish fireworks display.

In the distance, he saw the badly damaged *Concordia*, the massive ship just sitting in space, biding its time. If he wasn't mistaken, his past self would be sitting in the captain's chair right now, getting ready to put his last-ditch plan into action.

His suspicions were confirmed when he heard his own voice come over the loudspeaker. He remembered this moment vividly—it was his first command to the Earth fleet, the bluff he knew the enemy was listening in on that he'd used to draw out Tringrall's ancestors.

"Remaining Earth ships, your attention please! Prepare to activate the Death Bringer!" it said.

As the order came, all the enemy ships stopped firing and moved to retreat, fearing that humanity was about to fire a superweapon that didn't actually exist. But there was one ship out there that would still be firing on the others. This was the moment when his past self was on the bridge, surveying every square inch of space to identify the right ship to attack, the one with Tringrall's ancestors on it, which, if destroyed, would wipe him from existence and undo all the damage his sabotage had caused.

Geoff looked around and extended an arm toward Zoë.

"Why don't you come over here and have a look at this?" he said. "There's nothing to be afraid of."

Zoë didn't look particularly convinced.

"Come on," Geoff said, reaching toward her. "It's perfectly safe."

Zoë took a few slow steps forward, approaching the window with caution as though it were the edge of a cliff face. Eventually, she pressed her hands against the glass and leaned forward, staring in wonder at what she saw like a small child looking into an aquarium for the first time. "Oh my God," she said.

"You see that big ship in front of us?" Geoff said, pointing toward the *Concordia*. "That's the ship I told you about—the one I commanded two years ago. Right now, I'm standing on the bridge of that ship, trying to spot a particular craft that I need to destroy."

Zoë turned to Geoff. Her eyes were wider than he'd ever seen them before. "It's real!" she exclaimed. "It's really real!"

"That's right," Geoff laughed, taking her hand.

In front of them, the *Concordia*'s engines began to power up, a bright blue glow emanating from the rear of the craft. Slowly but surely, the ship began to move, the battered hull creaking like the bones of an old man prising himself out of a chair.

"Ah—here we go," Geoff said, rubbing his hands together enthusiastically. "This was the part I wanted you to see, when I set the *Concordia* on a collision course with the enemy ship."

Zoë wasn't really listening. At this moment, her mind was still coming to terms with the fact that she was in space, and that Geoff had actually been telling the truth all along about being a Time Rep. She was so stunned, he probably could have said anything to her at this point and she wouldn't have reacted, no matter how outrageous the statement.

"I don't believe this," she said, raising her hand to stroke the back of her neck.

"None of our weapons were working," Geoff continued his story regardless of whether Zoë was paying attention or not, "so I had to ram the *Concordia* into the alien ship in order to destroy it."

"Geoff," Zoë placed a hand on Geoff's shoulder to steady herself, "this is amazing. I can't believe it."

In front of them, the *Concordia* began to accelerate faster, the massive ship using every last drop of energy to catch up with its target. Just as Geoff had remembered, the ship they were standing on began to drift into the path of the flagship, and within seconds they had a full view of the bridge as the *Concordia* heaved toward them.

"There!" Geoff said, leaning close to Zoë and pointing her line of sight toward the bridge's main window. Sure enough, there was his past self, sitting in the captain's seat, looking ahead in horror at the ship that had just drifted in front of the *Concordia*'s path. "Can you see me?"

"Well I'll be damned," Zoë said, nodding. "It's you! Can he see us?"

"I don't remember seeing us, so I guess not," Geoff said. "At the time, I was a little bit more concerned with getting this ship to move out of the way."

Sure enough, it wasn't long before an order from his past self was broadcast throughout the ship.

"Get out of the way!" his past self said. "I can't hit it if you're in the way!"

"See?" Geoff said.

"What was that?" Zoë said.

"That was me ordering this ship to move," Geoff explained.

"This is extremely confusing."

The two of them stood transfixed by the window, watching as the *Concordia* narrowly avoided colliding with the ship they were on and maintained its pursuit of the enemy craft. Even though Geoff knew the outcome of this chase, he still felt his body tensing up in anticipation, and when Tringrall's ancestors began to accelerate away from the lumbering *Concordia* and it appeared all hope was lost, he still felt nervous, as though there were still a possibility that he might not succeed in catching them up.

But then the came his past self's master stroke—the *Concordia* activated its tractor beam, the enemy flying saucer was stopped in its tracks, and within seconds, the two ships crashed into each other spectacularly, with the enemy saucer ricocheting back out into space and folding in on itself before exploding in a brilliant flash of light.

Geoff turned to Zoë. "This is the best bit," he said, squeezing her hand. "Watch what happens now."

With Tringrall's ancestors destroyed and Tringrall himself erased from existence, the space-time continuum got to work undoing all the damage caused by his act of sabotage. Conveniently, this meant that all the ships that had been destroyed by the Varsarians began to restore themselves to pristine condition, with burnt-out wreckages and exploded craft unburning and unexploding before their very eyes. In front of them, the previously battered hull of the *Concordia* repaired itself, the giant gashes and scorch marks healing over as though they had never happened. Even the corridor Zoë and Geoff were standing in fixed itself, the cracks in the walls joining back together again, the floor and ceiling straightening out almost instantaneously. Someone in an insurance company somewhere was no doubt breathing a very large sigh of relief at this point.

Geoff smiled as he watched the fleet repair itself again— seeing it do this for the second time really was incredible. He could only imagine what Zoë must have been thinking, but he hoped it was something along the lines of: *Wow—Geoff wasn't lying! He really did save the world! I am seriously impressed with this man, and will now ask him if he would like a big kiss!*

Needless to say, that wasn't what was going through Zoë's mind in the slightest.

It was only a matter of seconds before Earth's battle fleet was back up to full strength, and as the last of the alien forces were being wiped out by an invigorated enemy, she turned to Geoff and gave him a look he'd never seen before.

"My God, Geoff," she said, letting go of his hand and taking a step back from the window. Her voice was quivering as she spoke, her wide eyes looking at him from a new perspective. "I can't believe it! Everything you said was true."

"That's right," Geoff replied. "And you have no idea how hard it's been keeping that a secret from you."

• • •

Since there was no point sticking around to see the rest of the Varsarians being wiped out, Geoff used the Sat-Nav to bring them both back to present-day London. But he didn't want to go back to the house—now that she knew the truth about who he really was, he wanted to take Zoë somewhere nice, somewhere he could confess his true feelings toward her, somewhere romantic. The house wasn't really ideal for that sort of thing, not least because a) you needed an ordnance survey map to navigate your way through each room, and b) even if you found a clean spot (which you wouldn't, but let's pretend for argument's sake), you were probably never more than two meters away from a stray sock.

And stray socks were a real mood killer when you were in the middle of telling someone how much you loved them.

No—he needed to take her somewhere special.

He knew he was probably going about all this a little quickly, but he couldn't help it—he was in love with Zoë, and he had been desperate to tell her how he really felt for years. And what better time to do that than after showing her how he had saved the world?

That sort of thing was pretty impressive, right?

Of course, Geoff understood that just because Zoë had seen him save the entire human race from extinction, it didn't mean she felt the same way about him.

He knew that love didn't work that way.

And she was pretty fussy, after all.

And so, after dismissing a number of non-romantic locations to confess his feelings, like the comic book section in

135

Forbidden Planet and outside the local chip shop, Geoff decided to take Zoë to a quiet area at the top of the hill in Greenwich Park, just next to the Royal Observatory. As romantic spots go, this was hard to beat—the hill offered an amazing view across the whole of London, there were no stray socks in sight, and being the site of the Prime Meridian, the place had a certain connection with time that Geoff felt was rather poetic.

They materialized on top of the hill, just as the sun was setting.

"Here we are," Geoff said, taking a few steps forward and letting his eyes wander across the London skyline. "Back on planet Earth."

He could see the beautiful dome of Saint Paul's Cathedral, peeking over the horizon. The spike of the Shard, piercing the sky like a lone stalagmite. Tower Bridge, which he remembered he would still be visiting at some point in the near future. And in front of him, Canary Wharf, with its chunky skyscrapers lit up in the twilight like giant advertisements for how to waste energy.

Zoë was breathing heavily, her hand pressed to her chest. "I still can't believe this," she said, padding over to a nearby bench and sitting down.

"How are you doing?" Geoff said, sitting down next to her.

"How am I doing?" Zoë said, turning to face him. "How am I doing? Geoff—I've just found out that you can time travel! That the planet was nearly destroyed two years ago by an alien invasion! I've just been into space and back! It's quite a bit to take in! How do you think I'm doing?!"

"I don't know. That's why I asked."

Zoë shut her eyes, scrunching her face up as tightly as she could for a few seconds and clenching her teeth.

"Look—I'm sorry if I scared you, okay?" Geoff said, placing his hand on her shoulder. "It's just—I didn't know what else to do. I had to show you I was telling the truth."

Zoë opened her eyes and shot to her feet, ignoring Geoff's hand falling away from her shoulder as she stood up.

"Okay—I'm fine," she said, breathing in slowly. She rested

her hands by her sides and breathed out again as if she were doing a relaxing yoga move. "I'm fine."

"You sure?" Geoff said.

"Absolutely," Zoë said. "A little overwhelmed, maybe, but I'm good. Sorry—this has just all come as a bit of a shock, you know?"

"I understand," Geoff said. "I didn't believe it either when Time Tours first told me about time travel. Nearly walked out the door. But it's pretty neat, right?"

"Neat?" Zoë said. "Neat? Geoff, this is incredible! It's the most amazing thing I've ever seen!" She walked over to him and looked down at the Sat-Nav. "You mean to tell me that thing allows you to travel to any time or place?"

"That's right," Geoff said. "We can go anywhere and any *when* we like."

"Unbelievable," she said, straightening up and looking around. Behind her, the roof of the Greenwich Observatory was reflecting the last rays of sunlight as dusk began to set in. "So why did you bring me to Greenwich? Was there something else you wanted to show me?"

"No," Geoff said. "I just thought this would be nice, you know?"

"Nice?"

Geoff swallowed. "Yeah."

"Nice for what? Are we having a picnic?"

"Um…I dunno," Geoff said. "I guess I thought…uh…"

He couldn't believe it. After building this moment up in his mind so much, he was scared to say anything.

And with Zoë now linked to the tablet, if this went wrong, there was no way of undoing a mistake he made with her anymore. Unless he disconnected her, if he rewound time, she would have the same memories he did. And he couldn't do that, because he didn't have any more serum.

"Are you okay?" Zoë asked.

"I'm fine," Geoff said. "I'm fine. Listen—do you mind if we just sit here for a while?"

"You want to just sit here?" Zoë said.

"Yeah. Is that okay?"

Zoë shrugged her shoulders. "I guess," she said. "But all this has got me a little worked up, you know? Can't we go and visit another time period or something?"

"You want to go somewhere else straight away?"

"Don't you?" she said, looking out across the London skyline. "Geoff—we can go anywhere! We can visit ancient Egypt, we can go and see what it was like in medieval times, we can go to the future—the list is endless!"

"I know it is," Geoff said. "I know. It's just that I thought…"

Zoë looked at him. "You just thought what?" she said.

Geoff stood up and walked toward her. "What did you think of what I just showed you?"

"What do you mean?"

"Well, you know that part where I saved the world from an alien invasion?"

"Yes."

"What did you think of that? It was pretty good, right?"

Zoë smiled and tilted her head to one side. "If you were trying to impress me, Geoff, you did a pretty good job," she said. "Is that what you wanted to hear?"

"Uh…yes." Geoff blushed. "Yes, it was." He felt a bit stupid now, forcing Zoë to say something.

"You know, maybe we *should* sit here for a while," Zoë said, walking over to the bench. "I get the feeling we both need to calm down a little."

And so that's what they did. For about five minutes, neither of them said a word. They just sat on the bench in silence, watching as the sun set on the horizon.

"Geoff?" Zoë said eventually.

"Yes?"

"There's one thing I still don't understand."

"Oh? What's that?"

"Well, you said you'd been working as a Time Rep for two years, right?"

"Yes, that's right."

"If that's the case, why did you wait until today to show me all this? Why didn't you tell me about your job straight away?"

"It's a long story," Geoff said. "For the last two years, I wasn't allowed to. My old company was worried that if anyone from the twenty-first century knew what I did, there was a risk that it could change the course of history. It was only today that I joined a new company called Continuum. Thanks to the Sat-Nav they gave me, I can go back and do whatever I like."

"Like showing me the moment you saved the world."

"Exactly," Geoff said. "That was the first thing on my list."

"Really?"

"Yeah."

"Well, I have to say I'm very flattered," Zoë said, shifting her weight on the bench slightly. "But of all the things you could have chosen to do, why did you want to do that first?"

"Because ever since I became a Time Rep, I've found it so frustrating to talk to you," Geoff said. "You're one of my closest friends, and I couldn't tell you any of this. Do you have any idea how hard it has been keeping this all a secret from you?"

"And do you feel better now that you've shown me all this?"

"Yes," Geoff said. "I guess so…it's just…"

Zoë put a finger to Geoff's lips. "I know what's going on here, Geoff. I know what you're trying to do. Just give me some time to think about it, okay?"

Geoff nodded.

"Now," Zoë said, standing up from the bench and taking a few steps toward the edge of the hill. "Let's go somewhere else, shall we? But this time, I'll choose, okay?"

"Okay," Geoff said, standing up and joining her at the edge of the hill, Sat-Nav in hand. "Just name the time and place and I'll take you there. How about we see if your band ever makes it? Wouldn't that be interesting?"

"I suppose," Zoë said, looking down at her feet and kicking a small stone. "But it seems so silly to go and see something like that now, given what we could use this thing to do."

Geoff frowned. "What do you mean?"

"I don't know. It's just, after being in space, it seems a bit of an anticlimax to go down the pub and watch the band play. I want to experience something else that will blow my mind. Something I've never seen before."

"Are you sure?" Geoff said. "Because you didn't handle going into space that well, if I'm completely honest."

Zoë frowned at him. "I'm sure," she said.

"Okay. If you want to see something that will really amaze you, this device has got just the thing."

"And what's that?"

"It can make time speed up."

"Speed up?"

"It's really incredible to watch, like fast-forwarding a video. Why don't we travel to the future, but instead of jumping straight there, why don't we watch how London changes over time? From here, we'll have a great view of the city. We'll be able to see all the new buildings go up in minutes, see the landscape change as the city gets more and more built up."

"Sounds amazing," Zoë said. "Let's do it."

"Right," Geoff said, looking down at the tablet. "Let me see if I can remember how this works." He pressed the WHEN icon, and then hovered his finger over the fast-forward button.

"I think this is it," he said. "Are you ready?"

"I'm ready," Zoë said, and walked over to the edge of the hill to take in the view.

Geoff did the same. "Here we go," he said, holding the button down.

Just like before when he had used the Sat-Nav to speed up the passage of time, things began to happen in front of them at a vastly accelerated rate. As the date on the screen counted up through the decades and then the centuries, Zoë and Geoff watched in awe as the London skyline rapidly evolved before their eyes. Some areas stayed remarkably similar over the years, with Saint Paul's Cathedral remaining completely untouched. Other areas changed dramatically. Three new bridges sprang up over the Thames, Canary Wharf's roster of skyscrapers quadrupled, and by the twenty-fourth century, the Millennium Dome was replaced by an enormous theme park.

By the twenty-seventh century, there were no signs of the old transport infrastructures of the city. With the advent of flying cars in the twenty-sixth century, which now streaked across the sky in organized lanes of red and white headlights, it appeared roads and railways were obsolete. Eventually, most of the roads and tracks were converted to long stretches of parkland, intersecting every few hundred yards and making the city look much greener, with lines of tall trees replacing most of the bands of gray and brown that had been there before.

After a matter of minutes, they finally reached the thirty-first century, with the city looking both familiar and unfamiliar at the same time. Some parts of it looked identical to the London of the twenty-first century; other parts looked totally different.

"Well, here we are," Geoff said.

"Wait," Zoë said, holding his finger down on the button. "Keep going! This is incredible! I want to see what happens next."

"Okay," Geoff said, keeping the button pressed down.

And so they watched as the city continued to grow. Geoff looked down at the tablet—another fifty years had passed, and the city was still changing, with buildings rising and falling in a cycle. There was a strange rhythm to it, as though each part of the city was destined to be rebuilt at a certain point.

However, by the time they reached the mid-thirty-second century, the evolution of the city began to slow down. For a moment, Geoff wondered if he wasn't pressing the fast-forward button hard enough, but it wasn't that—the years were still counting up quickly; it was the city that wasn't changing that much. Not only that, but the bright lines of traffic that had consistently streaked through the sky for hundreds of years started to weaken, as though fewer people were now traveling. By the end of the thirty-second century, something looked to be very wrong indeed. There was no traffic in the sky at all, and the city wasn't changing in the slightest. The only thing that was different was the greenery throughout the city and the parkland around them, which was now becoming hugely overgrown. It was as though there hadn't been anyone tending to it for years.

Then in the distance, a few of the taller skyscrapers began

to erode away and collapse, as if they had fallen into disrepair. It appeared that, like the greenery, people weren't attending to the upkeep of the buildings, either.

"Geoff?" Zoë said, looking around at him. "What's happened? Where is everyone?"

"I don't know," Geoff said. He could feel his heart beating faster.

He took his finger off the fast-forward button and watched as time immediately flowed at a normal speed again.

They were now standing in foot-high grass, overlooking a decaying, deserted city. According to the Sat-Nav, it was early evening. At this time of day you would normally be able to see thousands of buildings lit up as far as the eye could see, but there were no lights anywhere—just a gray, lifeless skyline, slowly withering away to nothing.

Either there had been a massive power cut and the entire city had gone to try and sort it out, or something was very wrong here.

"What's going on?" Zoë said. "Where is everyone?"

"I don't know," Geoff said.

"Geoff, I don't like this."

"Oh, wait a minute," Geoff said, tapping his forehead with the palm of his hand in that way people do when they've just remembered something. "I know what this is."

"You do?"

"Yes, I do. Or at least, I think I do. If I'm right, then there's nothing to worry about."

"And if you're not right?"

"If I'm not right, it still might not be that bad. There might be a perfectly reasonable, non-worrying explanation."

Zoë didn't look convinced. "The entire city is deserted and you think there's a perfectly reasonable, non-worrying explanation?" she said. "It looks pretty bad to me, like everyone's died or something."

Geoff shook his head. "No, no no no. I don't think that's what happened. You remember that supercomputer I told you about? The one that predicted the future?"

"Yes."

"Well, that computer always said that humanity would one day leave this planet to explore other galaxies. We must have just passed the point in history when that happened, that's all."

"I don't know, Geoff," Zoë said, walking over to an area that was a little less overgrown. "This doesn't feel right."

"I'm pretty sure there's nothing to worry about," Geoff said. "Pretty sure. All that's happened is that mankind has gone to explore other worlds. And while this looks bad now, with everything falling apart, in the future, once all these old buildings erode away, Earth will revert back to being a beautiful garden world."

"Hmm," Zoë said. "If you say so. But it still feels a little bit strange to me."

"Well, why don't we look it up?" Geoff said, pressing the WHAT button on the Sat-Nav. "Will that make you feel better?"

"You can do that?"

"Yeah—this thing can tell us exactly what happened."

Geoff found the page describing why everywhere appeared to be deserted and began reading it to himself. At first he just thought the explanation would confirm what he already knew—that mankind had left the planet to explore other galaxies.

Unfortunately, it didn't say that at all.

And contrary to what he had told Zoë, the real explanation wasn't a perfectly reasonable, non-worrying one.

In fact, it was kind of the opposite.

"Well?" Zoë said, peering over the Sat-Nav to try and read the screen for herself. "What does it say?"

Geoff looked at Zoë and sighed.

He handed her the Sat-Nav to read the explanation for herself. "There's been a complete and utter disaster, and we've got to do something about it."

Zoë took the Sat-Nav from him and started read aloud. "In the early thirty-second century, the population of the world had become completely addicted to the Continuum experience," she said. "To cope with this extraordinary demand, Continuum launched an ultra-premium holiday package. This meant that instead of people using Continuum to go on holiday and come back again, they were now allowed to disappear into their own alternative timelines and never come back. This package became so popular, it was decreed to be a basic human right for someone to be able to spend their entire life within the Continuum experience if they wished. To cope with demand, the world's entire manufacturing capabilities were dedicated to producing enough serum and Space and Time Navigation tablets to cater to the entire population of the planet. Within fifty years, over half the population had used Continuum to disappear into their own timelines forever, and by the end of the century, only a few remnants of humanity remained."

She handed the tablet back to Geoff and looked him in the eyes. "I don't think I can read any more," she said.

"Me neither," Geoff said. "Who would have thought that something like this could become so popular, it would end up swallowing up the entire population of the planet? It's worse than the bloody Pokémon craze."

"So what are we going to do?" Zoë said.

"I don't know, but first of all, we need to get out of here and warn someone."

Geoff pressed the WHEN button, selected the date he had joined Continuum, and pressed EXECUTE.

Nothing happened.

"Well, what are you waiting for?" Zoë said.

"I don't understand," Geoff said, pressing the EXECUTE button again. "It's not working."

"Not working? What do you mean it's not working?"

"I mean it's not working!"

"Have you tried turning it off and on again?"

"This isn't an office laptop, Zoë! I don't think it works like that!"

"So what the hell do we do?"

"I don't know," Geoff said. He kept pressing the button again and again, but nothing happened.

"Hang on," Geoff said, this time moving the slider back

to rewind time, rather than just trying to jump straight back. "Maybe this will work."

He pressed the EXECUTE button again, but still nothing happened. This time, though, a message came up on the screen. It said:

**FINGERPRINT
IDENTIFICATION REJECTED.**

ACCESS DENIED.

THIS DEVICE MAY ONLY BE USED BY A MEMBER

OF THE CONTINUUM CUSTOMER SUPPORT TEAM.

PLEASE WAIT FOR ASSISTANCE.

"Customer support team?" Zoë said. "Who the hell are they?"

"I don't know," Geoff said, closing the message. "But given that we've just found out something a tad controversial about Continuum, I doubt they'll be like the nice lady who pops up when you press the Kindle's Mayday button."

At that moment, the hologram of Jennifer Adams appeared in front of them, the image once again cast in a blue, pixelated light.

"Bloody hell!" Zoë said, jumping back. "What the hell is that?"

"Oh, don't worry," Geoff said. "It's just a hologram."

"Who is she?"

"Her name's Jennifer Adams. She's the boss of Continuum."

The hologram stepped forward and smiled at them. "Dear valued customer," it said. "It appears your Sat-Nav is experiencing technical difficulties. Please wait here while we send someone to assist you."

"Not blooming likely," Geoff said, tugging at Zoë's sleeve. "Let's find somewhere to hide before they show up."

They turned to leave, but the hologram quickly materialized in front of them again in a puff of blue dots.

"Please, remain where you are," the hologram smiled.

Zoë looked at Geoff. "What do we do?" she said.

"Don't worry," Geoff said, leading her toward the hologram. "It's only made of light. We can walk right through it."

But as Geoff walked up to the hologram to do just that, it reached out and pushed him hard in the shoulder, sending him tumbling to the ground. Somehow, this thing was capable of touching after all.

"Please, remain where you are," the hologram repeated, smiling vacantly in their direction. "A member of our customer support team will be with you shortly."

"Are you okay?" Zoë said, helping Geoff to his feet.

"I'm fine," Geoff winced, rubbing his shoulder.

They turned to run in another direction, but every way they faced, the hologram just appeared in front of them, repeating the same instruction.

Stay still.

Someone will be with you shortly.

In the end, the two of them gave up trying to run. Instead, they just sat together on the ground, overlooking the ruins of their once great city.

Every few minutes the hologram of Jennifer Adams would repeat her message, and after hearing it for the tenth time, Geoff and Zoë began to wonder if anyone from this mysterious "customer services team" was ever going to show up at all.

But someone did show up eventually.

And it wasn't who Geoff was expecting.

THIRTEEN

When Geoff tried to picture what someone who worked in customer support would look like, he imagined a thin, nerdy-looking guy, with thick, black-rimmed glasses and a couple of spots on his face. A nice harmless kid, a bit like the ones you see working in PC repair shops. His name would be something like Derek, his voice wouldn't have broken yet, and he wouldn't have been particularly intimidating. He would be the kind of person who ironed his pajamas.

Knowing Geoff's luck, though, he and Zoë were probably going to be met by a complete behemoth of a man. Someone well over six feet tall, with a shaved head, unpleasant four-letter words tattooed across his knuckles, and a muscular frame so large he probably needed an HGV license just to move his own body. This man's name wouldn't be Derek, though—it would be a sinister, harsh-sounding name, like Slater.

Harry Slater.

Harry "Skullcrusher" Slater.

In the end, the person who came to meet them wasn't Derek, nor was it Harry "Skullcrusher" Slater.

It was William Boyle.

"Good afternoon," William said as he materialized out of thin air. He was wearing different clothes from the last time they had met, and he looked to be a good few years older than before. His thinning hair was starting to show flecks of gray, his face had wrinkles around his eyes and mouth, and he looked like he'd lost a bit of weight.

In his left hand he was holding his own Sat-Nav, and in his right hand he was holding the strange gun he had had before, which he pointed directly toward Geoff and Zoë.

"A member of our customer support team has now arrived to assist you," said the hologram of Jennifer Adams. "Thank you for you cooperation."

And with that, the hologram disappeared in its customary puff of blue dots.

"On your feet," William said.

They did as they were told.

"*You're* a member of Continuum's customer support team?" Geoff said, positioning himself between William and Zoë.

Zoë leaned forward to whisper in Geoff's ear. "Do you know this guy?" she said.

"Once I'd visited every Time Rep to tell them about Continuum, I had to do something to keep myself busy," William replied. "Traipsing backward and forward through time starts to get a little boring once you don't have a purpose anymore, so now I do this."

"What, you go around threatening people?" Geoff said.

"I enforce Continuum's terms and conditions concerning the use of the Space and Time Navigation device," William replied.

"Terms and conditions?" Geoff said. "What terms and conditions? You told me Continuum would give me the freedom to go wherever I wanted! Let me change whatever I pleased!"

"You *can* change whatever you please," William said. "As long as you do it within the terms and conditions of use."

Geoff looked at Zoë, then back to William again. "But we never agreed to any terms and conditions of use."

"Yes you did," William replied. "They flashed up for a quarter of a second when you first used your Sat-Nav. They clearly stated that by continuing to use the device, you agreed to be bound by Continuum's full terms and conditions of use."

"A quarter of a second?" Geoff said. "That's not enough time to notice any terms and conditions, let alone read them!"

"Then you shouldn't have agreed to the terms and conditions," William smiled.

Geoff couldn't believe how unfair this was. It was even worse than those social networks that insist on having eighty pages of terms and conditions that they know no one is going to read. Because who the hell wants to understand about signing away their privacy before logging in to see what the most popular brand of chocolate chip cookie is today?

"Fine," Geoff said. "So what did we do wrong?"

William looked down at his Sat-Nav to read aloud from the screen. "You are both in violation of section 19, paragraph b of the 'future intentions' addendum."

"Section whatty whatty of the what now?" Geoff said.

"Section 19, paragraph b of the 'future intentions' addendum states as follows: 'The user agrees not to use the Sat-Nav to acquire, learn, discover, ascertain, realize, or deduce any knowledge about the future intentions of the Continuum organization.'"

"That's the most suspicious-sounding clause I've ever heard," Geoff said. "No wonder Continuum doesn't want anyone to actually read these bloody conditions of theirs! What's it say in section 19 paragraph c? 'The user agrees not to tell anyone that the Continuum organization is actually extremely dangerous, and will one day bring about the end of humanity'?"

"So you did read them after all!" William said.

"Does it really say that?"

"No," William said. "Section 19, paragraph c states that any user who can be convinced that they've guessed the exact wording of a clause is a gullible idiot."

"Does it really say that instead?" Geoff said.

"Oh, boy," William said.

"So, mister customer support man," Geoff said, reaching down to the ground to pick up his own Sat-Nav. "Are you here to fix this?" The device was still stuck on the WHEN screen, with the arrow positioned all the way back to the beginning of the slider.

"No," William answered. "As I said before, my job is to enforce Continuum's terms and conditions concerning the use of the Space and Time Navigation device. And can you guess what the standard procedure is for people who violate section 19, paragraph b of the 'future intentions' addendum?"

"They're given a complimentary meal in the Continuum staff restaurant and released?"

"No."

"They have to pay a very small fine as a token gesture, and then they're released?"

"No."

"They're made to guess what the correct procedure is for violating section 19, paragraph b for the rest of their life?"

"No."

"Okay, I give up."

"I'll tell you," William said. "The standard procedure is for the two of you to link up with my Sat-Nav by drinking this." Still holding his gun, he placed his Sat-Nav down on the bench next to him, and with his free hand took two bottles of the red liquid out from his pocket. "Once you are linked up, I will then rewind time on my device, taking the two of you with me back to a special Continuum facility."

"And what will happen to us at this facility, exactly?" Geoff said. "Does it have a day spa? Will we get a nice massage and things like that?"

"Not really. You'll both get your memories wiped."

"Ah."

"And then you'll be released onto the street with no knowledge of ever having visited Continuum."

Geoff thought about what they'd just been told. Based on what he knew about how these things worked, if William linked them up to his device and rewound time, all that would happen would be that he would return back to his time, and Geoff and Zoë would move in reverse along the timeline they had just experienced as far back as William's slider was set. If he thought about it, there wasn't actually anything to worry about.

"Sounds fair," Geoff said. "Shall we get on with it, then?"

"I know what you're thinking," William said, holding up the bottles. "And you're wrong, actually. This serum is different from the one you drank. Once this stuff links you to my Sat-Nav, your exact movements up until now won't happen in reverse when I rewind back to the beginning of my timeline. With this serum, you stay right by my side."

"Damn," Geoff said. He needed a plan.

He tried to think of some way out of this situation, but before he could come up with any ideas, Zoë was marching up to William, her arms crossed. "How can you do this?" she said, looking at him. "You've seen what will happen to the world if we don't stop this! Continuum is going to bring about the end of humanity! Doesn't that make you feel anything?"

"Don't come any closer!" William said. "Step back, or I will shoot!"

"Zoë!" Geoff said, rushing over and pulling her back. "Get away from him!"

"No!" Zoë said, struggling in Geoff's grip. "This is the end of the human race we're talking about! There must be something we can do!"

William appeared to be sweating, his breathing a little heavier. "Trust me," he said, "there's nothing you can do."

It was at this moment that Geoff noticed a faint scar on the side of William's face. He hadn't noticed it when William was younger, so it must have been caused at some point later in William's life. Then Geoff had a thought. He'd always assumed William's new job had just turned him into a bit of an asshole. But what if this outward confidence was something else? What if it was a defense mechanism of his, covering something up?

"William—this special facility you mentioned," Geoff said, narrowing his eyes. "Have you ever been a guest there yourself?"

"Be quiet!" William said, holding out the bottles for them to take. "Be quiet and drink your serums!"

"What did they do to you there?"

William lowered his voice. "There's nothing you can do," he said, his eyes looking up at the sky for a moment. "They are watching. Now, take your serums."

"What do you mean they're watching? How can they be watching?"

"Trust me—they are. They are watching everything you do, all the time. Now, take your serums."

Geoff tucked his Sat-Nav under his arm and took the bottle from him. "Are you really going to make us do this?"

"I'm afraid so," William said, offering the other bottle to Zoë. "You too, miss."

"No," Zoë said, folding her arms over her chest. "I refuse."

"Zoë?" Geoff said, grabbing her arm and pulling her toward him. "What are you doing? Take the bottle!"

"I can't, Geoff," she said. "We can't let him do this! There has to be another way!"

"There is no other way," William sighed, aiming his gun at Zoë. "Please. I don't want to do this, but you should be aware that if you refuse to ingest your serum, I am authorized to use lethal force."

Zoë looked down at the tablet William had placed on the park bench earlier, then back up at Geoff. He knew that look— she'd had an idea.

William held his weapon steady. "Miss!" he said. "Please, take the serum!"

"You're actually going to kill her if she doesn't?!" Geoff said.

"Like I said, they are watching," William replied. "And they won't let me leave anyone behind. Either you come back with me to have your memory wiped, or you don't come back at all."

"Zoë," Geoff said, turning her body by the shoulders to face him. "Please do as he says. Take the serum. We'll figure this out, you'll see."

Zoë's eyes were welling up with tears. She wrapped her arms around his neck, pulled her body toward his, and buried her head in the cup of his shoulder, sobbing.

Or at least, that's how it would have seemed to William.

"Now's our chance," she said, turning her head to whisper in Geoff's ear. "When I distract him, swap the things round."

Before Geoff had a chance to process what Zoë had just said to him, she marched over to William and snatched the serum out of his hand.

"You've made the right choice," William said.

"Have I?" Zoë said, moving to her left to draw William's

attention away from the bench where he'd left his Sat-Nav. "Have I?"

With William looking the other way momentarily, Geoff looked down at the Sat-Nav he had placed on the park bench and immediately realized what Zoë was trying to do. The screen looked identical to the one on Geoff's device. It was on the WHEN page, and the arrow was positioned at the beginning of the slider with the EXECUTE button flashing. Given that his own Sat-Nav was rejecting his fingerprint, he assumed he wasn't going to be able to just pick up William's one and use it, but maybe that wasn't what she was thinking. Maybe she'd thought that if he could swap the devices, when William pressed the EXECUTE button, his fingerprint would automatically be authorized, and Geoff and Zoë would unexperience everything that had just happened from their perspective. If she was right, their timeline would undo itself completely and send them both right back to the beginning of their journey.

But he didn't want Zoë to have any memory of this, and if he disconnected her from his device before swapping it, he knew she would forget everything. The reversal of time would just leave her posting letters in Woodview Gardens with no memory that any of this ever took place.

At least, that's what he thought would happen, based on his understanding of the rules of the Sat-Nav's use.

There were just two problems—first of all, if this worked, Zoë wouldn't just forget her encounter with William and the disturbing sight of London. She would also forget everything Geoff had told her about who he really was. She would forget seeing him save the world, and all his hard work would be undone. On balance, though, he thought it best for her never to have experienced any of this, no matter what the cost to himself.

The second problem was that this sequence of events was probably the exact sort of thing that caused him to have that nasty encounter with a bullet at half past three in the afternoon. He supposed he would just have to cross that bridge when it came to it—and that bridge would be Tower Bridge, most likely.

Zoë was still distracting William, her eyes flashing toward

Geoff every few seconds to see if he was going to make the switch.

Once he thought he understood what Zoë's plan was, Geoff moved quickly, holding the red button down on the back of the Sat-Nav to disconnect Zoë. The button was small, round, and plastic, so fortunately it didn't need fingerprint recognition to work. After three seconds, a message flashed up saying USER DISCONNECTED. Next, he dismissed the message, made sure the arrow on the WHEN screen was positioned at the very beginning of the slider, and reached over to swap his device with the one William had left on the bench.

At that moment, though, William began to turn around to see what Geoff was doing. He was done for.

But Zoë thought quickly.

"Hey!" she shouted, jumping up and down to draw William's attention away from Geoff. "You know what I think of your stupid serum?" she said, raising it above her head. "THIS!"

And with that, she threw the serum to the ground and stamped on it, the red liquid seeping into the ground like a pool of blood draining through the soil beneath their feet.

This definitely got William's attention, and Geoff was able to make the swap without him noticing. But without a serum, what was going to happen to Zoë now?

"No!" William cried, looking down at the broken bottle. "Why did you do that? Do you know what you've done?" He took a moment to regain his composure. "I'm so sorry," he said, wiping his eyes with his free hand as he looked down the sights of his gun at Zoë. "But you've given me no choice. I have to."

"Wait!" Zoë said, holding her arms out. "Now, hang on a second."

William gave a quiet sniff and continued to look down the sights of his gun at Zoë.

"Geoff?" she said, looking over at him.

"Wait!" Geoff said, running forward. "She doesn't know what she's doing! Don't you have any more serum to give her?"

"I'm sorry, Geoff," William said, not taking his eyes off Zoë.

"Well, can't she have mine?" Geoff said, looking down at the unopened bottle in his hand.

William lowered his weapon. "Yours?" he said. "You would give her your serum?"

"Yes," Geoff said. "Yes, I would."

"But if you did that, you know I'd have to kill you, right?" William's eyes looked up at the sky again, as if he were matching the gaze of someone looking down on them. "No one stays."

"I know," Geoff said.

"Geoff," Zoë said. "You don't have to do this."

"Yes I do," Geoff said.

But just as he was about to hold out the serum for her to take from him, he remembered the one piece of advice his future self had given him on the phone earlier that day: "When the time comes, don't save Zoë."

He thought about those words for a moment.

Was this a mistake?

Then it hit him—he was still connected to his Sat-Nav, meaning any injuries he sustained to his body wouldn't undo themselves. Zoë, on the other hand, would be fine. With her body disconnected, if she died, she would come right back to life when time was sent into reverse.

Now he understood what his future self had meant: he didn't need to save Zoë, because if her idea of swapping the Sat-Navs worked, she would have already saved both of them herself.

He retracted his hand and held the serum close to his chest.

"Geoff?" Zoë said, looking at him in shock.

Geoff didn't say anything. He desperately wanted to tell her that everything would be okay, but he couldn't. Instead, he just raised his eyebrows slightly and tilted his head toward the Sat-Nav on the bench. Zoë narrowed her eyes and gave a slow nod. She probably didn't fully understand what he was trying to tell her, but she seemed to realize that he wanted her to trust him.

Now all he needed to do was pretend to betray her.

This wasn't going to be easy.

"I'm sorry, Zoë," Geoff said uncomfortably, looking down at the serum. "But you can't have this. I don't want to die."

And with that, he took the bottle, unscrewed the cap, and poured the liquid down his throat. He hoped that drinking this new serum didn't cancel the effects of the first one—he needed to still be linked to his own Sat-Nav, and if he wasn't, Zoë's plan would fail.

Now it was Zoë's turn to put on a performance for William. If this whole charade was to be convincing, she needed to appear angry at what Geoff had just done. And terrified.

Then again, she was probably already terrified.

Zoë yelled, "What have you done?"

William raised his weapon again, pointed it toward Zoë, and sighed. "Sometimes I wish I was a Time Rep again," he said. "Things were so much simpler."

Zoë turned to run, but it was too late. William looked down the sights of his weapon and pulled the trigger. Geoff was expecting the whole park to echo with the piercing sound of a gunshot, but instead, the gun made a strange noise like a burst of static.

And that wasn't the only thing unusual about the gun. As the bullet hit Zoë square in the back of her head, he had only a brief moment to witness the fatal wound it inflicted on her as she immediately vanished into the ether.

William quickly turned to point his gun at Geoff. "I'm sorry," he said, picking up the swapped Sat-Nav from the park bench. Geoff sucked in his cheeks and straightened himself up. At this point, he didn't know how he should be behaving. He knew he should be acting distraught, but at the same time he knew that if this worked, Zoë would be fine.

"What happened to her just then?" Geoff said, looking at the spot where Zoë had been standing before she disappeared. "Where did she go?"

William sighed. "I shot her with a temporal bullet."

"A temporal bullet?"

"It sends the target to any point in time on impact."

"So where did she go?"

"That's none of your concern," William said, looking down at the screen of Geoff's Sat-Nav in his hand. He didn't appear to have noticed the swap, but that was only half the trick. If the device didn't immediately activate without needing some sort of extra verification, this would all be over.

"I think it's time for you and me to leave," William said, looking at Geoff. "Are you ready?"

"Ready," Geoff said.

"Good," William said. "If it's any consolation, it won't be so bad for you back at the Continuum facility."

"And why's that?" Geoff said, his heart pounding inside his chest with anticipation as he waited for William to press the EXECUTE button.

William raised a hand up to the scar on his face and looked Geoff in the eyes. "At least you won't remember any of it."

And with that, William pressed EXECUTE.

Geoff hoped to God this was going to work.

FOURTEEN

What happened next was probably one of the most bizarre things Geoff had ever experienced in his life—even more bizarre than the time he'd coincidentally picked up the phone to ring Tim at the exact same moment that Tim had decided to ring him. For a moment he couldn't understand how this was possible. Had his phone developed its own artificial intelligence with psychic powers? And how had the universe conspired to put Tim at the other end of the line at the exact point he'd chosen to ring him? This freaked him out for about twenty-five seconds until he realized the whole thing was a coincidence, and about ten minutes later he'd forgotten the incident had even occurred.

At the time, though, it was pretty strange.

But this was in a different league.

The first thing that happened as time went into reverse was that William unpressed the EXECUTE button, and Geoff's heart rate began to calm down again. After a few snippets of reverse conversation, William took his gun out of its holster and aimed it at thin air. In front of him, Zoë appeared out of nowhere, and Geoff was suddenly overcome with a huge feeling of joy as he watched her being unmurdered, the bullet that had hit her in the back of the head shooting back out of her healed skull and returning to the gun it had been fired from like a homing pigeon returning back to its coop.

After that, Geoff lifted the empty bottle to his lips, and undrank the serum. However, just as Geoff had observed when William had injected him, the serum didn't actually come back out of his mouth again. It appeared this serum was equally immune to the time-manipulation effects of the Sat-Nav, and the same was true of the serum in the bottle Zoë had stamped on—when she unstamped on it, the liquid didn't emerge from the earth again and go back inside the bottle.

And so, time continued to reverse itself.

William left them, time reversed itself back to the present day, and before he knew it, he was back in space again with Zoë, looking out of the window at the moment Geoff killed Tringrall's ancestors, allowing all the damage to Earth's battle fleet to be undone.

But this was where things got really weird, because going through all this backward meant he and Zoë were actually watching time reverse itself in reverse.

And this was difficult enough to say, let alone understand.

What it meant was that instead of watching Earth's battle fleet put itself back together, the ships that had previously been undestroying themselves and unexploding everywhere were now doing the opposite; they were destroying themselves and exploding everywhere. Almost the entire fleet was completely decimated in a matter of seconds, and the void of space was suddenly littered with the floating dead bodies of servicemen and women, and charred spacecraft debris.

Seeing backward time running forward at this moment was like watching a massacre, and there was nothing Geoff could do about it. And given that his body was forced to behave in the exact way it had behaved when time was running forward, only in reverse, he couldn't even close his eyes.

And he was smiling the whole time.

He was smiling as the *Concordia* unrammed the ship with Tringrall's ancestors on board. He was smiling as the ship they were on drifted back into the flagship's path. He was smiling as the *Concordia* ground to a halt in the middle of space, its engine wash fading to nothing. In front of him, his greatest achievement was quickly undoing itself, and all he could do was stand there and smile.

Soon afterward, he was back at 23 Woodview Gardens, then he was in the street again, surprising Zoë. Then he was in the restaurant, uneating his cheeseburger. It felt a bit unhygienic to rewrap a burger in its paper after removing it from his mouth and then handing it back to the cashier to put back with the other burgers from the kitchen, but it was probably no worse than what they did at the kebab van down the local high street. Probably.

Next there came the tutorial, backward, and before he knew it he rematerialized in the small, underground room at Continuum where he'd first drunk the serum.

The end of his journey brought him face to face with Jennifer Adams again, who was smiling at him the same way she had done just before he'd left.

He knew time was about to start flowing forward at any second.

And he knew this meant he was probably about to get shot.

Maybe if he could disguise the fact that he was back, he might be able to change his future. If they didn't know he'd discovered the truth about Continuum, he might be able to get away unharmed, right?

As he thought about how he might try and pretend nothing had happened, Geoff performed his final reverse act before time started to flow forward again: he breathed in slowly, and lifted his finger off of the Sat-Nav's screen to reveal the button that said BEGIN.

And begin it did.

EIGHT

"From now on," Jennifer said, "the fate of the world is in your hands. All you need to do is ask yourself one question: What will *you* change?"

She smiled, just as she had done before.

As far as Geoff could tell, she looked completely unaware that Geoff had already been and come back.

Geoff rested the Sat-Nav down on the table, took a step back, and sneaked a look at his watch.

Three twenty.

Ten minutes until his back had an appointment with that bullet, unless there was any way to change things.

Jennifer tilted her head to one side. "Something the matter?"

"What's that?" Geoff said, looking up. He knew he had to appear relaxed, so he adopted what he called the "Xbox avatar pose," which basically meant putting all his weight on one leg and leaning to one side. "No, nothing's the matter. I'm fine."

Jennifer's eyes looked to the left, then to the right, then directly at him.

"Really," he insisted. "I'm fine."

"Did you change your mind?"

"No, not at all," Geoff said. "I wonder if I might use the loo first."

Jennifer blinked. "The loo?"

"Yeah. It's a bit embarrassing, but I really need to go. Dodgy cheeseburger I ate earlier, I think."

Jennifer narrowed her eyes at him. "A dodgy cheeseburger."

"Yeah. I think it's repeating on me."

"No problem," she said. "The bathroom is just down the hallway and on the right."

"Thanks," Geoff said, turning to leave the room. He tried not to move too quickly, so as not to arouse suspicion.

"Oh, before you go," Jennifer said, "do you mind leaving that spare serum I gave you here?"

"The spare serum?"

"Yes. We don't like people carrying it around with them outside of the Continuum experience. I know your friends at Time Tours have already stolen a couple of bottles to analyze, along with a Sat-Nav or two, and I wouldn't want them getting hold of any more. You understand, right?"

"Sure," Geoff said, taking the bottle out of his pocket and putting it on the table. "Here you go."

"I knew it," she said.

"You knew what?"

Jennifer picked up the bottle and showed it to Geoff. "This bottle is empty."

Geoff swallowed. He'd forgotten that the serum wouldn't have returned to the bottle when Zoë undrank it. This was a bit of a giveaway that he'd already returned from his journey, unless he could think of a clever excuse.

"So it is," he said.

"When I gave it to you a moment ago, it was full."

"Was it?"

"Yes, it was." She put the bottle down again. "Care to explain?"

"Are you sure it was full?" Geoff said. "Maybe you gave me an empty one by mistake?"

"What?"

"You know like when you buy a game in the shop and the cashier forgets to put the disc in the case? That happened to me once—I got home with a new game, and the bloody disc was missing. Couldn't believe it. Maybe it was something like that?"

"Maybe," Jennifer said, taking a step toward him, "Or maybe you've already been into your Continuum experience and come back out of it again. Maybe you've just reversed your way right back to the beginning and you thought I wouldn't notice."

Geoff nodded.

Then he nodded a bit more.

Now he was nodding too much.

He stopped nodding.

"Yes," he said, taking a step back. "Yes, that is another possibility. But that's not what's happened here."

Jennifer didn't look convinced. "So why are you trying to leave all of a sudden?" she said. "Did you see something while you were gone, perhaps? Something that maybe you shouldn't have?"

"I don't know what you're talking about," Geoff said, taking another step back toward the door. "I just need the loo."

"Nonsense! Out with it! What did you see?"

Geoff thought about carrying on with his "I really need the loo" charade—in fact, he even considered wetting himself to really complete the illusion. In the end, though, he thought he might try and appeal to Jennifer's better nature, not least because he didn't want to walk around in wet trousers for the rest of the day. And besides, if the future success of Continuum really was responsible for bringing about the end of humanity, surely she would want to stop that from happening, right?

"Okay, okay," Geoff said, holding his hands up. "You're right. I've already been and come back."

"That's better," Jennifer said. She appeared to calm down a little now that she felt Geoff was being honest with her. "And what did you do?"

Geoff sighed. "First of all, I went to see Zoë—you know, the girl we talked about? I showed her the moment I defeated the Varsarians. I didn't quite manage to tell her how I really felt about her, but at least it was something."

"I'm very happy for you." Jennifer's voice was flat and emotionless. "Then what happened?"

"Next we traveled to the future," Geoff said, "Only, I think we traveled forward in time a bit too far."

"*How* far forward did you go?"

"Far enough to see what Continuum eventually does to the planet." Geoff took a step forward and looked Jennifer right in the eyes. "You remember how your supercomputer predicted

163

that humanity would one day set off to explore other galaxies, leaving the Earth to turn back into a beautiful garden world? Well, thanks to your company, that doesn't happen anymore. Humanity doesn't set off to explore the universe—instead, everyone becomes addicted to Continuum and disappears into their own alternate timelines. Isn't that horrible?"

Jennifer laughed. "Oh dear." She shook her head. "Tell me—that story about humanity leaving the Earth to explore other galaxies…"

"Yes?" Geoff said. "What about it?"

"Who told that to you?"

Geoff thought about this for a moment. "I think it was Eric," he replied. "Why?"

"Because it's not true," Jennifer answered. "Never was."

"What do you mean it's not true?" Geoff said.

"I mean it's made up. A lie. A fabrication. That's what people mean when they say something's not true."

"I don't believe you," Geoff said. "How do you know that?"

"Because I'm the one who made it up in the first place," Jennifer replied. "I'm the one who first told that story to Eric, seventeen years ago."

"What?"

"You know the future you saw with all the crumbling buildings? The future where the city is deserted? Well, that isn't some sort of alternate reality caused by the success of Continuum. What you saw has always been destined to happen. My supercomputer back at Time Tours predicted this years ago, only Eric never knew, because he was too lazy to get his hands dirty running all the initial predictions. That idiot left everything completely up to me. I was the one who had to write up all the reports on why the Earth appeared deserted at the end of the 100,000-year prediction cycle, so when it showed me that I would one day set up the most successful company in history and put Time Tours out of business, obviously I covered it up. I've always known the real reason for Earth being deserted in the future; I've always known it was because of the popularity of Continuum. I couldn't let Time Tours know that, though, so I fabricated a story about humanity leaving the universe to explore other galaxies."

"But why in good conscience would you want any of this happen?" Geoff said. "You've seen the impact that Continuum eventually has on the world—it brings about the end of all mankind!"

"Does it?" Jennifer said. "That's one way of looking at it, but I prefer to see it as *freeing* all mankind. Thanks to Continuum, humanity is finally able to break free from the shackles of existence, and spend the rest of its days roaming through time, changing things however it pleases. Don't you see? Once everyone is inside Continuum, no one makes another mistake ever again. Continuum doesn't just give power back to the people. It makes them like *gods*. Isn't that wonderful?"

Geoff couldn't believe what he was hearing. Without the threat of failure, how would anyone ever feel a sense of achievement? And if people could change something just because they didn't like it, how would anyone have the motivation to do anything anymore?

"But people *need* to make mistakes," Geoff said. "Won't everyone get bored if they know that everything they do is just going to work out exactly as they want?"

"Don't be so stupid," Jennifer said. "It will be paradise. And since I know the success of Continuum is already predestined, there's absolutely nothing you can do to stop it."

"But won't Continuum ultimately go bust if it eventually makes all of its customers disappear?"

"Yes. Yes, it will."

"So you're telling me your business model is to go out of business?"

Jennifer sighed. "This isn't about the success of Continuum as a business. It's about so much more than that. Don't you see? The Continuum project is an altruistic one, and it always has been. It isn't about making money—the dream is to free us all."

"You mean freeing people to turn into psychopaths like William Boyle? I watched him kill thousands of people without thinking twice, and it's all because your precious Continuum made him lose perspective on the importance of human life. With the power to do whatever he liked, the people he killed might as well have been ants! Is that what you want humanity to become? A bunch of savages with no moral compass whatsoever?"

"I don't care how people choose to spend their time in Continuum. All I care about is that they are free."

Geoff nodded. "Well, that's all very noble, but I still think you've lost your mind. What you're talking about isn't a dream—it's a nightmare. And since there's no point trying to reason with you, I think now might be a good time for me to run away."

"I don't think so," Jennifer said. She turned around, reached under the table, and began feeling around for something.

All of a sudden a very loud, recurring buzzing sound started to go off, and the room was bathed in a deep red light. Either Jennifer had the sudden urge to develop some photographs while listening to a strange dance track, or she'd triggered an alarm by pressing a button under the table.

He decided he wasn't going to stick around to find out which of those scenarios was true, and bolted out of the door faster than someone being told that their newly married friends were about to arrive with hundreds of wedding photos to show them. He was afraid to admit it, but these circumstances looked more and more like they were playing themselves out exactly as they were destined to. Maybe he should just accept that he was going to be shot on Tower Bridge and have done with it.

But Geoff was getting ahead himself. First of all, he needed to find a way out of Continuum's basement, which was proving to be even harder than trying to find the secret exit in the ghost houses in *Super Mario World*.

He ran down this hallway and that, sometimes coming across a dead end, other times running into an area he didn't recognize and having to turn around. It had been bad enough following Jennifer through the twisting corridors and passageways, let alone trying to find his way back to the lifts on his own. And it was even harder when the place was lit up in a pulsating red glow, with klaxons going off everywhere and the sound of a general commotion heading his way. Presumably, this was the sound of more nice gentlemen from Continuum's "customer support team" on their way to meet him and say hello.

And then kill him.

When Geoff finally thought he had his bearings, the unthinkable happened—he bumped straight into someone roaming the corridors, just as he'd turned one of the last corners before reaching the elevators. It was an older man, perhaps in his late forties or early fifties. He was very overweight, with long hair, baggy eyes, and terrible skin, his arms puckered with hundreds of horrid needle marks like a drug addict. He had a jittery disposition that suggested something wasn't quite right with him in the head.

As they bumped into each other, the man screamed at the top of his voice, his high-pitched wail cutting through the sound of the overhead klaxon in a way Geoff hadn't thought possible. But this wasn't a scream of fear—the man was smiling inanely, as though his mind were overflowing with joy. After recovering from the sudden bump, he ran over to Geoff and hugged him.

"G-give me your tie!" the man muttered.

"What?" Geoff said, waving a hand under his nose. This guy had seriously bad breath.

"Give me your tie!" the man repeated. He reached for Geoff's tie and yanked it straight off.

"Hey!" Geoff said.

"I got it!" the man said, holding the tie over his head and dancing on the spot. "I got it!"

Geoff didn't have time for this. If this guy wanted his tie, he could keep it. It wasn't even his anyway.

After running around a few more corners, Geoff finally came across the elevators, running up to them and jabbing the call button with his fist. Within seconds, one of the elevators opened its doors, and Geoff dashed inside.

"Ground floor!" he said.

The elevator didn't do anything.

Geoff bobbed up and down on the spot impatiently in the hope that this would somehow activate the elevator.

It didn't.

"Ground floor!" he said again.

This time, the elevator reacted to his voice and the doors began to close. As they did, he noticed a group of men turn the corner at the other end of the corridor outside and run toward him. There must have been six or seven of them, each wearing full body armor and carrying weapons, just as William Boyle had done when he'd showed up in the future. In fact, for a moment he thought one of the men actually *was* William, which he knew wasn't beyond the realm of possibility.

Fortunately, the doors slid shut before the men were able to catch up with him, and the elevator began to ascend to its destination. Cocooned inside the lift, Geoff was treated to some nice, gentle elevator music, played on a xylophone.

Geoff looked at his watch.

Three twenty-seven.

It seemed to be taking forever for the elevator to reach the ground floor, so much so that the music was able to complete three full loops before the doors opened. As they did, Geoff ran out into the bustling lobby and looked around. The exits were right the way over the other side of the room, right past the reception desk, the seating area, and all the corporate stands trying to sell holiday activities.

Noticing a few more members of Continuum's customer support team on either side of the lobby, Geoff thought it best if he tried to make his way out of the building as inconspicuously as possible. He tried to blend into the crowd, not moving too quickly so as to stand out, but he had only moved a couple of meters when he heard another elevator open behind him, and seven or eight armed men in body armor poured out.

Jennifer Adams was standing behind them. She noticed Geoff immediately, pointed right toward him, and whispered some orders at the men. The men holstered their weapons and quietly followed behind, as if not to draw too much attention to themselves.

Geoff began to move a little faster, sidling his way past groups of excited tourists, families carting their luggage this way and that, and crowds of people wearing huge backpacks. Behind him, the customer support team did the same.

When he had made it as far as the large rotating *C* in the middle of the lobby, the number of people around him began to grow thinner, and he was able to move quicker. By the time he was approaching the reception desk over on the other end of the lobby, he was almost jogging.

Jeanette, the attractive receptionist who had welcomed him earlier, noticed him leaving. "Mr. Stamp?" she said, standing up from her seat. "Where are you going? Didn't you take the job?"

"I'm afraid not," Geoff replied. "I have a slight difference of opinion with your management."

Jeanette frowned at him before noticing the number of men closing in on his position from behind. "Hey, wait!" she said. "Come back!"

At this point, there wasn't much point trying to disguise the fact that he was running for dear life, so he started to sprint, barging his way past more and more people before diving through the revolving door and out onto the street. It was quite sunny outside, and for a moment Geoff had to raise his hand up to his eyes while his vision adjusted to the light.

Continuum's office was located on the north bank of the river Thames, right next door to the Tower of London. A few hundred meters to his left stood Tower Bridge, and a few hundred meters to his right was London Bridge.

If he wanted to try and change history, he knew he could run toward London Bridge instead of Tower Bridge, but what was the point? It was fairly obvious things were happening exactly as they were supposed to, so why should he bother to resist? And in any case, he knew he would survive being shot, as his future self had been well enough to phone Tim just before he left for Continuum. But there was still something bothering him about all this. Didn't this mean his knowledge of future events was influencing what he was choosing to do? Had he not known his destiny, would he have done something differently? And what did that say about his free will? He felt like a sheep being herded into a pen of causality, with his knowledge of future events the sheepdog.

However, in the time it had taken him to have this little philosophical debate in his head, one of the pursuing men had been able to catch up with him, and wrestled him to the ground right outside the building.

So much for things being predetermined.

Geoff was flipped onto his back by the man, the side of his face pressed hard against the cold pavement.

"Hold still, Geoff," the man said.

Geoff couldn't believe it.

It was William Boyle, but he was younger again, like the one he'd encountered at Canary Wharf. There was no scar on the side of his face, and certainly no look of conflict in his eyes. This was William Boyle before he had tried to cross Continuum.

"William!" Geoff said, trying desperately to wriggle free. "Listen to me! You've got to let me stop them!"

William smiled. "And why would I want that, Geoff?" he said.

All around them, a few people in the street looked on nervously. Some appeared to be unsure as to whether they should be intervening or not.

"In the future, they do something to you too!"

"What?" William said, his smile fading. "What do you mean?"

But before Geoff had a chance to say any more, Jennifer Adams emerged from the revolving doors, followed by the other men. She looked exhausted.

"Get back!" William shouted. He dug his knee into Geoff's stomach. "This is a Continuum security situation! Everything is under control."

"Help me!" Geoff screamed. "Continuum is going to destroy everything! We've got to sto—"

But that was about as far as Geoff got, because the next thing he knew, William had pressed one of his hands over his mouth. Geoff looked William in the eyes. He wasn't smiling anymore as he had been when he'd first tackled Geoff to the ground. What Geoff had just said had clearly rattled him.

"Hold him down," Jennifer said, kneeling next to Geoff and reaching inside her coat pocket. Behind her, the other men had cleared a wide perimeter around them.

"Get his mouth open!" Jennifer said, taking a blister pack of pills out of her pocket and popping one out of the wrapper. It was bright pink and shaped like an elongated football. "We need to wipe his memory immediately."

Geoff assumed that the pill was unlikely to be some aspirin she was going to offer him to ease his current discomfort, and more likely to be something to bring about this whole memory-wiping business. Not being overly keen on the idea of losing his memory, Geoff clamped his mouth shut as tight as he could. Unfortunately, all William had to do to get it open again was hold Geoff's nose until it was impossible to breathe. When Geoff was finally forced to open his mouth, Jennifer dropped the pill inside, and William clamped his mouth shut, rattling his head between his hands until he swallowed.

"There," Jennifer said, wiping her brow. "Let's get him up."

William lifted his knee off of Geoff's chest and offered him a hand to pull him to his feet.

But at that moment, a man ran out of the crowd, slamming straight into William's side and sending him flying. "Run, Geoff!" the man said.

Geoff tried to make out who this person was, but for some reason his vision was extremely blurry. Maybe it was the pill.

But he didn't have time to worry about that now—this was his chance to get away. Despite the fact that his eyesight was worse than if someone had tried to substitute small slices of cucumber for contact lenses, Geoff leapt to his feet and started running.

"Stop him!" he heard Jennifer shout. "Shoot him if you have to, but we can't let him get away!"

Geoff kept running as fast as he could, but after a few seconds he was overcome by a crippling wave of dizziness, his surroundings spinning around worse than if he'd just decided to visit a kaleidoscope museum after downing five pints.

A few moments later and he'd completely lost his bearings. He couldn't tell which way he was heading anymore—all he could see was a blur of colors in front of him, with the sound of angry car horns blaring in his ears from all around.

He kept on running, but it wasn't long before he couldn't remember why he was running anymore. In fact, he couldn't remember anything. So he stopped running and looked around. To one side, he could see a long stretch of water beneath him, though he didn't know this strange liquid was called water anymore. Back where he had just come from, a number of men were running toward him, only he didn't know they were called men anymore. They were just things with arms and legs. The things with arms and legs were making loud noises and pointing some guns at him, but just as he'd forgotten what water and men were, so too had he forgotten what guns were.

Then there was some shouting.

He felt very confused about everything, and turned to look at the water.

What was happening to him?

What was that sudden burst of static he could hear?

Why was there now a sharp pain in his back?

And why was everything around him melting away to nothing?

NINE

The next thing Geoff knew, everything around him began to take form again, except his surroundings looked ever so slightly different. If he had had the mental capacity to put these differences into words, he would have said that although his location looked the same, the people around him were different, the traffic going over the bridge he was on was different, and the weather was different. Where it had been a bright sunny day a moment ago, now the sky was overcast, with a light drizzle coming down from above.

If Geoff's mind had been firing on all cylinders (or even on half a cylinder, for that matter), he would have realized that this was the moment he was waiting for, when he had traveled back in time to yesterday.

Everything had come full circle.

Unfortunately, Geoff didn't realize that, because thanks to the pill Jennifer Adams had forced him to swallow, he couldn't remember a thing. He had no knowledge of what had just happened, no memory of who he was, and in general, his mental state was comparable to that of a small, underwatered pot plant.

"My God!" a voice said. "Is that who I think it is?"

"It is!" another voice said. "That's Geoffrey Stamp!"

"Where did he come from? And what's the matter with him?" came another voice.

"Looks like he's drunk," somebody said.

Geoff spun around on the spot trying to focus on the source of the voices, but he wasn't having much luck. Instead, he decided it would probably be best for everyone if he just collapsed on the ground and closed his eyes, which he did rather impressively, spooling his body across the pavement as though someone had just let all of the air out of him.

As his vision faded to black, the last thing he heard was a single voice shout out, "Somebody call the police!"

Which they did.

ELEVEN

"Sorry I'm late," a voice over by the door said. "What did I miss?"

Geoff strained his head to look toward the voice, but his view was blocked by a number of people, all crowded around him. He now thought he recognized a few of the faces, but he couldn't be sure. With his head raised, though, he was able to look down at his own body, which he noticed was draped in a green sheet of some description. For a moment he thought there might be a better description for the sheet, but he just couldn't remember what it was.

For a moment nobody said anything. They all just looked awkwardly at the man who had just arrived.

"So...what's happened?" the man asked. "I haven't done something wrong again, have I? I mean, I swear I haven't told a soul what I do for a living, or—"

"Geoff...you might want to come over and have a look at this," another man interrupted, motioning the man who had just arrived to come toward them.

Geoff's head was beginning to ache, so he rested it back down again. To his side, he could see that the man had moved close enough to look at his face.

The man stopped still and looked around at everyone.

"Is that who I think it is?" the man said, extending his index finger slowly toward Geoff. The man looked to be in his late twenties, with thick chestnut hair, pale skin, and a round face. He was an average height, with a skinny build and narrow shoulders, and the more Geoff looked at him, the more he couldn't help but think he looked extraordinarily familiar.

He just couldn't remember why.

"I don't know," the other man said, walking across the room to stand next to the one who was looking over him. "Who *do* you think it is?"

And so it continued, with Geoff experiencing everything his past self had seen, but this time from the other perspective.

While an army of doctors, physicians, and surgeons frantically tried to work out why their patient was about as capable of rational thought as a piece of cheese was capable of driving a bus, Geoff's mind began to wander aimlessly, his unconscious drifting from one dream to another like an unmoored boat floating across a lake in whichever way the current decided to take it.

First of all, he dreamed about a limited-edition meal deal from his local pizza restaurant. It was called the Geoff Box, and it was amazing. In the box you got a large pizza, *twenty* pieces of garlic bread, *fifteen* chicken wings, a massive pile of potato wedges, and *three* dips. In fact, you got so much food that the meal had to come in three separate boxes. Over time, people from all over London regarded it as the best limited-edition meal deal anybody had ever created, and it became so popular that it won several awards, including the coveted "best limited-edition meal deal" award. Ultimately, the Geoff Box made it onto the restaurant's permanent menu, and the owner of the restaurant was so grateful to Geoff that he got free pizza given to him for the rest of his life. There was a problem, though—every time Geoff went to eat his free pizza, he noticed that it came with lots of little pink pills sprinkled on top, shaped like elongated footballs. No matter how many times he tried to eat the pizza, something would put him off, and he would end up spitting everything out again.

A few moments later, Geoff found himself floating in space, only he wasn't inside a spacesuit—he was just wearing his regular clothes, like someone who'd left the airlock of a space station without really reading up on this whole space thing. He was pretty sure this oversight would normally present a bit of a problem in terms of not being able to breathe, but for some reason he felt fine, as though he were just drifting through the sky like a balloon. All around him, thousands of spaceships were in the middle of blowing up, but everything was completely silent and moving in extreme slow motion, the bright explosions happening at a fraction of the speed they would normally. Geoff watched as giant frigates broke apart spectacularly, swarms of fighter craft imploded on themselves, and alien flying saucers crashed into each other. At this speed though, the destruction looked quite gentle, as though the very fabric of time had turned into a thick, gloopy syrup that reality had to wade through in order to get anything done.

As he drifted through the floating wreckage, looking around at all the different spacecraft in various stages of destruction, he felt strangely relaxed, as though he were watching a peaceful ballet. The dead bodies drifting around him no longer looked like dead bodies—they looked like graceful dancers, pirouetting in one synchronized movement across the stars. And the giant explosions no longer looked like giant explosions—the powerful flashes looked like a beautiful light display, dazzling some sort of cosmic audience watching from afar. However, as Geoff took in this fantastic vista of light and sound, his insides began to hurt a little. He didn't think much of it at first, but after a few minutes he was in extreme pain, clutching his stomach in agony. He began unbuttoning his clothes to see what was causing him so much discomfort, but when he finally ripped his shirt open, he was horrified to see a huge gash running vertically down his chest. There was no blood that he could see, but his body looked as though it had been surgically cut open.

This must have been about as much as his unconscious could bear to imagine, as Geoff soon found himself leaving space altogether, and standing at the top of a big green hill, overlooking a sprawling city. His stomach no longer hurt, and when he looked down at himself, he could see his shirt was buttoned up again.

To his left, he noticed a girl about ten meters away, with long dark hair. For a moment she looked as though she was running away from him, but as Geoff continued to watch, he realized she was moving backward, which meant she was actually getting closer. The girl appeared to have a nasty wound in the back of her head, and just as she looked as though she was coming to a halt, a large bullet burrowed out of her skull and shot toward him through the air. As had happened when he was in space, Geoff perceived all of this in extreme slow motion.

The girl turned to face Geoff, her head completely healed. She looked angry and was screaming something at him, but no matter how hard he tried, he couldn't make out what she was saying. Then he realized that the bullet that had emerged from the back of her head was heading directly through the air toward him. He thought about dodging out of its path, until he noticed that it wasn't actually moving toward him as such—it was moving toward the gun he was pointing at the girl, which he just realized he was holding. The next thing he knew, the bullet had disappeared down the barrel of the gun in a reverse muzzle flash, and his finger released the trigger.

He lowered the gun, and walked toward the girl. She just stood there crying, but her tears were flowing back up her cheeks and into her eyes. When he was standing right in front of her, he said something in reverse. He couldn't hear exactly what he was saying, but whatever it was, it must have been quite nice because by the time he'd finished talking, the girl looked happy, with no signs that she'd ever been upset.

Then Geoff leaned forward, slipped his hand around the girl's back and pulled her toward him. They looked each other in the eyes for a few seconds, then kissed. It should have been a moment of pure ecstasy, but something didn't feel right. Geoff could feel something moving up his throat; something small, round, and hard. The sensation was quite unpleasant, and he felt his face beginning to contort into a frown. The next thing he knew, the small round thing was rolling around inside his mouth, before he felt it getting sucked out between his lips into the mouth of the girl.

He stopped kissing her and took a step back.

The girl looked at him and smiled. As she did, Geoff noticed she was holding a small pink pill in between her teeth.

And that was the last he saw of the girl with long dark hair before his surroundings melted away again, this time changing to a plain white room. Geoff was just standing in the middle of it, wearing nothing but a surgical gown, his feet bare. For some reason, he felt absolutely exhausted, as if he'd just been for a run.

The place was so white that he couldn't tell where it ended.

He began walking in the hope of finding an edge, but instead of walking forward, he walked backward. He wasn't entirely sure why he was doing this, but he decided to just go with it.

As Geoff continued to walk, he began to notice a small crack running along the ground. At first it was barely noticeable, no wider than a human hair, but the farther he walked, the wider the crack became, and the wider the crack became, the faster he began to move. Soon, the crack was so wide that he found himself breaking into a backward run, and as he did, he could feel the floor beginning to vibrate violently with each footstep, the two sides of the crack splitting farther and farther apart. Geoff was now sprinting backward, yet instead of feeling exhausted, the farther he ran, the more energy he felt he had. Finally, at the moment when he couldn't run any faster, everything around him shattered like shards of glass in a giant greenhouse. The floor gave way, the ceiling caved in, and he found himself falling.

There was something odd about the way he was falling, though—if memory served him correctly (which it wasn't really doing at the moment, but he decided to ignore that), when most people fell, they usually fell downward. That was kind of how gravity worked, wasn't it?

In Geoff's case, though, gravity appeared to be reading its job spec upside down, because he was actually falling upward toward a big bright light.

What's more, as he fell he began to remember things.

He remembered his name.

His job.

His email password (*geoffisgreat1*, all lowercase.)

He remembered Zoë.

And by the time he had reached the light above him, he finally began to remember everything else.

He finally remembered the truth about Continuum.

And that he needed to change his password to *geoffisgreat2* in three days' time, because it was going to expire.

TWELVE

"There," a voice said. "I think that's it."

"You sure?" somebody else replied.

"I think so. His neural pathways are restoring themselves now. With any luck, he should regain his full memory within a matter of minutes."

"And you're telling me that all that was done to him with this little pill?"

"That's right. We found it inside his stomach when we cut him open. Fortunately, it was only partially digested, so it hadn't taken full effect. Had he gotten here a few minutes later, though, there might not have been a way to save him. You brought him to us just in time."

"Jesus. Who would have thought something this small could wipe his memory?"

"The pill doesn't work like that, Dr. Skivinski. It didn't wipe his memory—it just stopped him from being able to access it."

"So you're telling me all his memories should be intact?"

"That's right. When Mr. Stamp ingested the pill, a chemical was released that created a barrier around all his thoughts and experiences, locking them away from the rest of his mind. Even his most basic brain functions were blocked, from his ability to understand language to the processing of visual images. For all intents and purposes, that pill was able to turn him into a vegetable in a matter of seconds."

"Bloody hell."

"Trust me—this man is lucky to be alive. The damage to his mind was so great, it's a miracle his body even knew how to breathe."

"But you say you were able to repair it?"

"We think so. Once we were able to isolate the chemical compound released by the pill, all we had to do was synthesize an antidote, which began to break down the barriers forming in his mind the moment we administered it."

"And what about the wound in his back?"

"Oh, that was easy. The bullet missed his spinal column by a few inches and didn't puncture any major organs. We were able to stop the bleeding and heal the wound up with some regeneration gel in a matter of minutes. When he wakes up, he should feel just fine—"

Geoff opened his mouth and made a noise that sounded a bit like a cross between a long yawn and a zombie moaning.

"He's waking up!" one of the voices said.

Geoff opened his eyes. He was lying faceup in a bed, his head nicely cushioned on a big, comfy pillow. To his left, he could see Eric standing over him, leaning against the back of a chair. To his right, a man he didn't recognize was scribbling furiously on a clipboard. That's not to say the man looked angry about what he was scribbling—he was just doing it very quickly.

Geoff groaned again and moved his elbows to lift his body into a more upright sitting position. As he rested his back against the headboard, he noticed that a long white curtain had been pulled around the bed, making it difficult for him to see the rest of the room.

"Wait here," the man on the right said. "I'll get the others."

He stood up, put his clipboard on the chair, and ducked through a gap in the curtain. As the curtain parted, Geoff caught a glimpse of the room beyond. He saw cream walls. A few other beds. Medical equipment. A couple of nurses. Unless this was a movie set designed to look like a hospital ward, he was in a hospital ward.

"I don't believe it," Geoff said. "It's happened again! Why is it that every time I come to the future, some psychopath tries to wipe my memory and I end up in hospital?"

"I don't know," Eric said. He walked over to the other side of the bed, picked up the clipboard that the man had left on the chair, and sat down. "But it seems to be a nasty habit of yours."

"Well, it needs to stop," Geoff said. "Do you have any idea how inconvenient it is when people try and make me forget things all the time?"

"Please, Geoff—calm down. How are you feeling?"

"Okay, I guess," Geoff replied. But as he spoke, his mind was suddenly overcome with a flood of memories. He remembered what Continuum was really up to, how the world would one day become addicted to their technology, how Jennifer Adams needed to be stopped.

"Eric," Geoff said, "how long have I been here?"

"You mean in the hospital?" Eric replied, stroking his long white beard. "I'm not sure. Just under a day, I think. The doctors were operating on you throughout the night."

"Just under a day?" Geoff said. "You mean it's tomorrow already?"

"What are you talking about?" Eric said.

"When you found me, I'd traveled back in time by one day, right?"

"Right."

"So do you mean to tell me it's been almost a full twenty-four hours since I arrived?"

"Yes, almost," Eric replied.

"My God," Geoff said. "Quick—what time is it?"

Eric looked at his watch. "I make it eleven forty in the morning."

"Jesus—I need to get to a phone," Geoff said, tossing his sheets to one side and swiveling his body out of the bed. "There's no time to lose!"

"Hold your horses," Eric said, placing a hand on Geoff's shoulder and pushing his body back against the headboard. "You're not going anywhere. Not until the doctors say you're okay."

"You don't understand. I need to speak to Tim!"

"Oh I understand, son," Eric said. "I understand that you were this close to having your entire memory erased!" He pinched his index finger and thumb together, leaving the teeny-tiniest gap between the two to show how close he meant.

"Now, please, let's just wait for the doctors, okay? Let's see what they say."

"I feel fine, Eric," Geoff said. "Really, I do."

"Your phone call can wait," Eric said. "Do you have any idea what kinds of injuries you just sustained? Have you *seen* the thing they removed from your back?"

"No, but I'm guessing it was a bullet, right? Quite a large bullet?"

Eric blinked. "How did you know that?"

"That was the thing that sent me back to yesterday. It's called a temporal bullet, and it's fired from a kind of gun that can program each shot to send its target to a particular point in time on impact."

"Huh," Eric said. "Do you have any idea who shot you?"

"No, but it must have been someone from Continuum."

"Continuum, eh? We thought this was something to do with them. What were you doing there, anyway?"

"Tim sent me to spy on them—he wanted me to find out why they were hiring so many Time Reps when they didn't really need them, and what they might have had to do with my future self appearing on Tower Bridge with a bullet in his back. It turns out the only reason they are interested in hiring Time Reps is to put Time Tours out of business, but while I was there I discovered a much darker secret. Something horrible. I tried to get away, but some goons from their customer support team gave chase. In the commotion, one of them must have shot me."

"But that doesn't make sense," Eric said. "If these guns work as you say they do and can be programmed to send the target anywhere in time, why would they send you back to a point like this, when you could still warn others about what was about to happen? Why not send you somewhere you couldn't do any harm, like the distant future?"

"I don't know," Geoff said, "but speaking of the distant future, I have a question for you."

"Fire away," Eric said.

"Nice choice of words, considering I've just been shot."

"Sorry," Eric said. "I meant—go ahead. Ask your question."

"While I was at Continuum, I had a long chat with an old friend of yours."

Eric sighed. "You mean Jennifer."

"Yes—Jennifer Adams. She told me something about your supercomputer, and I wanted to know if it was true."

"What did she say?"

"Well, you know how the computer's simulation shows the Earth being completely deserted in 100,000 years' time?"

"Yes?"

"You once told me that that was because one day, humanity would leave Earth to explore other galaxies, right?"

"Yes, that's right."

"Okay. So here's my question: have you actually seen that happen in the simulation?"

"What?"

"I mean have you personally seen the moment when humanity leaves the Earth to explore other galaxies for yourself? Did you watch that moment with your own eyes?"

"Not exactly," Eric said, rubbing the back of his head. "I didn't really have time to watch all the simulation footage generated by the computer. But the reports are very clear, and I have it on good authority that—"

"Jennifer lied to you," Geoff said, folding his arms over his chest.

"What?"

"She's the one who told you that story, right?"

Eric looked at the floor. He said nothing.

"Well, she made it up. Earth doesn't eventually become deserted because humanity leaves this world for a better one. It becomes deserted because the entire population of the planet gets addicted to her Continuum experience, and disappears into their own fantasy timelines. Jennifer discovered that this was going to happen back when she was working at Time Tours, running all those simulations of the future for you. Knowing you would probably try and stop this from happening if you ever found out the real reason the planet appeared deserted in 100,000 years' time, she covered the whole thing up, writing false reports about humanity flying off to distant galaxies to throw you off the scent."

"That's impossible," Eric said.

"No it isn't," Geoff said, looking the old man in the eyes. "In fact, I saw it for myself when I tried out the Continuum experience. That's why Jennifer tried to wipe my memory, and why they tried to kill me when I almost escaped. In the future, humanity doesn't go off to explore other galaxies—it simply vanishes without a trace into millions of alternate realities, where mistakes can be undone, dreams can be realized at the push of a button, and all achievements are worthless."

"I don't believe it," Eric said. "That little—"

At that moment, the curtain surrounding Geoff's bed was pulled back by the man who had run off earlier. He was accompanied by twenty or so men and women, all wearing white coats.

"Out of this man's way!" Eric said, pulling Geoff out of the bed and helping him to his feet. "He needs to get to a phone right away!"

THIRTEEN

Eric escorted Geoff over to a small office on the other side of the ward. Inside the office there was a small desk, a rather uncomfortable-looking chair, a clock on the wall that had just struck quarter to twelve, and a phone.

"You make your call," Eric said, holding the door open. "I'll keep the doctors busy." And with that, he left Geoff alone, closing the door behind him.

Geoff sat down behind the desk, shifting his weight around to try and find a comfortable position to be sitting in. When he realized that wasn't going to be possible, he picked up the phone, held the receiver to his ear, and dialed Tim's number.

After three rings, Tim answered.

"Good afternoon, Tim Burnell speaking," he said.

"Tim?" Geoff said. "It's me!"

The other end of the phone went quiet for a few seconds. If Geoff remembered rightly, this was the bit where Tim had turned to him and said "It's you," and he'd misheard him say "It's Hugh," and they had to clear all that up.

The next thing he heard was his own voice shouting down the phone. "ARE YOU ALL RIGHT?"

"Tim," Geoff said, "I've remembered everything! The reason Continuum are—"

"Geoff, hold on a minute. I've got the other Geoff here as well. Are you sure it's okay to talk like this with him here?"

"Yes, it's fine. I remember being in the room the whole time while you had this conversation with me, so it should be fine."

"I see," Tim said. Geoff then heard him say to his past self, "He says he remembers being in the room when I was on the phone with his future self, so it must be okay for you to be here now."

"So I can stay?" he heard himself say in the background.

"Apparently."

"Oh, hold on a second," Geoff said. "You told me to sit down on the other side of the room, so I probably should ask you to make me do that."

"But he says I told you to sit down over there," Tim said.

"Okay," he heard himself say.

There was a moment of silence. Presumably, this was the moment when he trying not to sit down at all.

"Tim—tell Geoff I'll talk to him later," Geoff said.

He listened to Tim and Geoff argue in the background about whether Geoff should sit down or not, before Tim's voice finally came back on the phone.

"Okay," Tim said. "You can talk now."

"You know how it didn't make sense why Continuum wanted to hire Time Reps? Well, I went to their offices to find out what they were up to, pretending I was there for a job interview. You were right, Tim—Continuum isn't interested in employing any of us to be Time Reps at all! The only reason they want to recruit us is to steal everyone away from Time Tours, and put you out of business."

"Who told you this?" Tim said.

"Jennifer Adams."

"You met with Jennifer Adams herself?"

"That's right," Geoff said. "And she told me everything."

"I knew it," Tim said. "So what did they ask you to do for them instead?"

"Nothing," Geoff said.

"Nothing?"

"She just gave me one of those Sat-Nav things, and said I could go back and live the rest of my life inside the Continuum experience, changing whatever I liked."

"I see," Tim said. "So what happened next?"

Geoff explained everything.

"That bloody…" Tim trailed off. "Well, that certainly explains everything," he said. "But how come—"

"I know, I know," Geoff said. "If they wanted to get rid of me, why did they only send me back one day, giving me a chance to warn you? Why didn't they send me somewhere like the distant future, where I couldn't do any harm? I'm afraid I don't know the answer to that."

"I see," Tim said eventually. "Well, I think you and I need to get over there right away, don't you?"

"No, not yet," Geoff said. "First of all, we need to let your Geoff go to Continuum and find all this out for himself. If we don't, I won't be here to tell you all this, and we'll have one of those nasty paradox things."

"Of course—you're right," Tim said. "We need to let your past self do his thing first, otherwise you won't be speaking to me now. Good thinking."

Suddenly, Geoff heard his own voice down the other end of the phone. "Okay," it said. "I've had just about as much of this as I can take. Will someone tell me what the hell is going on?"

"Geoff," Tim said. "Your past self has lost his temper over here. Didn't you say you were going to speak with yourself?"

"I guess I did," Geoff said. "Look, can you come and pick me up? I'm not sure where I am exactly—some sort of hospital, I think, but we need to make sure we're there to apprehend Jennifer Adams the moment one of her goons shoots me in the back on Tower Bridge."

"Okay," Tim replied. "After I send Geoff to Continuum, I'll come and pick you up from the hospital."

"Also, do you think it might be worth going to the police?" Geoff said. "These guys were all armed with those weird guns, so it would probably be a good idea to have some backup rather than just turning up and saying, 'Hey! Stop it!'"

"Good thinking," Tim said. "After I come and get you, we'll go over there and explain the situation. Hopefully they should be able to help us."

"Okay. Ooh—and one other thing—can you get me a Coke? I'm really thirsty."

"Uh…sure."

"You won't forget?"

"No, I won't forget! Look, here's Geoff for you."

Geoff swallowed. This was the part of the phone call he was dreading.

He wasn't so much bothered about telling himself not to save Zoë.

He just hated listening to the sound of his own voice.

FOURTEEN

It wasn't long after Geoff had gotten off the phone to himself that Tim turned up to take him to the police station. Geoff was so hyped up by the time they arrived, he half expected them to devote every officer in the city to help apprehend Jennifer Adams once he'd explained what she was up to. Unfortunately, their reaction to him trying to report a crime that hadn't been committed yet actually turned out to be one of slight bafflement. It didn't help that the officer at the front desk wasn't really taking them that seriously, but then who could blame him? Geoff's story was about as believable as the time he'd tried to convince Tim he could give up tea for lent.

He'd lasted eight minutes.

"Let's go through this one more time," the officer said, raising his elbows onto the desk and propping up his head in his hands. They'd been going through this for at least two hours now. The officer was red-faced and quite overweight, his greasy hair mopped over his head like a drooping weed. His uniform didn't look like it was particularly comfortable, and bulged in odd places as though his body were a balloon that had been overinflated.

"There really isn't time for this!" Geoff said, looking down at his watch. It had just gone three o'clock. "Don't you understand? In less than half an hour, someone is going to try and kill me!"

"You don't say," the officer sighed, his eyes heavy. "That's terrible."

"I don't know how many more ways we can explain the situation, officer," said Tim, who had been able to keep a little more calm than Geoff over the course of the conversation.

"Like we said, at three thirty this afternoon, someone from Continuum is going to attempt to murder my friend here. That's all there is to it."

"And who would that be again?"

"I already told you—I don't know," Geoff said. "I didn't see the shooter, but it was definitely someone from Continuum."

"You didn't see the shooter?"

"Not exactly."

"And why is that?"

"My vision was blurred."

"Your vision was blurred."

"That's right."

"And why was it blurred?"

"Because these people drugged me!"

"So you were on drugs at the time?" the officer said.

"Yes!" Geoff said. "I mean no! I don't know what they gave me! All I know is that they held me down and forced me to swallow a pill."

"They forced you to swallow a pill."

"Yes!"

"What was the pill? Ecstasy?"

"No!"

"Speed?"

"No!"

"Aspirin?"

"Look, all I know is that whatever they gave me, it made me really dizzy!"

"And it erased your memory," Tim said.

"That's right," Geoff said. "It also erased my memory."

"So if you were forced to swallow a pill that made you lose your memory, how come you remember swallowing it?"

"Our team of doctors at Time Tours were able to provide an antidote," Tim said. "If they hadn't, Geoff would have been a gibbering wreck by now."

"Uh-huh," the officer said. "A gibbering wreck, you say?"

"That's right."

"And you're sure this antidote worked?"

"What's that supposed to mean?" Geoff said.

The officer leaned back in his chair and rested his feet up on his desk.

"Look at this situation from my perspective for a moment, boys," he said. "It's a quiet afternoon. You are sitting behind this nice desk, doing the crossword in the paper. Twelve down is proving a bit tricky, but otherwise the afternoon hasn't been that taxing. Then all of a sudden, two guys show up. They say that they are here to report an attempted murder, except the victim looks fine, they don't know who the shooter is, they don't know the type of gun used, they admit to being on drugs at the time, and best of all, the crime hasn't happened yet. That's not exactly the sort of thing you want to be rushing into the captain's office with, now, is it?"

"Look, I know how crazy this must sound," Geoff said, "but I'm not making it up! Jennifer Adams is dangerous! You have to arrest her!"

"For the last time," the officer said, "we can't just go up to one of the world's most successful businesswomen and arrest her! What's the charge?"

"Attempted murder!"

"But you said you don't know who shot you!"

"Okay then—assault!"

"You mean the assault where you remember being forced to swallow a pill that made you lose your memory?"

"Conspiring to wipe out the human race!"

"That's not even a charge!" the officer said, "And I think I've just about had enough of this."

"How about this," Geoff said. "Did I mention there was this old guy who stole my tie?" He pointed at the absence of a tie hanging around his neck, as if this somehow proved it had been stolen.

"What?"

"While I was trying to escape from the Continuum building, this crazy man ripped my tie off of me and started dancing around, holding it over his head! I'd be wearing that right now if it wasn't for him!"

"So?"

"So that's theft, right? Can't you arrest them for theft?"

"Tie theft?"

"Yeah!"

"You want me to arrest one of the most successful businesswomen in the world because someone in her building stole your tie?"

"That's right."

The officer's face was starting to go a little more red. "You have exactly ten seconds to leave before I arrest you for wasting police time," he said.

"But—"

"Ten!" The officer said, beginning his countdown.

"Please!" Geoff said.

"Nine!"

"Geoff, forget it," Tim said. "We're just going to have to deal with this situation ourselves."

· · ·

Unfortunately, the delay at the police station meant that Tim and Geoff hadn't had a chance to work out what they were going to do when they arrived at the Continuum building. In fact, by the time they had found a parking space that was reasonably enough priced so that you didn't need to take out a small mortgage for the parking meter, there were only a couple of minutes to spare before Geoff knew he would see himself step out of those revolving doors and get wrestled to the ground by William Boyle.

They hid behind a large tree on the other side of the road from the Continuum building and waited.

"You know that man whole stole your tie?" Tim said while they waited for Geoff to emerge.

"Yeah?"

"How old would you say he was?"

"I don't know," Geoff replied. "Late forties, early fifties. He wasn't in great shape, so it was hard to tell. Why do you ask?"

"No reason. I'm wondering if that might have been

the scientist who used to work for Time Tours. The one she's supposed to have convinced to leave with her and set up Continuum."

"I wouldn't know," Geoff said. "But if that was the kind of person she wanted working for her, it's a miracle Continuum ever became successful. I mean, dancing with my tie over his head like he'd just won a gold medal? That guy was bonkers."

"Well, you know what they say," Tim said. "The difference between genius and insanity is measured only by success."

"And by whether or not you like stealing random items of clothing and dancing around with them over your head," Geoff added.

"I suppose there's that too."

"Okay, so what's the plan?" Geoff whispered.

"I have no idea," Tim said. "I think we're going to have to make this up as we go along. One thing is for certain, though—until you get shot and sent back in time, we mustn't interfere with anything that happens. If we do, it's paradox city, population: us. After that, though, it's fair game. I say we wait for the right opportunity, then try and apprehend Jennifer Adams somehow."

"How do you apprehend someone?" Geoff said. "I've never done that before."

"Me neither," Tim said. "But it can't be too difficult, can it?"

"Look!" Geoff said, pointing toward the revolving doors.

Tim stopped talking and looked around.

The past version of Geoff had just stepped outside, holding a hand up to his face to shield his eyes from the light. He looked around for a few seconds and began to make a run for it; however, in the time it had taken him to get his bearings, William Boyle had managed to catch up with him and wrestle him to the ground, grabbing his legs in a swift rugby tackle and throwing him to the ground. Geoff struggled not to look away as he watched William flip his past self onto his back, pressing the side of his face against the pavement.

"Hold still," he heard William say as a number of passersby began to gather round. After a brief exchange of words between the two of them, he watched William's smile fade. This must have been the moment he'd tried to warn William that one day he would fall foul of Continuum.

Suddenly Geoff had a thought. William had appeared totally comfortable working for Continuum until Geoff had placed that seed of doubt in his mind. What if William had gotten in trouble with Continuum because of what Geoff had told him?

He didn't have time to give that much thought, though, as before he knew it, Jennifer Adams had emerged from the revolving doors, followed by the other men.

It wasn't long before William had dug his knee into Geoff's stomach, the men had cleared a perimeter around them, and Jennifer was trying to force him to swallow the pill.

Geoff watched as his past self tried to resist opening his mouth.

At that moment, he felt Tim tap him on the shoulder.

"You know, I've just had a thought," Tim said. "You remember the person that rescued you at this point?"

"Yes?"

"What if that was me?"

"What?" Geoff said, watching as his past self was forced to open his mouth to breathe, allowing Jennifer to drop the pill inside. This was very uncomfortable to watch.

"Didn't you say the person said 'Run, Geoff!'?"

"Yes."

"Not 'Geoffrey,' but 'Geoff'?"

"Yes."

"So this person knew your name?"

"I guess so."

"Son of a bitch," Tim said, running toward the crowd.

"Where are you going?" Geoff shouted. In front of them, William was just lifting his knee off of his past self's chest to help him up.

"Remember what I said about not interfering with this course of events?" Tim called back to Geoff, pushing through the crowd.

"Yeah?"

"Well, ignore that! Interfere as much as you like!"

And with that, Tim slammed into William's side, sending him flying into a wall.

"Run, Geoff!" Tim said to Geoff's past self.

Geoff watched as his past self leapt to his feet and did exactly as he was told, running away from everyone as fast as he could.

"Stop him!" he heard Jennifer shout. "Shoot him if you have to, but we can't let him get away!"

Unfortunately, his past self didn't really look like he could see where he was going, and this suspicion was confirmed when he ran right across a busy road, narrowly avoiding lane after lane of fast-moving traffic. Geoff could barely watch as cars on either side of the road swerved to avoid him, slamming on their brakes, and all around, drivers honked their horns in that way people do when they want to make it sound as though their car is very angry about something.

His past self kept on running once he had made it to the other side of the road, but it was clear by now that the drug was seriously impairing his vision. In fact, the more he ran, the more he looked extraordinarily unsure as to why he was even running in the first place.

A few meters back, Jennifer Adams and most of her men were in pursuit, although they had to leave William behind, as he was still recovering from being hit by Tim, supporting his body against the wall with one arm as he struggled to get to his feet. Tim was lying next to him, looking a little bit dazed—if he didn't move soon, William would have him.

But that wasn't going to happen.

Geoff realized this was his chance for some payback. He ran over to William, clenched his hand into a tight fist, and smacked him in the face as hard as he could.

William collapsed on the ground in front of Geoff, unconscious.

The punch hurt like hell, but Geoff was so worked up after landing such a killer blow, he didn't even notice it.

"Sorry," Geoff said, standing over William's limp body as

he shook the pain out of his hand. "I know you were forced into it, but you deserved that."

"Well done, Geoff!" Tim said, getting to his feet. "You really knocked him out cold!"

"Thanks," Geoff said. "I'm not really a man of violence, but that felt really, really good."

Tim looked down at William, then at the gun he was holding.

"What is it?" Geoff said.

Tim picked up the gun and looked at it. "I think we've got a problem," he said.

"Problem?" Geoff said. "What problem?"

"This is the thing that fires those temporal bullets, right?"

"That's right," Geoff said. "I think you can program it so the bullets send the target back to any point in time you like. Why?"

"You remember we were wondering why Continuum sent you back to yesterday? Why they didn't send you to a more remote time period where you couldn't raise the alarm? Well, it turns out that's exactly what they were trying to do."

"What's that now?" Geoff said.

"Look at this."

Tim held the gun on its side so Geoff could read the display. To his horror, the screen said AD 1,000,0000.

"So what does this mean?" Geoff said. "You think one of their bullets malfunctioned or something?"

"No," Tim said, looking around at where Geoff's past self had gotten to.

Despite not having any sense of direction, Geoff's past self was still running as fast as he could away from everyone, toward Tower Bridge. He'd done remarkably well, considering his condition.

Tim began fiddling with some buttons on the side of the gun. It turned out the controls were quite obvious, and he was able to change the target date to yesterday with ease.

"Shit," Tim said, grabbing Geoff by the shoulder. "We've been looking at this all wrong! Continuum wasn't who shot you today—it was us!" He started running toward Tower Bridge as well.

"What?" Geoff said, following closely behind.

"It's the only explanation!" Tim said, looking back. "Don't you see? Sending you back by one day was the only way to warn us about what was going to happen! The person who shot you wasn't trying to kill you—they were trying to save you!"

"Well, shooting me in the back is a funny way of saving me!" Geoff said. "Can't we think of a less painful way of dealing with all this, like perhaps shooting all the other men instead? That's how this sort of thing normally works, right?"

"There's too many of them!" Tim said, running faster. "Trust me—this is the only way!"

By now, Geoff's past self had covered quite an amazing distance considering he might as well have been running with a blindfold on. He'd made it right to the end of the street and turned right, running along the road that led up onto Tower Bridge. By this point, though, the drug was clearly hindering Geoff's ability to put one foot in front of the other in rapid succession, and he began to slow down. Jennifer and her men were only a few paces behind, but Tim and Geoff were catching up fast.

After a few more seconds of running, Geoff's past self looked as though this whole running malarkey had suddenly become far too complicated an activity for his brain to deal with anymore, and he came to an abrupt halt in the middle of the bridge, standing near the railings and leaning over to catch his breath. Then he just stood there aimlessly, swaying like a drunkard, watching as everyone ran toward him, and then he turned away to look down at the river.

"Don't shoot him!" Jennifer shouted at her men. "Holster your weapons! Holster your weapons!"

The men did as they were told, slotting their guns into a compartment in their armor.

"Okay," Jennifer said. "Now, let's take him in."

However, just as the men from Continuum began to move in to grab Geoff, Tim pushed past Jennifer, knocking her to the pavement. He barged his way through her men, pointed William's gun directly at Geoff, and fired a single, well-aimed shot.

At that moment the air filled with a sudden noise of static. The bullet struck Geoff's past self in the back, and he vanished into thin air instantaneously. The effect looked exactly the same as when William had shot Zoë, with Geoff's body evaporating into nothing as though it had just disappeared into the ether.

"Yes!" Tim shouted, punching the air as Geoff caught up with him. "I got him! I got him!" He ran over to Jennifer, pulled her to her feet, and pressed the gun to the side of her head. On the road next to them, cars screeched to a halt and people jumped out of their vehicles, running to the safety of somewhere where there weren't lots of people with guns.

"Don't move," Tim said to his new hostage.

"I won't," Jennifer said.

"Good," Tim said.

"But tell me," she continued, making a quick gesture to her men to take out their weapons, "what are you going to do now?"

FIFTEEN

Geoff and Tim watched as Jennifer's men took out their guns and showed them the end that the bullets usually came out of.

After putting in all that effort to save his past self from being sent to an inconvenient time period, all that had happened was that they'd now found themselves in the exact same predicament.

Typical.

"What *are* we going to do now?" Geoff asked.

"I'm not entirely sure," Tim replied, holding Jennifer close to him, the barrel of his gun pressing against her temple. "I didn't think this far ahead, to be honest."

"Oh," Geoff said. "Well that's a bit annoying."

"I cannot believe you two morons!" Jennifer shouted, apparently feeling more frustrated with her present situation than concerned about the fact that she had a gun held to her head. "What exactly were you hoping to achieve by coming here?!"

"We're here to stop Continuum," Geoff said, walking in front of Jennifer, his hands resting on his hips like a dad giving his son a lecture about not walking on the roof of the garage. As he moved, the men around him moved their guns to follow, but none of them looked like they were ready to shoot. He hoped they wouldn't try anything while their boss was in danger, unless of course they wanted to try surrendering, which would have been acceptable.

Something told him that wasn't going to happen, though.

"We cannot allow the world to get addicted to Continuum," Geoff said. "The future of the human race depends on us shutting you down!"

"Oh dear," Jennifer sighed, turning her head as much as she

could within Tim's grip to look at them both. "Look, I'm not entirely sure how many times I need to explain this to you, but there is nothing you can do to stop Continuum, okay? Nothing. The success of Continuum has already been determined. The supercomputer at Time Tours already predicted its future dominance years ago, and you've seen the future with your own eyes. It is the destiny of the human race. It is meant to be."

"I don't believe you," Geoff said. "There has to be a way to stop this from happening."

"No, there isn't."

"Why not?"

"Because if you did, you would create a paradox."

"Not those stupid things again," Geoff said. "Why do they always turn up when you least want them?"

"How will stopping Continuum create a paradox exactly?" Tim said, loosening his grip on Jennifer a little.

"Think about it," Jennifer replied. "The only reason you think you need to stop Continuum is because when Geoff went forward in time, he saw a world where everyone had disappeared into the Continuum experience. However, if you *do* succeed in shutting Continuum down, that future will never transpire, meaning you will never have seen the future you are trying to prevent, correct? Then you wouldn't have any reason to try and stop Continuum, so you won't stop it, and it will exist again. That, my friends, is a paradox."

Tim looked like he was about to open his mouth to say something, but decided against it.

"Don't you see?" Jennifer added, "Destroying Continuum will simply create an endless loop of cause and effect, which could endanger the very fabric of the universe! What you want to do may actually be worse for the future of mankind than the very thing you are trying to prevent!"

Geoff thought about what Jennifer had said for a moment.

"That's not necessarily true," he said. "When I was in Continuum, the future I saw was based on a timeline where I had gone into Continuum myself, right? If that's the case, I could still have seen a future where the world was deserted, because the computer was taking into account the fact that I was using Continuum myself to travel back and forth through time, rather than stopping that future from transpiring. So in theory, it should still be possible for me to stop Continuum in the real world, without it affecting what I saw inside it. Isn't that right?"

This time it was Jennifer who thought about what Geoff had said for a moment.

"But without Continuum," she said, "you wouldn't have been able to use the Sat-Nav to see that alternate timeline! If you destroy it, you'll lose the memories that sent you down this path in the first place!"

"No I won't," Geoff said. "Thanks to that serum, I can destroy Continuum and still remember why I needed to do it."

Tim was nodding to himself. "That was very good," he said. "You may actually be right."

"Yes, I admire your logic," Jennifer admitted, "But that still doesn't change what the supercomputer predicted when I was at Time Tours. In the future, this planet is deserted because everyone disappears into Continuum. I've seen it with my own eyes."

"But then again, you could be lying about that," Tim said.

"I'm not lying!" Jennifer cried. "Don't you understand? All this is supposed to happen! You cannot change what is already predetermined!"

Geoff clenched his fists.

His body began to tremble.

This was a similar sensation to the time he'd found out that LucasArts had been closed down.

In short, he was really, really angry.

"I can change whatever I like!" Geoff said. "I'm sick of people telling me what I can and can't do, how I'm allowed to behave and how I'm not. You tell everyone that Continuum is the only way people can change the world around them, that it's the only way they can fulfill their dreams. But you know what? I don't need your stupid Continuum to change the world. I don't need it to make my dreams come true. From now on, I'm going to behave however I like; I'm going to try and do things my way, no matter who says I can't, and no computer is going to tell me otherwise!"

He felt triumphant, like he'd just given a rousing speech to some troops on the eve of a big battle. Unfortunately, the only troops listening in this instance were the ones on the other side, and they all kind of wanted him dead, if they were being honest.

He was wasted on his audience.

"Okay, Geoff," Jennifer said, "okay." She looked at her men and smiled. "Lower your weapons," she ordered.

"Ms. Adams?" one of the men said, not taking his sights off Geoff.

"You heard me," Jennifer said. "Lower your weapons."

Reluctantly, the men did as they were told.

"Now, throw them in the river."

"Really, Ms. Adams," another man protested, "do you really think it's wise to—"

"Don't argue with me!" she said. "Do it! Throw them in the river now!"

Once again, the men did as they were told, throwing their weapons over the side.

"There." Jennifer looked at Tim. "I've discarded my weapons. Do you think you could do me the courtesy of lowering yours?"

"Wait a minute," Geoff said. "Why are you doing this?"

"I'm so confident about Continuum's place in the future, I'm going to let you go," she said.

"What?" Tim said. "You really expect us to believe that?"

"I do," Jennifer replied. "Please, put your gun away."

Tim looked at Geoff, who shrugged his shoulders in an "I have no idea what the hell is going on but maybe we should take the chance?" sort of way.

After a few seconds, Tim lowered his gun from Jennifer's head and let go of her.

"You're really just going to let us go?" Geoff said.

"That's right," Jennifer said, straightening the collar of her suit jacket and walking back over to her men.

"But why?" Geoff said. "You must know that the first thing

we're going to do once we get out of here is try and come up with a way of stopping Continuum."

"Geoff," Jennifer said, taking a few steps back toward him. "Like I said before—you cannot stop Continuum. It is an inevitable part of our future. It is unavoidable. Do you understand what those words mean?"

"I understand," Geoff said. "But I still refuse to believe I'm powerless to change things."

"Okay," Jennifer said, running her fingers through her hair, "I'm going to humor you for a moment. Let's say that I'm wrong. Let's say that the future of Continuum isn't set in stone, and that there *is* still a way to prevent it from taking over the world without causing a universe-ending paradox."

"Okay," Geoff said. "I like this game."

"*How* would you destroy it?"

"What?" Geoff said.

"I said: *how* would you destroy it? Where would you start? Continuum isn't like that Varsarian invasion you dealt with, Geoff—there isn't a silver bullet you can fire that just takes care of everything. Unlike that single flying saucer you destroyed that turned the tide of an entire battle, Continuum is very different. There is no central computer to break, or an important building to blow up, or a person to kill that would wipe Continuum out forever—Continuum is everywhere."

"Oh," Tim said. "Oh dear."

"Your eloquent friend understands what I'm talking about," Jennifer said. "If you destroyed our headquarters, Continuum would live on. If you killed me on the spot, Continuum would live on. If you sent a broadcast out to the whole world telling everyone how horrible we were, Continuum would live on."

"She's right, Geoff," Tim said. "I hate to say it, but she's right."

"No," Geoff said. "There must be a way."

"Think of it this way," Jennifer said. "Let's say you wanted to try and destroy the Internet. How would you succeed?"

Geoff thought about this for second.

"Give me a moment," he said, holding his finger up.

"The answer is you wouldn't succeed. Continuum is like the Internet—it's bigger than me, it's bigger than you, and it's bigger than all the vats of serum or piles of Sat-Navs that it uses. We have millions of people going on holiday every day, and even though they're only going on temporary vacations at the moment, it is quickly becoming something people can no longer live without, something that is becoming a part of our culture. That's why you'll never be able to take it away from the world. Never. You could destroy every factory that made Sat-Navs, wipe out all the labs that produce the serum for us, but it wouldn't matter—they would be rebuilt. Like it or not, Continuum is here to stay. The people demand it."

Geoff stood still for a moment, considering what Jennifer had just said. He walked to the edge of the bridge, leaned over the railing, and looked down at the river. She did have a pretty good point—Continuum was like the water flowing beneath him—pretty unstoppable. And even if Continuum could be destroyed, where the hell would he start?

"So I'll leave you with that little conundrum," Jennifer said, turning to leave. "But one of these days you're just going to have to face it—Continuum will eventually offer everyone the chance to disappear into their own personal paradise, and there's nothing you can do about it."

Geoff and Tim watched in silence as Jennifer began to walk back along Tower Bridge the way she had come, followed by her men.

"Oh, and one other thing," Jennifer said, looking back. "Did it ever occur to you that you might already be inside Continuum? That everything you know might just be part of someone else's fantasy? How do you know all of this isn't *my* creation, and that I've changed the past so that I get to run my own time travel company? How do you know I can't rewind all of this at any time?"

Geoff looked over at Tim and felt his heart stop. He hoped for the love of God that wasn't true.

"You're joking, right?" Geoff said.

"Yes, I'm joking," Jennifer said, giving him a smug smile.

"But I couldn't resist suggesting it, just to see the look on your faces! Anyway, good luck trying to destroy Continuum! And do let me know if you work out where to start!"

And with that last taunt out of the way, she left.

High up in the sky, the sun began to disappear behind a large black rain cloud. For a second, Geoff thought this was strangely apt, like a Charles Dickens narrative device where the weather changes depending on the tone of the story. In this case, though, the weather had absolutely no idea what was going on down below, and soon enough, the sun came back out again, shining even brighter than before.

It really was a lovely day.

Then Geoff had a thought.

It was a thought about what Jennifer had said just before she left: *Let me know if you work out where to start.*

"I've just found our silver bullet," Geoff said. "I think I've worked out a way to destroy Continuum."

SIXTEEN

"So where are we going?" Tim said, removing a large number of fliers that had been placed on the car windshield before getting in. He handed the fliers to Geoff and started the ignition.

"What's that place your tourists use to travel back in time?" Geoff said, looking down at the different pieces of paper Tim had handed him. One was actually advertising a flier-removal service.

"You mean the timeport?"

"Yeah, that thing. We need to go there."

"If you say so," Tim said, starting the car's ascent into the sky. "But something is bothering me."

"Really?" Geoff said. "Is it by any chance the fact that we've uncovered a plot to cocoon the human race away in their own personal fantasy worlds for the rest of eternity, and we're the only ones who can stop it from happening?"

"I meant besides that," Tim said, weaving the car in between two skyscrapers and joining a line of traffic flowing north. "Although I'll admit that's been bothering me too."

"What is it, then?" Geoff said. "Did you leave the oven on?"

"No, it's not that either," Tim said, giving Geoff a tired look. "It's just—don't you think it's funny how Jennifer chose to defuse that situation? Once I'd lowered my weapon, her men could have easily overpowered us, but instead she just let us go."

"So what?"

"Don't you think that's weird behavior?"

"I guess," Geoff said, looking at the cars flying in perfect formation either side of them. Looking down through the glass window at his feet, he guessed they must have been at least a couple of hundred feet up in the air. Flying in a car across

London was quite similar to driving along a road on the ground, only you never encountered any roadwork, cyclists, or potholes. Running out of petrol presented a bit more of a problem, though, as it wasn't just a case of pulling over—it was more like crashing over.

"So what's this brilliant plan of yours?" Tim said, moving into a perpendicular stream of traffic flowing west. In front of them, the sun was beginning to set, casting a beautiful red glow across London.

"First of all, Jennifer is right about Continuum being too big for us to destroy," Geoff said. "It's impossible."

"Sounds encouraging so far," Tim said, nodding. "Carry on."

"But she's wrong about me not knowing where to start. Continuum does have a weak spot."

"It does?" Tim said. "Where is it?"

"Not *where*," Geoff said, "but *when*."

"What are you talking about?"

"If we want to destroy Continuum, we need to prevent Jennifer Adams from ever inventing it in the first place. In short, the place to start *is* the start—the day she resigned from Time Tours."

"Hold on a minute," Tim said. "If you go back and stop her from leaving Time Tours to set up Continuum, won't that create a paradox? If she never invents Continuum, you won't have a reason to go back and stop her from inventing it."

"Yes, I will probably cause a paradox," Geoff said. "A big, hairy paradox with bad breath, fangs, and sharp claws, ready to rip the crap out of everything it touches. But you know what? I don't care. I don't care what people tell me I can and can't do anymore—and besides, defeating the Varsarians two years ago created a massive paradox as well, and that turned out all right."

"I guess."

"And I'm pretty certain we've already notched up one or two paradoxes today, what with everything we've been through, right?"

"Probably," Tim admitted.

"So one more isn't going to hurt now, is it?"

"Okay," Tim said. "But what do you intend to do? You can't just go back in time and say to her: 'Hi there, Ms. Adams, I know you're thinking about leaving to set up your own company, but have you ever considered pursuing a career in pottery?'"

"No," Geoff said. "That wouldn't work."

"So what are you going to do, then?"

"I'm not sure yet. But I was thinking about what you said about how she persuaded this other mystery scientist to leave with her as well. Didn't you say that person was instrumental in helping her invent Continuum's technology?"

"From what I know," Tim said, "by the time Jennifer resigned, she had a working prototype of the Sat-Nav, however she was struggling to create the serum needed to link the device to a person. But then she met this scientist who was able to solve that problem for her, and together they left to set up Continuum."

"Who told you this exactly?"

"They're just rumors. Rumors that have been floating around Time Tours for years. Nobody knows where they came from."

"Well, that's it then," Geoff said. "If I can go back and stop Jennifer from meeting that scientist, I can stop her from ever setting up Continuum, right? Maybe I could even find a way to destroy that prototype Sat-Nav…"

"I don't know about this," Tim said. "If I was the space-time continuum, I'd be pretty miffed about this plan. If you put a stop to the very technology that made you to want to go back, what will happen to you?"

"This isn't about me," Geoff said. "It's about stopping Continuum, and this is the only way."

Tim banked the car around into another lane of flying traffic and shook his head.

"I don't know," he said. "I still think that encounter we had just now ended a little too conveniently. What if…"

Tim paused for a minute.

"What is it?" Geoff said.

"I think she knows you were going to come up with this plan. I think she wants you to go back in time to try and stop her."

"What?"

"Think about it. Jennifer said herself that when she was at Time Tours, she watched a simulation of the future, which showed the world becoming addicted to Continuum. Who's to say she didn't watch more than that? Who's to say she didn't watch a simulation of this very conversation we're having back then? For all we know, she could have complete knowledge of everything we decide to do, and as much as you think you're following your own path, you may very well be acting exactly as she wants you to."

"I guess that's possible," Geoff said, "but why would she want me to go back? It's not like I'm going to hand over any technology or do anything that would help her create Continuum, is it?"

"I guess not," Tim said. "But something still doesn't feel right."

"I tell you what," Geoff said. "Before I go back in time, why don't we use the supercomputer to make sure this is the right thing to do? That way, we can be sure we're not playing into her hands."

"Good idea," Tim nodded.

• • •

"Isn't it going to be a bit busy?" Geoff said, looking at his watch as they came in to land at the timeport. "It's only five o'clock in the afternoon, and we'll need to commandeer the paradox scanning facility for me to make this trip, you know."

"It will be fine," Tim said.

They easily found a parking space on the roof of the facility, and as Geoff got out of the car, he could see why Tim wasn't concerned about how busy it would be. There were hardly any other parked cars to be seen, and when he walked inside the departure lounge, the place was mostly deserted.

"What the hell happened?" Geoff said, looking around

at the handful of people sitting on benches, waiting for their destination to flash up on the departures board. "The last time I was here, this place was ridiculously busy! You couldn't move for men dressed as cowboys going back to the Wild West, or women in Victorian gowns, going back to enjoy a nineteenth-century tea party, or men in suits of armor, or people in togas, or—"

"I told you times were tough, didn't I?" Tim said.

Geoff looked up at the departures board. Only a couple of time destinations were listed, with all the rest accompanied by the word CANCELLED.

"This is the effect Continuum has had on business," Tim said, leading Geoff across the lounge. "Hardly anyone uses us anymore."

Tim flashed some identification at the extremely bored-looking security guards to skip the various procedures normally required before entering the paradox scanning facility, and before Geoff knew it, he was back in the big, dome-shaped chamber looking up at the vertical shaft of light beaming down on a pedestal in the middle of the room. Before traveling back in time, every tourist had to stand in the light, which allowed the supercomputer to scan them.

"Okay," Tim said, sitting down at a terminal on the far side of the room. "What date do you want to go back to?"

"I need to go back to the day she resigned from Time Tours and convinced this other scientist to help her set up Continuum," Geoff said. "If I can prevent that from happening, we'll be in business. And she'll be *out* of business."

Geoff smiled wryly at Tim for a second, waiting for some sort of reciprocation.

Tim looked at Geoff as though he'd spotted a bit of dirt on his face but didn't want to say anything out of embarrassment.

Geoff blinked.

"Did you see what I did there?"

"Yes, I did," Tim said. "You have a singular wit."

"Thanks."

"Well, if you want to interfere with Jennifer leaving Time Tours, the best day to do it would be the night it happened."

"Sounds good," Geoff said. "How long ago was that exactly?"

"About seventeen years," Tim said.

"I thought you said Eric hired Jennifer to build the computer *twenty* years ago?" Geoff said.

"That's right, smartypants," Tim said, "But she didn't build it instantaneously, did she? This place took three years to complete, hence why I'm sending you back seventeen years. Understand?"

Geoff nodded.

"If the rumors are true, she resigned in the early hours of the morning right outside her office, just as everyone was getting back from the ceremony where Eric received his second Nobel Prize. If I send you back a couple of hours before that happens, say around midnight, you should have a good chance of interfering with her meeting that scientist, and perhaps destroying the prototype Sat-Nav."

"Sounds good to me," Geoff said.

Tim pressed a few more buttons on the computer terminal. "We're ready. All you need to do is step into the beam."

"What?" Geoff said. "I can't do that if I'm deliberately going back to change something, can I? It will turn red!"

"You have to step into the beam, otherwise the computer won't let you travel."

"I don't believe this," Geoff said, stepping up onto the pedestal and closing his eyes. He hadn't stepped into this light for about two years, and had forgotten how cool the light was compared to the rest of the room. "Can't you just hack the computer and let me through?"

Suddenly Geoff felt very hot again.

"No need," Tim said. "The computer says you're okay to travel."

Geoff opened his eyes. Sure enough, he was enveloped in a green light.

"But that doesn't make any sense," Geoff said. "If the light is green, that means the computer predicts I'm not going to change anything by going back, right?"

"Apparently," Tim said, "But like you said—this thing has been wrong before, right?"

"I suppose so," Geoff replied. "Shall we look at a simulation of what's going to happen if I go back?"

"Working on it right now," Tim said, tapping away at the terminal.

After a few seconds, a large screen materialized in midair in front of them. It showed Geoff walking straight to Jennifer's office and meeting her face to face.

"How come I know exactly where Jennifer's office is?" Geoff said.

"Probably because you just watched yourself walk there on this screen," Tim replied.

"That's a bit spooky."

They continued to watch the simulation.

The Jennifer on the screen looked much younger, perhaps in her early twenties. She had softer skin, wore her hair in a bob, and her eyes were hidden behind a pair of thick, black-rimmed glasses.

Inside the office, the atmosphere seemed quite polite. The Geoff onscreen made up some reason for being there, and then sat in a chair, talking to Jennifer as she sat behind her desk. She even made him a cup of tea. After a long conversation, she took what looked to be a completed Sat-Nav out of her desk drawer and gave it to Geoff. The moment Geoff had it in his hands, he smashed it on the floor, and as he did, the screen went blank.

"So it would appear you go back, convince her to show you the Sat-Nav, then destroy it, thereby preventing Continuum from ever existing. The moment the screen turned to static must be the moment you caused a paradox," Tim said. "I couldn't see any sign of that scientist she was supposed to meet though…"

"That doesn't matter," Geoff said, stepping down from the pedestal. "If destroying the Sat-Nav is all it takes to stop Continuum, that's all that matters. Now, where can I find a pair of those earphones I need to travel back in time?"

"There should be some spare ones in the departure chamber," Tim said. "Listen—I know the simulation shows you going back alone, but don't you think I should come back with you?"

"No," Geoff said. "I've got a different job for you."

SEVENTEEN

Geoff materialized in the middle of the paradox scanning facility, his body appearing out of nowhere in the dark chamber as though he'd just been added into a film scene by a special effects company. He removed his earphones, stuffed them in his trouser pocket, and looked around. The place was empty.

He had to say, it felt good to be traveling through time the old-fashioned way again rather than having to bother with all these serums and Sat-Navs, although he couldn't believe he was really starting to describe the time traveling earphones as being old-fashioned. For someone from the twenty-first century, these earphones should have been remarkable—one of the most amazing scientific discoveries ever known. To an old hand like him, though, they already seemed a bit dated. He guessed that was the problem with being human—no matter how remarkable something seems one minute, the next minute it's completely taken for granted. Two years ago, he'd thought that a pair of earphones that allowed him to time travel was incredible. Today, he was asking himself why they weren't time-traveling socks instead, which would have been far more comfortable.

Looking around, Geoff noticed a number of differences between the paradox scanning facility he had just left and the one he had arrived in seventeen years earlier. For a start, it was clear this place had only just opened—celebratory bunting hung down from the ceiling, the floor was littered with colorful tickertape, and various posters were hanging from the walls advertising Time Tours as "a brand new holiday experience!" Another thing Geoff noticed was that despite the facility having just opened, there were still a lot of construction materials lying around everywhere—tall ladders were leaning against walls, various pieces of equipment were draped with dirty sheets, and several areas were cordoned off with bright yellow tape that said WET PAINT. In fact, he could still smell the unmistakably nose-stinging scent, which hung in the air like a thick chemical fog.

In the center of the paradox scanning facility stood the familiar beam of light, shining down on the elevated pedestal, ready to scan whoever stepped into it. It being the middle of the night though, the beam was currently much dimmer than Geoff had seen it before. Maybe it was in standby mode or something. To his left, he saw a long corridor leading to the exit. If he remembered correctly from what he'd seen in the simulation moments earlier, this was the way he had walked when he was looking for Jennifer's office. So he started walking.

At this hour, the place was so quiet it made Geoff want to make stupid noises to see what the echo was like. He managed to resist, although his footsteps were quite loud, the noise bouncing off every surface like an enthusiastic dog being let off of its leash for the first time in days. Each footstep reverberated around so much that the sound came not just from his feet but from the left, the right, up above, and down below. It was like sitting in the cinema to watch one of those annoying films where the sound starts coming from all around you. Because having a frog going *ribbit* behind you during that swamp scene is really what immersive cinema is all about, right?

"Hello?" Geoff called out as he began to walk down the corridor. "Is anybody there?"

No answer.

"Hello?" Geoff repeated. "Can anyone hear me?"

Once again, there was no answer.

He supposed not too many people would be hanging around here in the middle of the night, so he thought it was understandable for nobody to reply.

Then he heard a very small squeak and got really scared, until he realized it was actually his nose whistling as he breathed. He tweaked his nose to get rid of it and kept walking.

Soon enough, Geoff reached the end of the corridor. In front of him was the security check area, with a set of frosted-glass doors leading to the Quarantine Chamber not far behind. To his left he noticed a door that said OFFICES above it. There wasn't really much else to say about this door. It was a pale lime green, it had a small chrome handle, and generally it looked a lot less jazzy than all of its other doormates. However, what made this door a lot more interesting than all the others was the fact that a crack of light was shining through the gap at the bottom.

Geoff walked over to the door, grabbed the handle, and opened it, just like he had done in the simulation.

Inside was another long corridor, albeit slightly narrower than the one he had just come from. The corridor was lit up by several long strips of fluorescent light, and the walls were drab and boring, a bit like the textures used in *Aliens: Colonial Marines*.

On either side of the corridor there stood a number of doors, each one spaced apart from the last by a few meters.

He knew Jennifer's office was the last door on the right, and sure enough, at the end of the hallway he could see a door that was slightly ajar, with light shining out onto the corridor from the inside. He headed toward it, his footsteps dragging on the carpet as though someone had coated the soles of his shoes with glue.

Despite knowing what was about to happen, he was a little hesitant.

He was nervous.

He had another nose whistle.

He got rid of the nose whistle again and kept walking.

As he got closer, he noticed a small plaque next to the doorway. It read:

> Jennifer Adams BSc, BTPh, PPQHSc.
> Senior Specialist Supercomputer Supervisor

That was a lot of *S*'s, like a snake.

Geoff tilted his head around the doorway and looked inside. Sure enough, Jennifer Adams was sitting at her desk, scribbling something down on a piece of paper in front of her. Despite having already seen what Jennifer looked like when she was younger, it was still fascinating to look at her now. With her hair in a different style and those glasses, she really looked very different. He had to keep reminding himself that this was the Jennifer Adams from seventeen years ago, and people can change a lot in seventeen years. Geoff was living proof of this—fifteen years ago he was halfway through puberty, and looked like a cross between a teenage boy and one of those limited-edition pizza box meal deals, only far less appetizing.

Geoff knocked on the door twice.

Jennifer threw her pen across the room in fright and leapt out of her chair.

"Goodness me!" she said, holding a hand to her chest. "You scared the living daylights out of me!"

"Sorry," Geoff said.

"That's all right," Jennifer said, straightening her glasses and moving over to meet him. "Please—come in."

Geoff stepped inside the office and looked around. Much like the office of her future self, this place was quite a mess, with papers spilling out of filing cabinets, notice boards bulging with notes pinned to them, and various pieces of old electrical equipment in boxes stacked up to the ceiling. In one corner of the room he could see a mini fridge, with a box of tea bags, a couple of mugs, and a kettle on top. Jennifer hadn't been lying when she'd told him earlier how this job had made her accustomed to being cooped up—the woman didn't even have to leave the room to make a cup of tea.

"Are you Jennifer Adams?" Geoff asked. He knew she was, but he had to keep up the pretense of not knowing who she was, just as he had done in the simulation. In fact, he knew exactly what he needed to say to make her hand over the Sat-Nav so he could break it.

"That's right," Jennifer replied. "Were you looking for me?"

"Yes, I was."

"Do you work here?" Jennifer said.

"Yes, I do," Geoff said. He supposed it was kind of true, even if his timing was a little off. By over a decade.

"Good to meet you," she said, extending a hand for him to shake.

"Likewise," Geoff said. Her handshake was a little less firm than before—she must have developed a stronger grip over the years.

"So, you appear to have me at a disadvantage," Jennifer said. "Who are you?"

"Oh, sorry," Geoff said, quickly trying to think of a false name. Had he thought about it, he would have realized he didn't really need to use one, but being put on the spot made him panic. "My name is Jean-Luc Picard."

"Jean-Luc Picard?" Jennifer said, raising her eyebrows. "What's that? French?"

"That's right," he said.

"Well, Jean-Luc," Jennifer said, walking back around to the other side of her desk and sitting down, "what can I do for you? And how come you're here so late? Aren't you supposed to be out with the others?"

"The others?"

"Yeah—tonight's the big night! The night Eric gets awarded his second Nobel Prize! I thought everyone was going to the ceremony with him to celebrate?"

"Not me," Geoff said, trying to think quickly. "If you ask me, you should be up there too, collecting that award with him."

Jennifer leaned back in her chair and smiled.

"I like you, Jean-Luc," she said, wheeling herself in her chair over to the kettle in the corner of the room. "Can I offer you a drink? A cup of tea, perhaps? I've just boiled the water."

"That would be lovely," Geoff said, watching as Jennifer plopped two tea bags into a couple of mugs and added the boiling water.

"How do you take it?" she said, removing the milk from the fridge.

"Milk and two sugars, please," Geoff said. "But not too much milk."

Jennifer added the milk, removed the tea bags, and stirred in two sugars. While her back was turned, Geoff sneaked a look at what she had been writing as he'd come in.

It was the beginnings of a letter of resignation, though he noticed a number of screwed-up pieces of paper to the side.

"There we go," she said, handing Geoff his tea and placing her own mug on the desk in front of her. "Now, what can I do for you?"

Here we go, Geoff thought, taking a quick slurp of his tea. *This is it.*

"I understand you are working on something off the books," he said.

Jennifer picked up her tea, wrapping her hands around the mug and blowing on the surface. "What do you mean, 'off the books'?" she said.

"I know you are working on a device that would allow tourists to go back in time and change whatever they like, without disrupting the space-time continuum."

"I don't know what you're talking about," Jennifer said.

"Yes, you do," Geoff said, taking another gulp of his tea. "It's a black tablet device, small enough to fit in your pocket. You're thinking of calling it the Space and Time Navigator, or the 'Sat-Nav,' for short."

Jennifer continued to warm her hands around her mug. "What did you say you did for Time Tours again?" she said.

"I didn't," Geoff said.

But then Geoff had an idea, taking inspiration from the rumors Tim had told him. Perhaps if he pretended that *he* was the scientist working on the serum, he could convince her to show him the prototype Sat-Nav. Then, once it was in his hands, he could destroy it, just as he'd seen in the simulation,

"Huh. Well, Jean-Luc, I don't know what to say. But if I was working on such a device, why would I want to talk to you about it?"

"Because I can help," Geoff said. "I know about the problems you are having with it. I know the device is complete, but you can't get it to synchronize with the user properly."

Jennifer narrowed her eyes.

"Go on."

"What if I told you I had access to a substance you could

use to connect people to this device? A base serum you could make infinite variations of to link different people to different devices? Would that be worth something to you?"

"This is a joke, right?" Jennifer said. "Did Eric put you up to this? Because if he did, it isn't very funny."

"This is no joke," Geoff said. "I'm being serious. You have the Sat-Nav, I have the serum. Together, we could leave Time Tours and beat them at their own game. Wouldn't you like that?"

Jennifer looked at Geoff for a few seconds before taking a sip of her tea. She put the mug down, took a small key out of her breast pocket, and unlocked the desk drawer to her right.

"I don't know how you know what you know," she said, taking a Sat-Nav out and placing it on the desk in front of her. "But your intelligence is very good. This is my prototype. The only one in existence."

"May I see it?" Geoff said, reaching over to pick it up.

"Be my guest," Jennifer said, giving it to him.

The moment Geoff had the Sat-Nav in his hands, he leapt out of his chair and threw it down on the floor as hard as he could, smashing the device to pieces.

"Ha!" he said, grinning at Jennifer. "I got you!"

He shut his eyes and waited for the space-time continuum to sort itself out.

He had done it.

Any minute now, he would disappear and exist in a world without Continuum.

But nothing happened.

Back when he'd been watching the simulation, it appeared as though things had changed immediately, but for some reason that wasn't happening now.

He kept his eyes closed a bit longer. Maybe the space-time continuum was experiencing a lot of changes at the moment and needed a few minutes to sort things out, a bit like when you ring a call center at lunchtime and they put you on hold. He imagined what the message might have been if he *had* been on hold: "The paradox you have created is very important to us. Please continue to hold while we sort out the mess you have made."

But still nothing happened.

He opened his eyes and looked down at the Sat-Nav. Maybe it wasn't broken enough. He twisted his foot into the broken circuitry, hoping that that would do the trick.

Still nothing.

He looked up at Jennifer and gave her a sheepish grin.

"I don't understand," he said, sitting down in his seat again and taking another sip of his tea. "This wasn't supposed to happen."

Jennifer leaned forward on her elbows across her desk and smiled.

"Yes it was, Geoff," she said. "Yes, it was."

EIGHTEEN

"W-what did you say?" he said. "How do you know my name?"

"I know everything, *Geoffrey Stamp*," Jennifer said.

"Everything?" Geoff said.

"Yes, everything," Jennifer said. "I know about Continuum, I know about your little encounter with my older self on Tower Bridge, and I even know about your plot to come back here and destroy the prototype Sat-Nav. You cannot get anything past me."

"But how?" Geoff said, taking his hands off her desk. "How do you know all this?"

Jennifer laughed. "How?" she said. "How? Geoff, for the last three years I have been building and testing the most advanced supercomputer in the world, running every possible simulation of the future that there is to simulate. While you and your friends have been running around trying to work out what's been happening in your time, I've been watching it all transpire on a computer screen back here, right from the comfort of this chair."

"But I don't understand," Geoff said. "When I watched the simulation before I came back, it showed—"

"—it showed you destroying the Sat-Nav and changing the timeline," Jennifer said, finishing his sentence. "I know. Like I said—I've had unlimited access to this computer since the day I built it. I knew you were going to watch that simulation—in fact, it was me who programmed the computer to cut it off at the right point to make you think you'd succeeded in changing history. But you didn't. You think that thing you broke is the only Sat-Nav I've got? Think again. And those rumors about how I'd invented the Sat-Nav and convinced a rogue scientist to leave Time Tours with me to set up Continuum? Who do you think started those?"

Geoff had heard that one of the cleaning ladies was a bit of a gossip, but in this case there was another name that sprang to mind.

"I'm guessing that might have been you," he said.

"Correct. Without those rumors, you might not have tried to come back here and stop it from happening, so I made sure everyone was whispering about the circumstances of my resignation, knowing one day the stories would find their way to you. So you see, this whole scenario was a massive setup with one purpose in mind—to get you to come back here."

"Balls," Geoff said, slumping back down in his seat.

"Balls, indeed," Jennifer said.

"But... what has all this got to do with me anyway?"

Jennifer laughed.

"Oh, you have no idea how important you are to the Continuum project," she said. "Without you, none of it will ever exist."

"Are you sure?" Geoff said. He didn't feel particularly important, but then he'd learnt from past experiences never to underestimate himself. "How does that work then?"

"Creating the Sat-Nav was no problem for me—electronics are my speciality, after all," Jennifer said. "But you said it yourself—the serum is proving to be a little more tricky. I'm having real problems synthesizing a substance that's immune to the way time is manipulated, while being able to link a user to the device."

"That does sound pretty hard," Geoff said. He had enough trouble making hot chocolate, let alone that sort of concoction.

"Fortunately for me, though," Jennifer said, "that's where you come in."

"Me?" Geoff said. "How can I possibly help you create the serum? I didn't bring any back with me."

"Yes you did," Jennifer said. "It's in your blood."

"My blood?" Geoff said, holding a hand to his throat.

"That's right. Over the past twenty-four hours, you have

been injected with it, and you've drunk it twice. Your body is riddled with the stuff—enough for me to create a base formula from which I can make as many unique variations as I need to supply every man, woman, and child on this planet."

"I don't believe this," Geoff said. "You mean to tell me that *I'm* the reason you were able to set up Continuum in the first place? All those people that end up disappearing into their own timelines in the future—all that happens because of me?"

"Bingo," Jennifer said. "That's why without you, Continuum would never have existed. You should have listened to your friend. He was right about why my older self just let you go without a fight on Tower Bridge. She let you go because she knew she needed you to come back here and give me your blood. And as for your plan to have your friend watch over this moment from the future to make sure everything goes to plan, I've taken care of that as well. Right now, he's watching a fabricated scenario of you entering your Continuum-free world, wondering why his own reality hasn't been altered. He won't figure out what I've done until it's too late."

Geoff looked down into his half-drunk mug of tea and sighed. After all that talk of not doing what people told him to do, of not allowing his life to follow the path laid out for it by others, everything he had done had actually been working against him.

His actions had created the very thing he was trying to stop. What an idiot.

That was why the paradox scan had turned green before he came back here—traveling back in time hadn't changed history; it had kept it things running exactly as they had been all along.

"I don't understand," Geoff said, his body completely deflated like a soufflé someone had forgotten to eat. "If you've known about this all along, how come there were times when you were acting all surprised about what was happening? Like when I first came back from my Continuum experience and you discovered I'd already used the serum?"

"It was all an act," Jennifer said, flicking a few strands of hair back. "I played my part in a course of events I knew would eventually motivate you to come back here."

"But if your plan all along was for me to come back here, why go to all that trouble of erasing my memory? And nearly getting me killed?"

"Think of it in terms of cause and effect. Cause: You lost your memory and got sent back in time with a bullet in your back. Effect: You came to Continuum to investigate what had happened to you. I had to let all that happen, because if it didn't, I never would have triggered the chain of events that brought you here tonight."

"But doesn't this whole situation create one almighty paradox?" Geoff said. "The only reason I lost my memory and got shot was because I came to Continuum to find out why I lost my memory and got shot! And more than that: if the only reason Continuum ever existed was because you were able to synthesize a serum from my blood that I wouldn't have in my body had I not come back in time, that means no one ever actually created the serum, right?"

"That's right," Jennifer said.

"So...how does that work, then?" Geoff said. "Isn't that a paradox? Why hasn't this situation resulted in the space-time continuum losing its temper and writing a very stern letter of complaint to both of us?"

"Because all the situations you have just described are not paradoxes, Geoff," Jennifer explained. "They are what are known in the scientific community as causal loops."

"Causal loops?"

"Yes," Jennifer said. "Basically, it's where the lines between cause and effect become a little blurred. It's the same principle behind how you knew the directions to my office, which only happened because you watched the way you walked in the simulation before traveling back in time. While you cannot pinpoint where your knowledge of those directions has actually come from, neither did you create a paradox, since the laws of physics have not been violated. Exactly the same thing has happened here—I am about to use your blood to synthesize a serum that wouldn't exist had you not traveled back in time with it inside you."

"There's just one problem," Geoff said, standing up and posing in as menacing a way as he could while still holding a cup of tea. "I may not be much of a fighter, but I'm bigger than you, and although I don't normally hit women, if you try anything, I'm happy to make an exception."

He had actually hit a woman before, when he was holding an umbrella over Zoë and a sudden gust of wind had made him accidentally punch her in the face. But that was an accident.

And she'd hit him back, so they were even.

"What are you saying?" Jennifer said.

"I'm saying, how exactly do you plan on getting a sample of my blood?" Geoff said, taking a gulp of his tea.

"Oh, I don't just need a single sample," Jennifer said. "I need access to your body for years and years before I have enough blood to go into mass production."

"What?"

"Every bottle of serum has some of your blood in it, Geoff," Jennifer said. "Why else do you think the liquid is red and tastes metallic? Oh, no—I need you alive and well fed to keep producing the stuff for me."

Geoff took another gulp of tea and laughed.

"There's no way I'm allowing that to happen," he said, taking out his earphones. He didn't feel particularly threatened at the moment. "All I need to do is put these earphones on and travel back to the future, and this is all over."

"I'm afraid you're too late," Jennifer said.

"Oh?"

"Remember that older man you bumped into back at the Continuum offices? The fat guy with the awful skin? I don't suppose you recognized him, what with the long hair and everything. But that was you, twenty years from now. You're about to spend the rest of your life locked up inside the Continuum building, giving me all the blood I need. After a few years you start to go a bit crazy, but that doesn't matter. What's important is that your blood just keeps flowing."

Geoff shuddered. Now that he thought about it, he could see a resemblance. He needed to get out of here right now, or at least immediately after he'd finished his tea. It would be a shame for it to go to waste.

"So how exactly do you plan on stopping me from getting away?" Geoff said, taking a final gulp of tea and putting the empty mug down on the desk. He took out his earphones and began placing them in his ears. "You'd need an army to stop me leaving right now."

"That's right," Jennifer said. "Or I'd need to trick you into drinking some sort of highly potent drug that makes you extremely open to suggestion."

"Exactly."

"Speaking of which, how was your tea?"

Geoff swallowed.

"My tea?"

"Yes."

"It was all right," Geoff said.

"No it wasn't," Jennifer said, walking over to him. "It was the best tea you've ever had."

"Now that you mention it, it was pretty delicious," Geoff said. "Best tea I've ever had."

Jennifer smiled.

"Drop the earphones," she said.

Geoff did as he was told. For some reason he was finding Jennifer to be incredibly persuasive, like the voice in his head that told him it was okay to watch entire DVD box sets without moving from the sofa.

"Wait," Geoff stammered, suddenly overwhelmed with a brief sense of panic. "What have you…done…to…"

He looked around desperately for something to defend himself with and grabbed the mug he had just put down. As far as weapons go, it wasn't ideal, but he could still do some damage with it.

"Ah yes, the mug. Think you can hit me with it?"

Under the circumstances, Geoff didn't fancy his chances much, but he got the feeling he was now in a considerable amount of danger and needed to do something, even if it was nothing more than hitting someone with a mug. So he swung it round toward Jennifer's face as hard as he could.

"Oh no you don't," Jennifer said, not even flinching.

As she spoke, Geoff felt his arm lock tight just before the mug was about to make contact. He couldn't move.

"Put the mug down, please," she commanded.

Geoff looked at her in puzzlement as his arm did what it was told.

"That's it," she said. "You see Geoff, everything you're about to do, I've already seen coming. Resistance is futile."

But Geoff clenched his teeth and drew on every shred of willpower to resist what she was telling him to do, The feeling of not doing as he was told was unbearable, but his efforts did appear to be making a difference. Slowly but surely, he began to raise his arm again.

"PUT THE MUG DOWN!" Jennifer shouted.

"N-no," Geoff said. "I...will...not!" And with that, his arm broke free of Jennifer's control, and he walloped her round the face with the mug with so much force that it shattered on impact, leaving a long, vertical cut under her left eye. This act of resistance was extremely satisfying, but also totally exhausting, so much so that he didn't think he'd have the mental capability to do something like that again. He dropped the mug to the floor and let out a sigh.

Jennifer clutched her cheek and scowled at him. It was funny—despite thoroughly deserving a smack in the face for everything she was about to do, Geoff still felt bad about hitting her. But given his life was in mortal danger and the future of all humanity was at stake, he was sure he would forgive himself.

It was at this moment that something happened in Geoff's mind—his memory of Jennifer changed. Now when he thought back to what her future self looked like, he remembered her having a feint scar under her left eye, exactly where he'd hit her just now. At the same time however, he could also recall an alternate future when it *hadn't* been there. It seemed that hitting Jennifer with the mug had demonstrated two things to him: firstly, it was still possible for him to change the future, and secondly, if that change *did* create a paradox, all that meant was that he could remember both scenarios.

There was just one problem: now that the drug had taken full effect, he was so open to Jennifer's suggestion, that he was completely powerless to take advantage of this newly acquired knowledge.

Jennifer dabbed the wound on her face with a tissue. "It seems I shouldn't have goaded you about the futility of your situation more than I did in the original simulation," she said, taking a step back. "Looks like that gave you a bit of extra determination. Make no mistake though—from now on, I'm sticking to the script."

Outside the office door, Geoff could hear a few people laughing and joking, like a bunch of students stumbling back after a pub crawl.

"Ah—that must be Eric returning from his awards ceremony," Jennifer said, holding the tissue to her face and walking over to the door. "Time for us to leave. Follow me."

"W-where are we going?" Geoff said, his feet shuffling toward her. He tried to his best to resist, but it was hopeless.

"I don't know if you're familiar with history," Jennifer said, "but this is the point where I famously tell Eric that I resign."

And with that, she marched out of her office, her head held high.

Geoff followed a few steps behind. He had absolutely no idea what to do.

At the other end of the corridor, a younger version of Eric had just entered through the door at the other end. He still looked pretty old, maybe in his sixties. One hand was holding a framed certificate that was presumably his Nobel Prize, and the other hand was wrapped around the waist of a young woman, who was presumably fond of old men who had just won Nobel Prizes. Eric was accompanied by a number of other people, all of whom looked like they weren't going to have a particularly great time tomorrow morning once the hangovers set in.

"J-Jensifer?" Eric said, looking up as she strode toward him.

He didn't sound particularly sober, and his eyes were glazed over like he'd left his contact lenses in a glass of milk before putting them in. "W-what are you shtill doing here?"

He removed his hand from the waist of the young woman and stood up straight.

"You know, Eric," Jennifer said, tossing her tissue to the floor and pushing her way through the drunken crowd of people. "I've been asking myself that very same question for quite a while. What *am* I still doing here? I mean, after the way you've all treated me, what THE HELL am I still doing here?"

"Now, Jennnnnsifer," Eric slurred, "com'on, we've talked about thish…"

All around, everyone else was completely silent, apart from one guy who couldn't stop hiccupping.

"No, Eric!" Jennifer said, tossing her hair back. "I'm sick of it! I'm sick of this place, I'm sick of this life, and I'm sick of putting in all the work, only for you to get the recognition!"

"What are you shaying?" Eric said, falling back against the wall of the corridor. "And who'sh shoes thish guy?" He looked up at Geoff, but he was so drunk there was no way he would remember his face in the morning.

"This is a good friend of mine," Jennifer said, looking around at everyone as they stared back at her. "He's another scientist from Time Tours who's leaving with me. And I promise you one thing—together, we're going to create something amazing. One day you'll be hearing from me again, and when you do, it will be because I'll be putting Time Tours out of business for good!"

Upon hearing those words, Eric slid down the wall and lay across the floor like a drunk old man who'd just won a Nobel Prize and then had to deal with some crazy woman resigning.

"Come on, Geoff," Jennifer said, calling him as though he were a small puppy that had run off to sniff a tree. She stepped over Eric's legs and dodged her way past the drunken Time Tours employees, leading Geoff through the door at the other end of the corridor.

"W-where are we going?" Geoff managed to say.

"Up to the roof," Jennifer said. "I've got a few friends waiting for us, and from there, we'll be flying across London to my temporary offices on the other side of town."

"I don't want...to..."

Jennifer looked back and tugged him closer to make sure he didn't fall behind.

"Don't be like that," she said. "Try and enjoy this little trip, okay? After all, it's the last time you'll be in the outside world for the rest of your life."

NINETEEN

The roof of the timeport demonstrated that over the course of a thousand years, the general design principles behind a car park hadn't changed particularly. It was exactly as you might have expected, really: a large, flat expanse of black tarmac, with five or six rows of parking bays marked out in straight lines of white paint.

Jennifer was standing over by a convoy of five parked cars, her head turned to look across the horizon. The cars next to her were all black sedans, and had dark privacy glass for windows, which prevented you from seeing inside.

"Come over here and admire the view," she said.

Geoff did as he told, walking over to where she was standing and looking at the London skyline.

"Doesn't the city look pretty from up here?" she said. "Why don't you take a moment to admire it for a second? This will be your last memory of the outside world, after all."

Geoff stared vacantly into the night. The sky was clear, the air felt warm on his skin, and in the distance he could see the many twinkling lights of office blocks and skyscrapers. Up above them, flying traffic streaked against a backdrop of stars in a blur of red and white light, like millions of differently colored fireflies whizzing backward and forward in perpendicular lines.

"Okay, that's enough," she said, motioning him to follow her toward the cars. "Come over here."

Again, Geoff did what he was told. His mind was a jumble. Part of him was screaming to resist Jennifer's orders, but at the same time he couldn't help obeying every instruction he heard. It felt as though his body were being controlled remotely, with his rational mind nothing more than a trapped passenger.

Jennifer tapped her hand on the roof of one of the parked cars. As she did, the doors of every car opened and a number of very large men stepped out. There must have been at least twenty of them, all wearing black suits and earpieces like secret agents charged with looking after a presidential motorcade. Each of them also had a handgun holstered at their side.

"Okay, you know why I've hired you," Jennifer said, standing before them with her hands on her hips, "and you've all watched the simulation of what is about to happen. By now, a man from the future named Timothy Burnell has realized what we're up to, and has worked out that this trip across London is our only moment of vulnerability. Be on your guard, and remember— if Geoff dies, Continuum dies with him. Whatever happens, I need Mr. Stamp to complete this journey alive."

The men all nodded and slipped back inside their vehicles.

"Come with me," Jennifer said, leading Geoff to the car in the middle of the convoy.

"Get in," she said, opening the back door.

Geoff obeyed Jennifer's instructions and climbed inside. The car had a luxurious white leather interior, with a bottle of chilled champagne resting in the middle of the seating well. As he sat down, he noticed someone sitting on the other side next to him, behind the driver's seat.

It was William Boyle again, although this time he looked even older than the man who had shot Zoë when they'd traveled to the future. This William was easily in his early sixties. What little hair he had left was completely gray, his skin was pale and wrinkled, and he looked unhealthily thin, his face gaunt.

"W-William?" Geoff said, straining against the influence of the drug to look the man up and down.

"Hello, Geoff," William said, trying to force a smile.

"H-how old are you?" Geoff stammered.

"I'm not sure anymore," William said, looking down at his wrinkled hands. "I've spent so much time here, there, and everywhere, I've lost track."

Jennifer leaned in and looked at William. "You remember what's about to happen?" she said.

"Yes ma'am," William replied, sitting upright as she spoke to him.

"Good. Be ready." She turned her attention to Geoff. "And as for you—don't go anywhere."

She closed Geoff's passenger door and walked around to the other side of the car.

Geoff couldn't believe it. All he had to do was open this door and make a run for it, but no matter how hard he tried, his body just wouldn't obey what he was telling it to do. He wanted to scream until his voice could take it no more, but in this state he could only manage an awkward groan through gritted teeth, a bit like the noise people make when they're having trouble getting the lid off of a stiff jam jar.

He watched as Jennifer opened the driver's door, sat down in the driver's seat, and fastened her seatbelt. He was still making his weird noise, which now sounded like the moment the jam jar lid was about to come loose.

Jennifer looked around. "Buckle up," she said.

Geoff stopped making his strange noise and fought the command with everything he had. And for a moment, he could feel his hand moving for the door handle instead of reaching for the seatbelt. He knew he had the power to change what was about to happen—hitting Jennifer around the face with that mug had proved it was possible—all he needed to do was think hard enough, and he could break free of whatever spell Jennifer's drug had cast over him.

"I said, buckle up," Jennifer repeated.

Geoff's hand moved away from the door handle, reached behind him, and grabbed the seatbelt, stretching it across his body and fastening it to his side. William did the same, his hands shaking as he pulled the strap across his body.

"Right, I think we're all set," Jennifer said, pressing a button on the dashboard. As she did, Geoff felt the car begin to vibrate beneath him, and his ears filled with a high-pitched sound as the antigravity propulsion system revved up.

Jennifer pressed another few buttons in front of her and gripped the steering wheel with both hands.

But then she paused for a moment.

William leaned forward. "Is everything all right, ma'am?" he asked. His voice sounded a little croaky, as if he were unwell.

"I think so," Jennifer said, looking around at Geoff one last time. "It's just…I don't remember him resisting what I was telling him to do like this in the simulations. And I can't help but feel that there's something different about him."

"Different?"

"Yes. But I can't put my finger on what it is…"

"Should we move to plan B?"

"No," Jennifer said, facing front again. "My plan is flawless. You just need to do your job, okay?"

"Yes ma'am," William said, sitting back again.

"Right," Jennifer said, releasing the handbrake to her side and pulling down on the steering wheel. "Here we go."

Geoff looked out of the window as the car began to ascend into the sky. The other cars did the same, surrounding their vehicle in a protective formation.

Once they had climbed a few hundred meters in the air, Jennifer pushed the steering wheel forward, and the car began to accelerate. She banked the vehicle to the right, and within a few seconds they had joined a stream of flying traffic heading north. Each car from the convoy took a position to the left, right, front, and back of them.

Geoff pressed his face to the glass and looked down at the streets below. They were very high up, and for a moment he felt as though he were looking down at an incredibly detailed model city, complete with lit-up buildings, moving traffic, and little people walking around.

"Here he comes!" Jennifer said, looking in her rearview mirror and gripping the steering wheel a little tighter.

At that moment there was a loud crash, and the roof of the car buckled in slightly.

Geoff spun around in his seat and looked outside. He could see another vehicle peel away from on top of them—a red sports car—and as he leaned forward to get a closer look, he could see that it was Tim behind the wheel.

"You all right?" Jennifer said, looking around.

"Yes, ma'am," William said.

"Not you!" Jennifer said. "Geoff—how you doing? Answer me!"

Geoff looked down at his body. He was shaking, but it wasn't because of nerves. He could feel himself starting to regain control. The more he focused on the idea that he still had the power to change history, the more he found himself able to fight the drug. But he didn't want Jennifer to know that.

"I'm fine," he said, putting on a docile voice.

"Good," Jennifer said, pushing down on the steering wheel. The car reacted by ducking down into another stream of traffic flying beneath them.

Geoff continued to sit still in the back seat as Jennifer sent the car through all sorts of crazy aerial maneuvers, weaving past flying lorries, buses, and cars at an incredible speed. All around, he could hear the blare of angry car horns, and there was the odd moment when he caught a glimpse of people in the surrounding traffic. Inside these vehicles, he could see drivers looking back at them angrily, and as his mental faculties began to return, he began to appreciate just how dangerously they were flying.

Then there came another bump, this time from underneath. This collision was much more violent than the last one, and as they were hit, Jennifer was forced to bank the car on its side to compensate. Geoff slid down toward the passenger door, his body pressed against the window like a sandbag. The direct view of the sheer drop beneath him was terrifying, but then he realized something—if he fell from this height, there was no way he would survive.

And as Jennifer said, if he died, Continuum would die with him.

Geoff finally knew what he had to do.

He had to get out of this car.

And preferably while it was in the air, since getting out once they were parked wasn't going to be particularly hazardous to his health.

This realization of how he could put an end to Continuum

was so powerful it completely overwhelmed whatever inhibitions the drug had placed on him, and he found himself in full control of his body once more. The simulations Jennifer had run might have made her think she was in control of everything, but it seemed the moment she had deviated from what she had witnessed and started teasing Geoff about what he was destined to do, she had set them on a new path—a path where Geoff was able to muster up the will to resist, and break free from her control.

"Where the hell is my protection?" Jennifer screamed, craning her head to look up through the windshield as she leveled the car off.

Geoff lifted his hand up to the door handle, but it was no use—the thing was locked.

William quickly realized what was going on and reached over to grab his hand.

"We've got a problem here, ma'am!" he said. "Geoff is trying to get leave!"

"Geoffrey!" Jennifer said, looking at him in her rearview mirror. "Listen to me very carefully! You are to stay completely still, okay? Do not attempt to leave the car."

Geoff said nothing,

"Do you hear me?" she said.

"You know what?" Geoff said, "I'm getting sick of people telling me what to do!"

Jennifer looked at William.

"Something's wrong!" she said. "This didn't happen in the simulation!"

William's eyes widened.

"It didn't?"

"No, everything's changed! You need to do whatever it takes to keep him there!"

William nodded and scooted across the back seat toward Geoff, wrapping his arms around Geoff's neck to stop him from moving. Geoff tried to wriggle free but it was no use—despite William appearing to be frail, in this position it was incredibly difficult to break free.

Out of the window to the left, Geoff watched as the red sports car came around once more, racing toward them again as if to ram straight into their side. However, moments before it was able to make contact, one of the black cars in Jennifer's convoy swooped down from above and slammed into its roof, knocking Tim off course.

"That's right!" Jennifer said. "Keep him away from us!"

Geoff followed the path of the red sports car through the sky, watching as it did an upside-down loop-de-loop and headed straight toward them again from below. The car in pursuit didn't seem to be capable of pulling off the same maneuver, and within seconds they were rammed again, the underside of the sports car scraping vertically along Geoff's side of the car.

As Tim made impact, the window next to Geoff shattered, sending bits of broken glass flying inside the car. Suddenly there was an almighty roar as the wind from outside rushed in, and William fell back.

Geoff looked over at the sports car, which was now flying parallel to them. Inside the cabin, Tim was looking back at him. He seemed to be shouting something, but Geoff couldn't make out what it was.

He tried the door handle again. To his surprise, when he pulled on it this time the latch clicked, and the door flung open. Tim must have damaged the lock when he flew into them.

Tim tried to match the movement of Jennifer's car, flying as close as possible as if to allow Geoff to jump from her car to his, but at that moment he was shunted from behind by one of the black cars and sent into an uncontrollable spin.

Geoff edged toward the door and looked down through the broken window. Tim appeared to be wrestling with the car to get it back under control, closely followed by two of the black cars.

But Geoff didn't need Tim to get back up here.

All he needed to do was jump.

"Oh no you don't!" Jennifer said, seemingly realizing his plan. She banked the car on its side so the open door was facing upward. As she did, the force of the wind ripped the door from its hinges and sent it tumbling toward the streets below.

Geoff fell back into the car and landed on William, who was pressed against the inside of the opposite passenger door facing the ground. Very quickly, he was able to reach around him and try the door handle. He felt the latch click—on this side, they hadn't bothered locking it.

"No!" William shouted, scrambling at Geoff to try and stop him from opening the door. "Fly level! Fly level!"

"Shit!" Jennifer screamed, looking around at them and tilting the car back the right way up.

As she did, the passenger door flung open. Geoff rolled over William, gripped the doorframe, and began to pull himself outside the vehicle. As he did, though, William grabbed his legs and started to pull him back inside.

But this wasn't enough to stop Geoff, who turned onto his back and began kicking wildly as though he were in his first swimming lesson. This made it very difficult for William to hold onto him, and his grip slowly began to weaken, allowing Geoff to stick his head and torso out of the car. All he had to do was lean back a little farther and he would fall.

"No you don't!" William said, lurching forward. He grabbed Geoff by the collar of his suit jacket and started pulling him back inside.

"William, listen to me!" Geoff said. "I can stop this! Do you hear me? I can stop all of this!"

"Continuum is everything to me!" William gasped, struggling to speak as he pulled Geoff back.

"Look at yourself, William!" Geoff shouted, pulling himself farther out again. "Is this what you imagined Continuum would give you? Leaving you old and frail, a servant to Jennifer Adams for the rest of your days?"

Jennifer looked back at William. "Don't listen to him, William!" she said, "Get him back in this car at once!"

William looked at Jennifer, then back toward Geoff.

"Please, William," Geoff said. "Let me go."

"What are you doing?" Jennifer said. "Pull him in right now!"

William's eyes gazed down once again at his old, withered hands, then back up at Geoff again.

"Let me go," Geoff said again.

William nodded, and loosened his grip. But as Geoff began to fall backward, Jennifer opened her door and reached out toward Geoff. Her hands darted toward his collar, but with no tie around his neck, she had nothing to grab onto. Had Geoff been wearing one, Jennifer would have easily been able to pull him back inside the vehicle and that would have been that, but instead, she began fumbling with the lapels of Geoff's shirt, desperately trying to keep hold of him somehow.

But it was no use. Jennifer just couldn't get a strong enough grip, and within seconds Geoff was completely free from the car and began to plummet through the sky toward the streets below.

"Nooooo!" he heard Jennifer scream from above him.

Despite the wind rushing in his ears and his eyes watering, Geoff experienced a brief moment of calm.

This was it.

This was the end of Continuum.

There was no chance he could survive a drop from this height, unless his fall was about to be broken by a number of inconveniently placed window canopies, hanging laundry, and tarpaulins before landing in a skip outside a bouncy castle factory.

Which would be seriously annoying after all that effort to get out of the car and kill himself.

From here could barely tell how high up he was, but for a while the ground didn't seem to be approaching him that quickly. He fell through low-hanging clouds, he fell through various streams of flying traffic, and he fell past the tops of the tallest buildings.

To his side, he noticed one of the black cars going into free fall as if to try and catch up with him, but it was no use—there was no way anyone would be able to get to him before he hit the ground.

In the last few seconds before Geoff became a two-dimensional object, time seemed to slow down. He wasn't sure if this was because in your last moments all kinds of crazy stuff was supposed to happen to your powers of perception, but nonetheless, everything seemed to move in slow motion.

He could now see the terrified faces of the people below, looking up at him as he fell. He could see cars skidding to a halt in the streets, with people climbing out and pointing to him. And he could see the fine texture of the paving slabs he was about to slam into.

He clamped his mouth shut, closed his eyes, and just hoped he wouldn't make too much of a mess.

But he already had made quite a mess, and the space-time continuum was now busy trying to work out how the hell it was going to clean this all up.

ONE

"Mr. Stamp?"

"Mmmm?"

"Mr. Stamp, can you hear me?"

"Mmmm…mmmm?"

"Mr. Stamp, please can you stop mumbling and open your eyes?"

Geoff didn't want to open his eyes just yet. He was still a little bit overwhelmed from the sensation of falling to his death, and needed a couple more seconds to compose himself. He did think it would be a good idea to stop mumbling, though.

He needed to think. What just happened? Wasn't he supposed to be Geoff pâté right about now? Why was he still alive, and where was he?

Maybe he wasn't alive at all.

Was he dead?

He soon came to the conclusion that a large number of these questions would probably be answered if he did actually open his eyes, just as he'd been asked to.

So he did.

Okay, so he was sitting in a room.

He was sitting in a small room, behind a gray desk.

It was quite bright in here, so much so that he couldn't quite see properly.

As more details of his surroundings filled themselves in as his eyes adjusted to the light, he realized that he knew this place—unless he was mistaken, this was that room at Time Tours where the man with the thin moustache had told him off for nearly creating a paradox when he'd almost told Zoë he was a Time Rep!

What the hell was he doing here?

He was so surprised, he didn't realize that the man with the thin moustache was actually sitting across the desk from him, albeit in a chair slightly to the right. There was also another chair directly in front of him, but it was empty.

"Mr. Stamp?" the man said. "Are you feeling okay?"

"Oh shit!" Geoff said, jumping out of his chair as though someone had just run an electric current through it. He suddenly realized why he was probably here—if his actions had succeeded in destroying Continuum after all, he had probably created the mother of all paradoxes, just as he'd suspected! He had no idea how much trouble he was in, but he knew this wasn't going to be good.

"Look, I'm sorry, okay?" Geoff said. "I'm sorry if I caused any trouble!"

The man looked at him quizzically. "What on Earth are you talking about, man?" he said, looking down at a clipboard in front of him. "You haven't caused any trouble!"

"I haven't?"

"Not that I'm aware of," the man said. "Unless you haven't shared something with us?"

Geoff narrowed his eyes and slumped back into his seat. "What about Continuum?" he said. "What happened to it?"

"Continuum?" the man said. "You mean the space-time continuum? As far as I'm aware, it's fine. We're still here, aren't we? Cause and effect are still the right way round, aren't they?"

"I don't mean the space-time continuum," Geoff said. "I mean the organization called Continuum."

The man looked at him blankly.

"You know?" Geoff said. "The holiday company that allows you to go back in time and change whatever you like."

"A holiday company that allows you to go back and change whatever you like?" the man laughed. "I've never heard of anything so ridiculous in my life!"

"What?" Geoff said. "But I thought you guys were really worried about them! Haven't they been stealing all your tourists? Isn't Time Tours on the verge of going bust because of them?"

"Are you kidding?" the man said, smiling. "Business has never been better! We've got more tourists going back to more historical periods than ever before!"

"So you're telling me there is no such company as Continuum?" Geoff said.

"That's right."

"Interesting," Geoff said, taking a moment to stroke his chin in that way people do when things begin to slot into place in their mind. Was it possible that his actions had actually succeeded in creating a new timeline in which Continuum never existed?

He certainly hoped so, because that would be marvelous.

"Are you taking any hallucinogenic drugs I should be aware of, Mr. Stamp?" the man said, "Because if you have, it may affect the verdict of the panel."

"Panel?" Geoff said. "What panel? What am I doing here?"

"You don't remember?" the man said. "You're here to find out whether your change request has been approved, aren't you?"

Geoff blinked. "My change request?"

"That's right."

"And what is that, exactly?"

"What is what?"

"A change request. What's that when it's at home?"

"Don't you remember anything?" the man said. "How can you not know what a change request is when you were the first Time Rep to volunteer for the trial?" The man removed a sheet of paper from his clipboard and slid it in front of Geoff. "Here's the form you filled in," he said, tapping the paper with his pen. "You remember filling this out, don't you?"

Geoff scanned his eyes over the sheet of paper quickly. At the top it read:

CHANGE REQUEST FORM V.1
THIS FORM IS FOR REQUESTING
A **CONTROLLED** CHANGE YOU
WOULD LIKE TO MAKE TO THE
SPACE TIME CONTINUUM.

Q1: WHAT WILL YOU CHANGE?

Well this was certainly new—it appeared to be a form that Time Reps could fill out, requesting permission to make a controlled change to the space-time continuum. Reading down the form, he could see that this one had been completed in his handwriting, and the request was very clear: he had asked if he could change the course of history by pursuing a relationship with Zoë.

"I remember now," Geoff lied, pushing the paper back toward the man. "Sorry about that. I don't know what it is, but I seem to be awfully forgetful at the moment."

But then, just as he was able to retain dual memories of Jennifer Adams with and without her scar, he began to remember things about this parallel timeline. He'd changed so much, though, that it was taking a moment for the blanks in his mind to fill themselves in.

"Don't worry about it," the man said, attaching the paper back to his clipboard. "These things happen."

"So you say this is a trial?" Geoff said.

"That's right," the man replied. "The ability for Time Reps to make small controlled changes has always been high on the Time Rep Council's agenda. We like to think we listen to you guys, so we've developed this trial. We still don't want you going around making massive changes willy-nilly, but if your request is sensible and able to be made under controlled conditions, we're happy to consider it."

"The Time Rep Council?"

Geoff thought about asking what that was, but as he searched the back of his mind, he realized he already knew. In this reality, Time Reps were represented by elected members of a council. They acted as a sort of union, putting forward issues from the workforce for the Time Tours management to deal with.

They finally had a voice.

At that moment, there came a knock at the door.

"Ah—that will be the Director of Change with the results of your request," the man said, turning toward the door. "Come in!"

Geoff looked up. The door opened, and in walked someone he wasn't expecting.

It was Jennifer Adams.

"Hello, Mr. Stamp," she said, taking a seat in the empty chair in front of him.

Geoff looked Jennifer in the eyes. She looked kind of similar to the older Jennifer Adams he had last seen on Tower Bridge, although her hair was now cut into a bob, much like her younger self had worn it. She also didn't have any sort of scar under her left eye, and still wore her black-rimmed glasses.

As he looked at her, Jennifer just sat there, politely returning his gaze. There was no malice in her eyes, no sign that she remembered anything about Continuum.

"Now, to business," she said, leaning forward on the desk. "I'm pleased to inform you that your request to pursue a relationship with your friend Zoë has been approved. There are a few minor changes that will happen to the space-time continuum as a result, but nothing too serious."

"Really?" Geoff said. "That's fantastic!"

"There is one condition, though," Jennifer said. "You still can't tell her what you really do for a living, do you understand? She can't know that you're a Time Rep, and she certainly can't know anything about the events of two years ago. Do you understand?"

"I understand," Geoff nodded.

"Good," she said, holding a hand out for him to shake. "Then there's nothing more for me to do than offer you my congratulations, and the best of luck."

Geoff looked down at her hand and hesitated.

This was very strange—one minute this woman was trying to kill him, the next she was making his dreams come true.

"Mr. Stamp?" the man with the thin moustache said, motioning him to accept Jennifer's handshake.

"Sorry," Geoff said, returning the gesture.

Her handshake was completely different this time from before—it was somehow firm yet gentle at the same time, and she brought her other hand up to clasp his hand from the other side.

"Very good," Jennifer said, turning to leave the room. "We'll keep an eye on the state of the space-time continuum as things progress between yourself and Zoë, but in the meantime, I wish you all the very best."

She walked over to the door and opened it, but before she left, Geoff wanted to say something.

"Ms. Adams?" he said, standing up from his chair.

"Yes, Mr. Stamp?" Jennifer said, looking around.

"Thank you."

Jennifer gave him a single nod and left the room, closing the door behind her with a click.

"What happens now?" Geoff said, turning to the man with the thin moustache.

"Now you can go back and ask your friend out," the man said, getting up from his chair and turning to leave.

Geoff suddenly felt nervous at the prospect of asking Zoë out on a date again, although he took some comfort in knowing that there was no way it could be worse than the last time he'd taken her out. This was, of course, assuming that she would agree to go on a date with him at all. Without the power of Continuum, Geoff couldn't tell her the truth about himself, and he had no way of changing things if this all went wrong. But then again, that was what made life exciting.

And at least she'd probably get through this date without dying.

EPILOGUE

"So, are you ready for this?" Tim said, straightening Geoff's tie for him.

"I think so," Geoff replied, looking himself up and down in his bedroom mirror. "How do I look?"

As well as granting him permission to go on a date with Zoë, Time Tours had also been kind enough to give him some money to purchase a smart suit—the first piece of clothing he'd ever owned that would actually allow him to get into a proper restaurant, which was where he had invited Zoë for dinner later that evening.

"You look great," Tim said. "Really dapper."

"What does *dapper* mean?"

"Smart. Stylish. You know—dapper."

Through a series of subtle questions over the last few days (and one not-so-subtle question where he'd just blurted out "What the hell happened to Continuum?"), Geoff had determined that, like everyone else, Tim had no memory of what had transpired over the last twenty-four hours. He didn't remember trying to stop the spread of Continuum; he didn't remember shooting Geoff in the back; he didn't remember anything.

Geoff found this extremely annoying, because he really wanted to talk to someone about all this. Why was he the only one who remembered what happened?

He'd also done a bit of investigation about William. He was still a Time Rep in seventeenth-century London, but through a future change request he was allowed to make, William was finally able to own a place of his own and start a family. He would eventually die in his early eighties, succeeded by many loving children. Children that were his of course, not just some random kids.

"So where are you taking Zoë tonight?" Tim asked.

"I thought I'd take her down the local pizza restaurant," Geoff said. "According to a leaflet that came through the door the other day, they've got this new limited-edition meal deal called the Glutton Box. In it you get a large pizza, ten pieces of garlic bread, twenty chicken wings, some potato wedges, and a dip…"

Tim looked at Geoff in silence for a moment.

"I am, of course, joking," Geoff said.

"Thank God for that," Tim said.

"You actually get eight pieces of garlic bread."

• • •

As it happened, Geoff had chosen to eat in a rather posh restaurant, but not one of those fine-dining affairs where the chef considers a decent portion size to be a small prawn balanced on a single pea, housed inside a porcelain teaspoon of tomato consommé. No, he had opted for a nice Italian restaurant on London's South Bank, overlooking the river Thames.

"This is nice," Zoë said, taking a sip of her wine. She looked great this evening, wearing a light summer dress and a silver shawl around her neck. She'd also chosen to wear her hair down in a style he'd never seen before, with a thin silver clip holding it in place.

Looking at her now was simply heaven. In fact, if he looked too long, he thought he might just forget the events of the past twenty-four hours, just like everyone else had.

Zoë really had that much of an effect on him.

She made all of his worries drift away.

Then again, it could have been the wine, which usually made him forgetful as well.

The waiter had kindly given them the best table in the house, right in the middle of the balcony overlooking the river.

It was a beautiful evening, the clear sky full of stars and glowing with a full moon.

"You like it?" Geoff said, looking down at the menu. He wanted to eat pretty much everything on it, but didn't think that would be particularly romantic.

"I love it," Zoë replied. "Who would have thought I'd ever get to eat in a place like this?"

Geoff frowned. "What do you mean?" he said. "Why do you think you wouldn't ever get to eat here?"

"I don't know," Zoë said. "It's just not what I'm used to, that's all. I feel like we're impostors, and that any moment from now, someone is going to come up to us and tell us we're not allowed to be here."

Geoff smiled. "Nobody is going tell us anything of the sort," he said. "Nobody is going to tell us what we're supposed to do, or where we're supposed to be, or how we're supposed to act. From now on, we do what we want to do."

Zoë smiled. "So, what have you been up to since I last saw you?" she asked. "Anything interesting?"

Geoff looked at Zoë. So much had happened over the last twenty-four hours, and he was dying to tell her everything he had just been through to be here with her.

But then the voice of Jennifer Adams echoed in his mind. Under no circumstances could he tell Zoë he was a Time Rep, or that he had saved the entire human race from an alien invasion two years ago. Both of those things were certainly impressive, but they had to remain a secret.

"Zoë," he said. "Can I tell you something?"

"Sure," Zoë said, leaning forward. "What is it?"

"I'm a Time Rep."

ACKNOWLEDGMENTS

Thanks to:

Mark Selby, Geoff Tachauer, Cammil Taank, and Adam Malinowski

Dan Geneen and Briony Singh

Lucy Ward and Erik Brown

PETER WARD was born in London in 1980. He was educated at William Torbitt Primary School, Ilford Country High School, and the University of Southampton, though not at the same time, because that would be ridiculous. His skills include making a fairly decent lamb korma from scratch, drawing X-Wings, and riding his bike with no hands. Oh, and writing.

He lives in London with his wife Lucy, a very small cat, and a spider that won't leave the kitchen that he has decided to call Dennis.

Time Rep: Continuum is his third novel, unless time travel is invented within his lifetime and he decides to go back and release some books other than *Time Rep* and *Note to Self* before this one.

NOTE TO SELF IS AVAILABLE NOW!

In a world where technology controls everything, sometimes your own handwriting is the only thing you can trust.

Richard Henley is an ordinary man leading an ordinary life, but when he finds strange notes in his own handwriting warning that someone is trying to kill him, he is sent on a journey to places he never knew existed. With an ominous and all-powerful organisation on his trail, his only hope is to trust unexpected allies, take control of his life, and uncover the truth about what happened to the girl he loved twenty years ago. A darkly humorous commentary on our app-obsessed culture, if Richard can stay alive, his world will never be the same again.

CPSIA information can be obtained at www.ICGtesting.com
Printed in the USA
BVOW08s1416240716

456681BV00006B/80/P